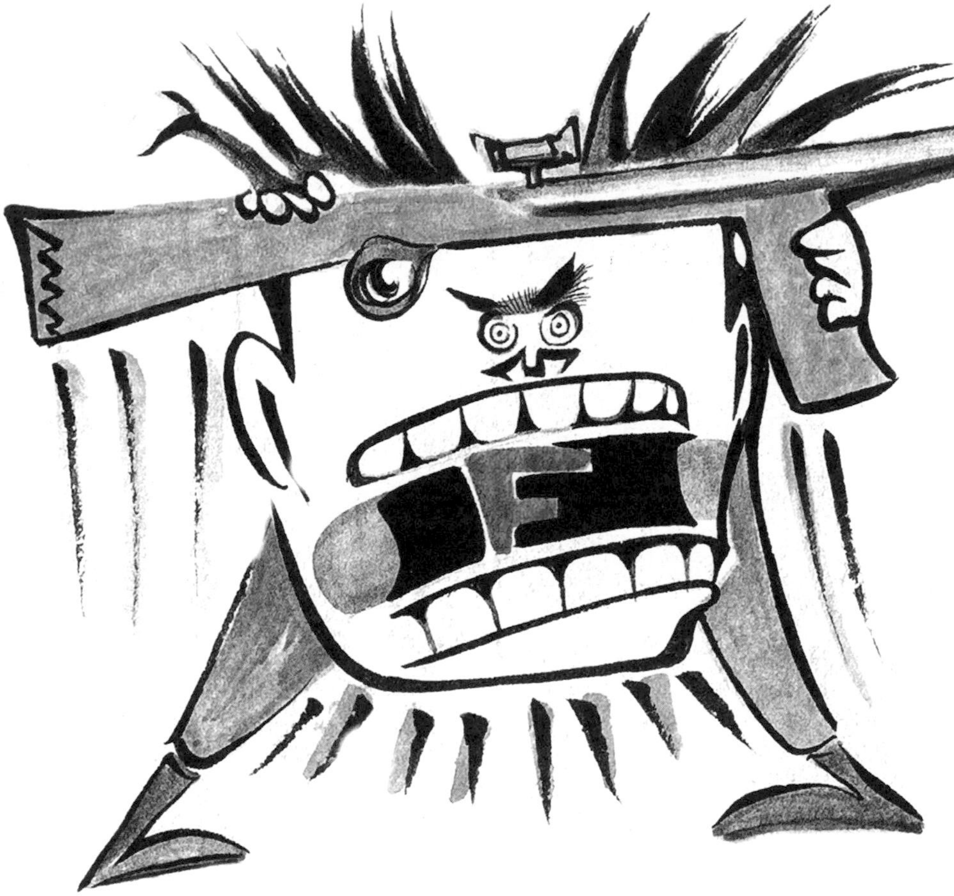
F

MICHAEL NICOLL YAHGULANAAS

CARPE FIN

A HAIDA MANGA

Carpe Fin is dedicated to the many who feel few
and to the strong who think themselves weak.

ACKNOWLEDGEMENTS

With appreciation to David and Emily for wit; Barry Gilson for thoughtfulness; Barbara Brotherton and friends of the Seattle Art Museum for believing; Fuyubi Nakamura, Ozu Washi and the Kubota family for kozo washi; Barbara Golden and Golden Paints for pigment; David van Berckel and the Opus team for a fast camera; Anton van Walraven for a table; Noah Carson for pushing the catalogue; Jake Litrell for digital mastery; Michiko Sakata for tasty delicacies; Gabe Sentlinger for generous humour and magnets; Anne Cameron for wise contemplation; Robert Bringhurst for sharing; Nanni Delores, Nanni Jane and Babs for anchoring; Launette for caring; and Mirella for refreshing life.

INTRODUCTION

The ragged edges of the temperate rainforest reach far out onto an island in the western seas. It is a place where one chooses to go ahead or turn back. Perched a thousand metres above the abyssal ocean floor, this rocky eruption is a refuge for the storm-tossed. Tucked and sheltered, I watched an old story emerge onto sheets of paper.

This story was old even when it was recorded as brittle paged text, but like life itself it has been refreshed through recitation. Seventeen years ago a brush in the hand of a watchman painted the first draft of the paper now in your hands. Seventeen months ago that same brush started a mural two metres high and six metres long. It is now in the permanent collection of the Seattle Art Museum. The mural became this book, the prequel to *Red: A Haida Manga*. *Carpe Fin* is an explanation of how the Carpenter was found alive on a rock in the middle of the ocean.

ONCE UPON A TIME THIS COULD BE A TRUE STORY...

A STEEL HULL PUSHES THROUGH NORTHERN WATERS IN AN EARLY FALL CHILL. IT CARRIES AN ASSORTMENT OF SUPPLIES AND A FEW PASSENGERS...

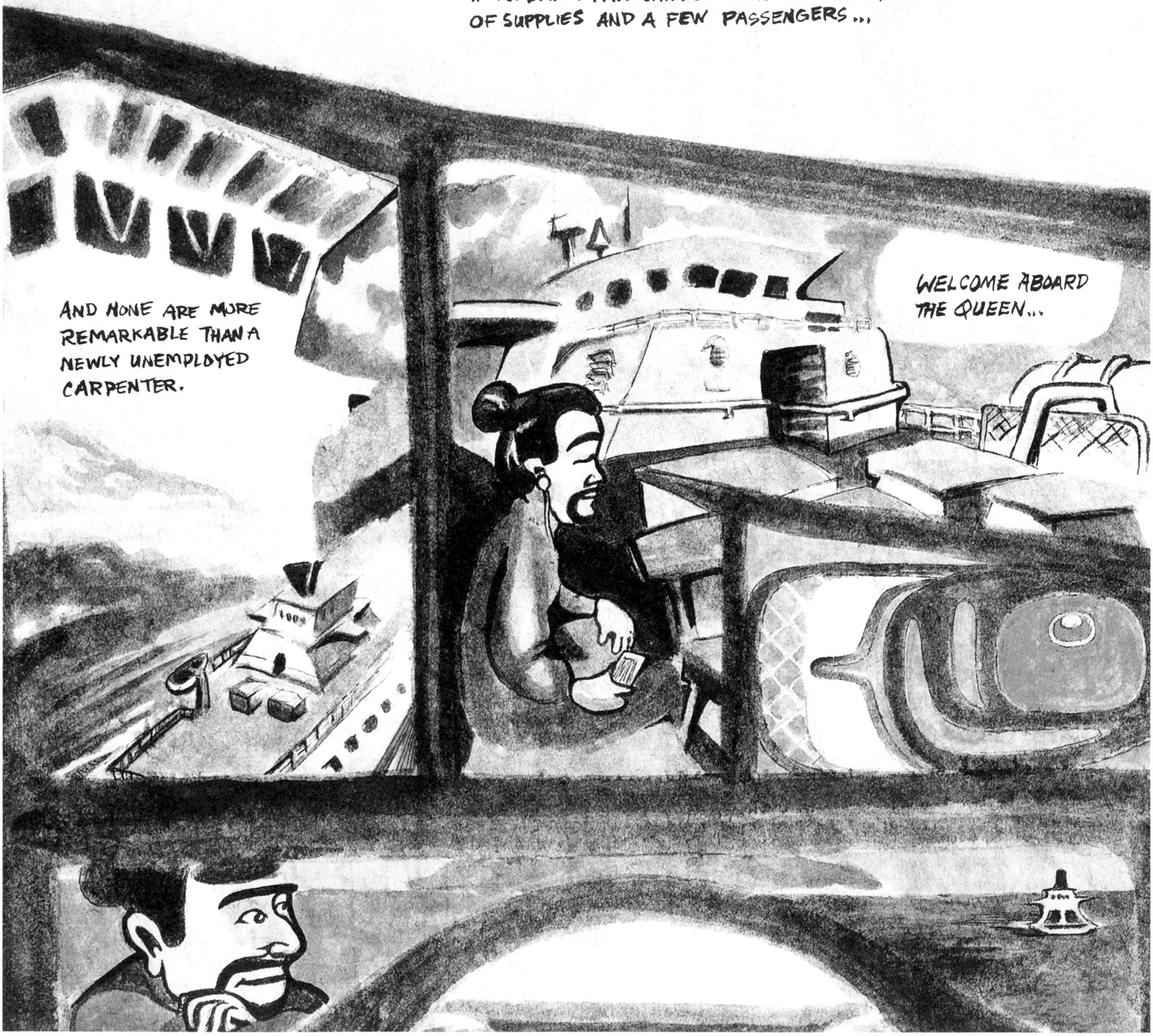

AND NONE ARE MORE REMARKABLE THAN A NEWLY UNEMPLOYED CARPENTER.
WELCOME ABOARD THE QUEEN...

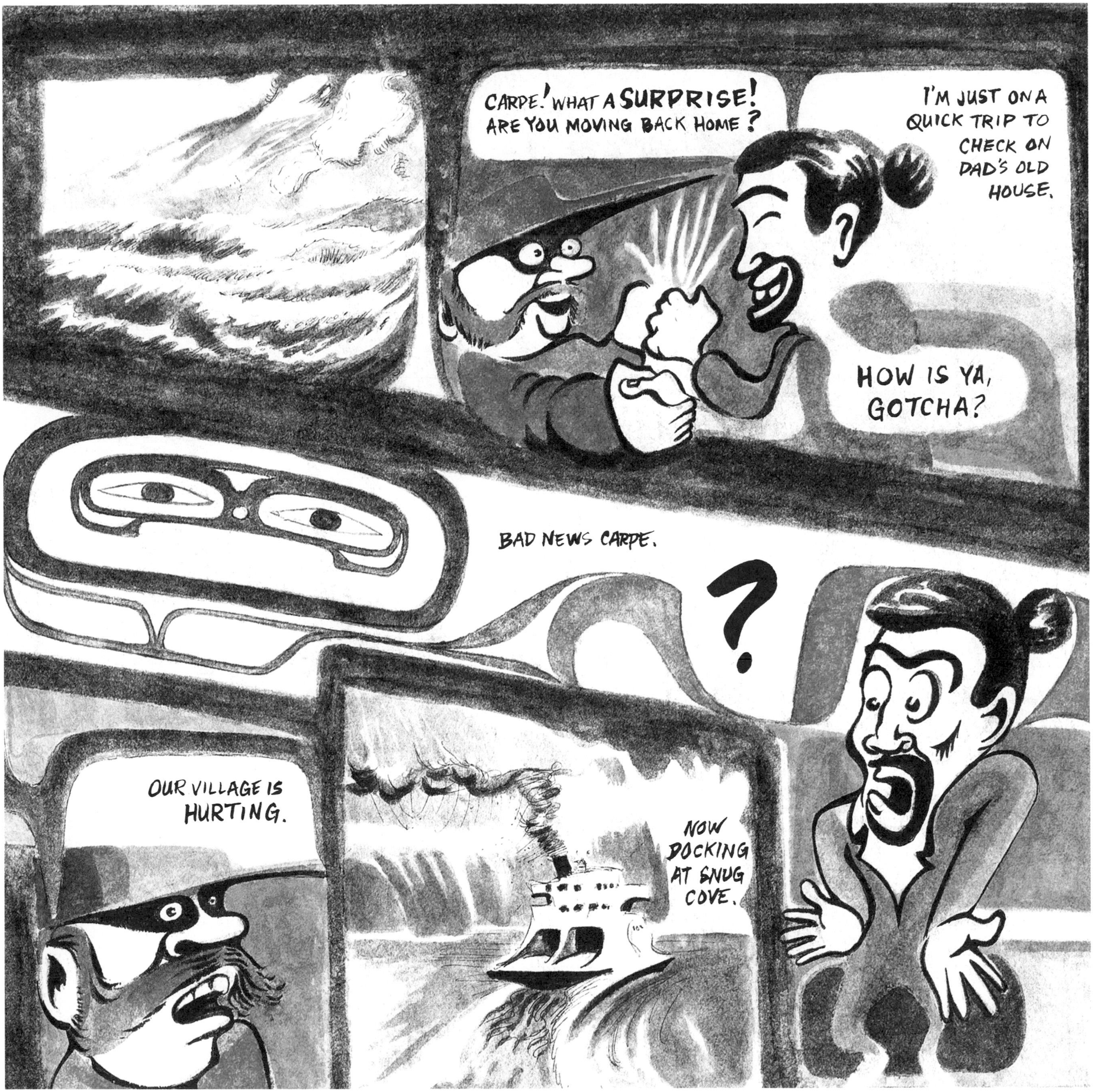
CARPE! WHAT A SURPRISE! ARE YOU MOVING BACK HOME?
I'M JUST ON A QUICK TRIP TO CHECK ON DAD'S OLD HOUSE.
HOW IS YA, GOTCHA?
BAD NEWS CARPE.
?
OUR VILLAGE IS HURTING.
NOW DOCKING AT SNUG COVE.

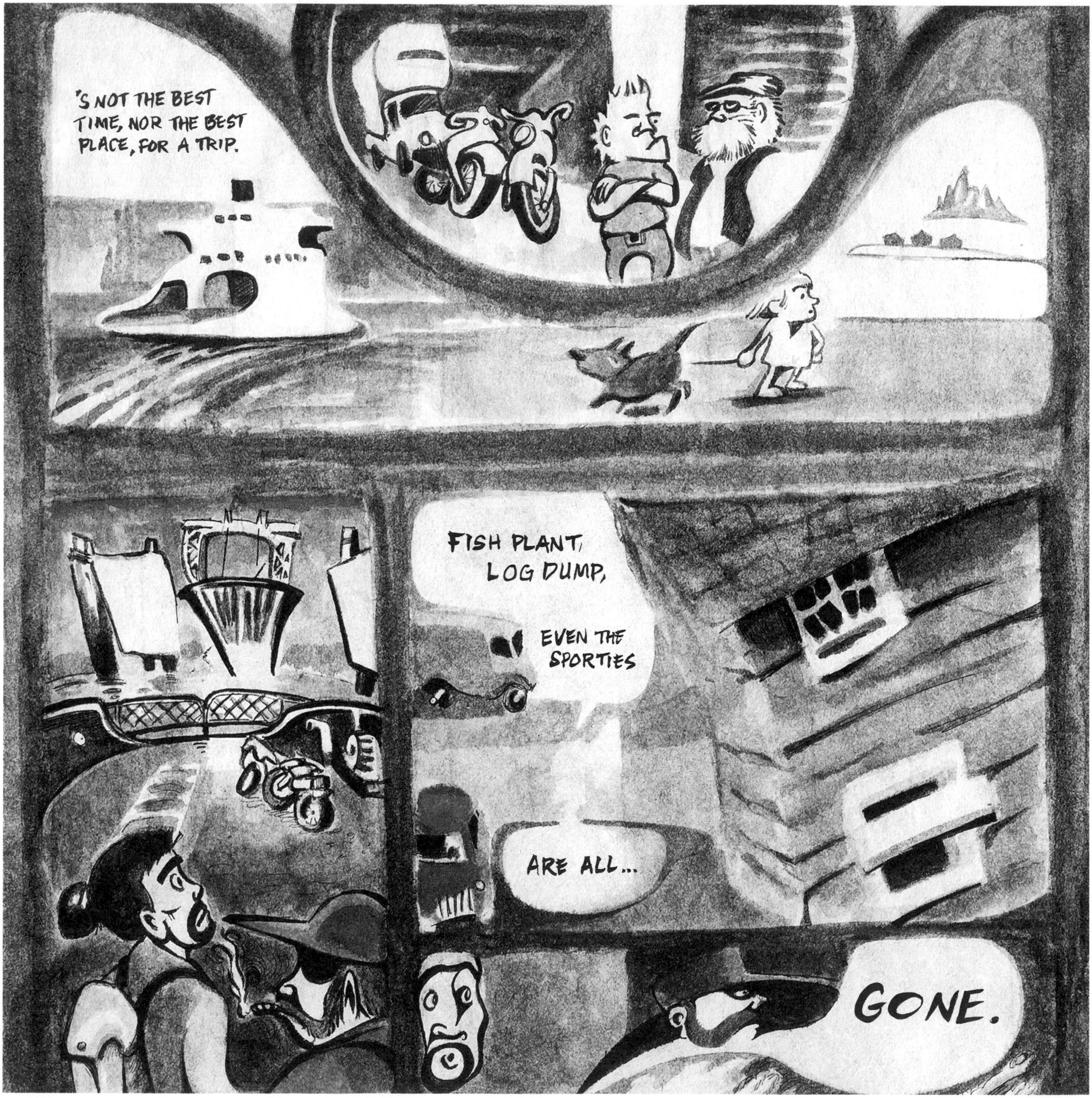
'S NOT THE BEST TIME, NOR THE BEST PLACE, FOR A TRIP.
FISH PLANT, LOG DUMP,
EVEN THE SPORTIES
ARE ALL...
GONE.

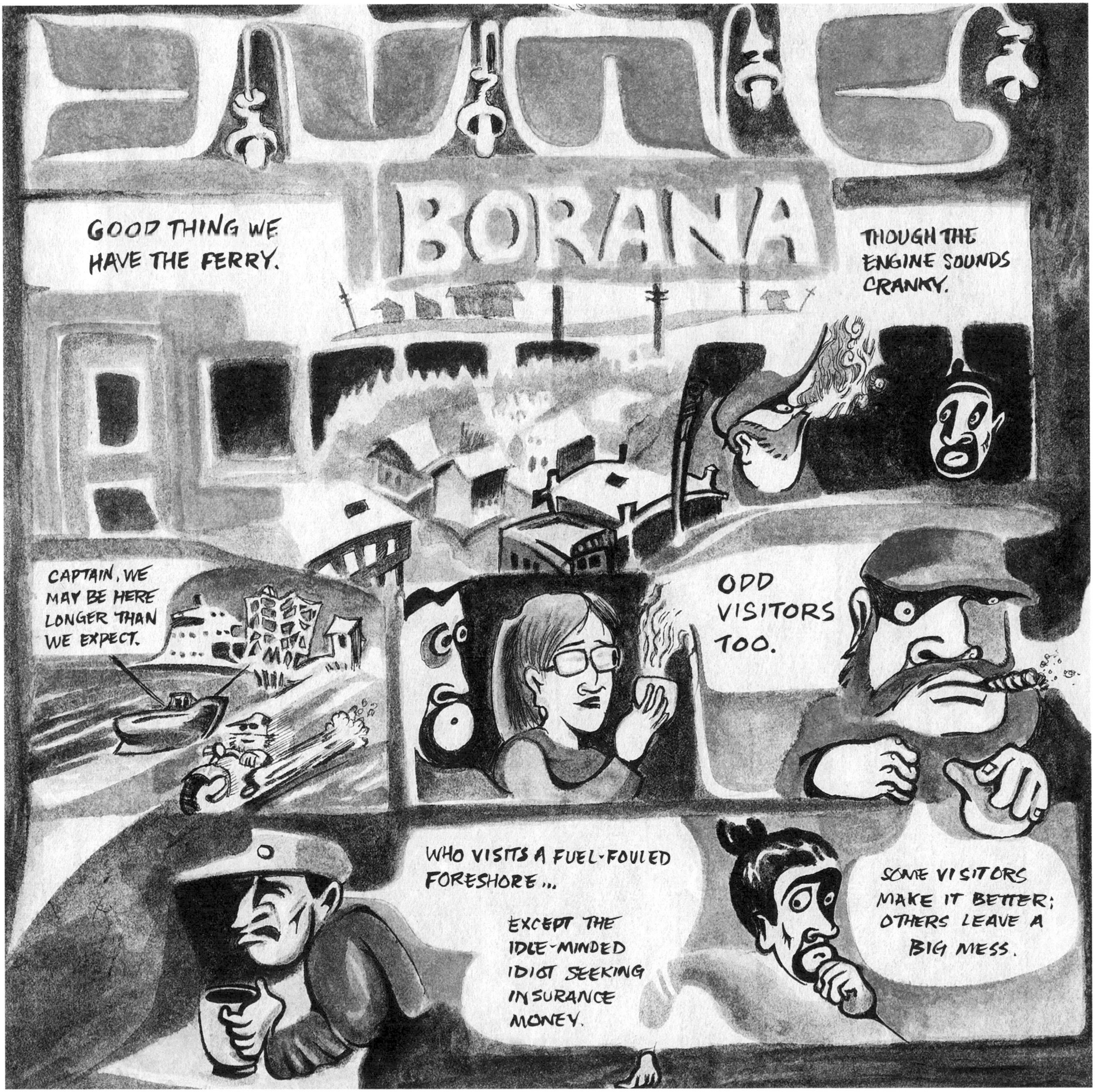
BORANA
GOOD THING WE HAVE THE FERRY.
THOUGH THE ENGINE SOUNDS CRANKY.
CAPTAIN, WE MAY BE HERE LONGER THAN WE EXPECT.
ODD VISITORS TOO.
WHO VISITS A FUEL-FOULED FORESHORE...
EXCEPT THE IDLE-MINDED IDIOT SEEKING INSURANCE MONEY.
SOME VISITORS MAKE IT BETTER; OTHERS LEAVE A BIG MESS.

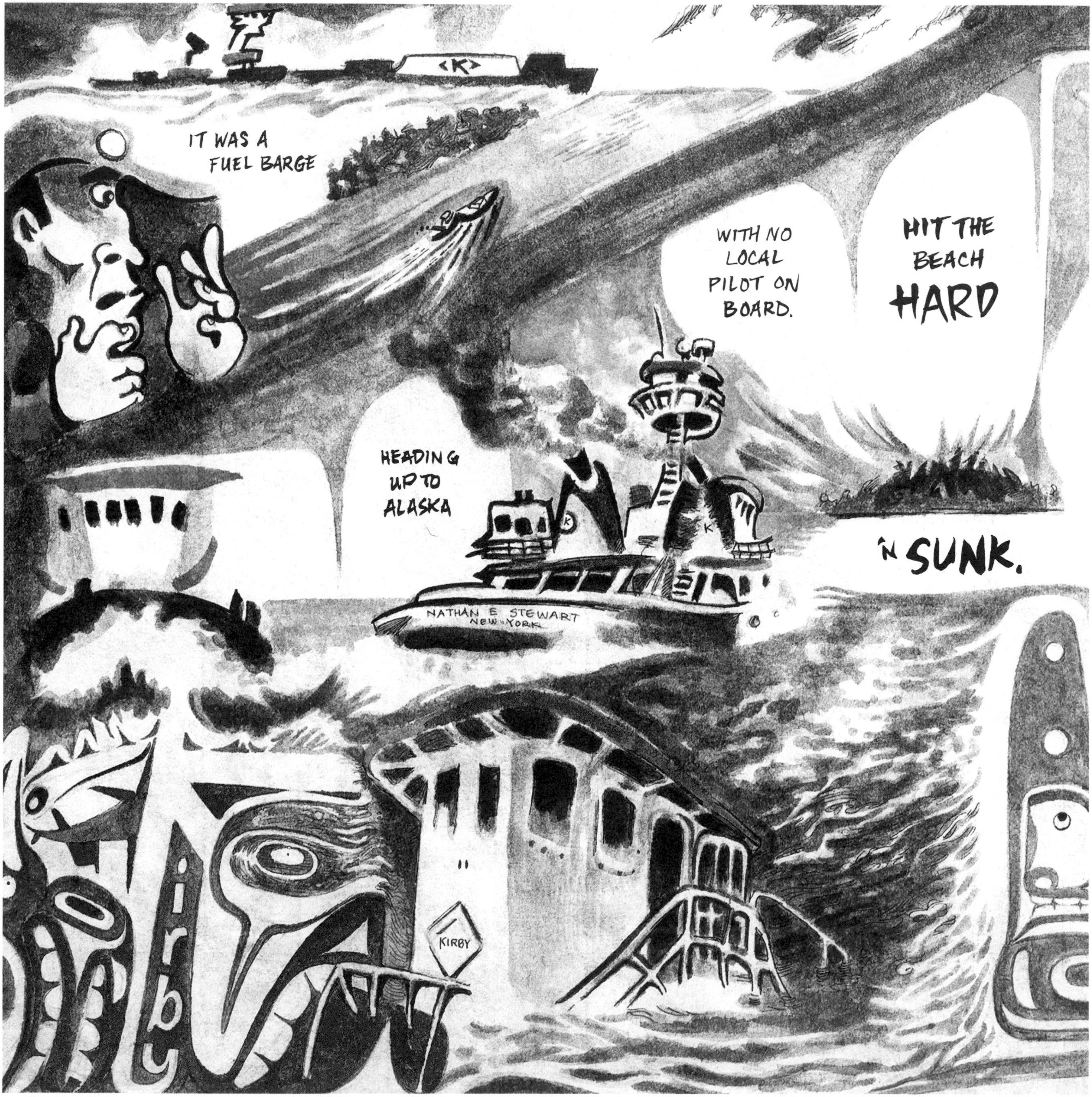

IT WAS A FUEL BARGE
HEADING UP TO ALASKA
WITH NO LOCAL PILOT ON BOARD.
HIT THE BEACH HARD
'N SUNK.
NATHAN E STEWART NEW YORK
KIRBY

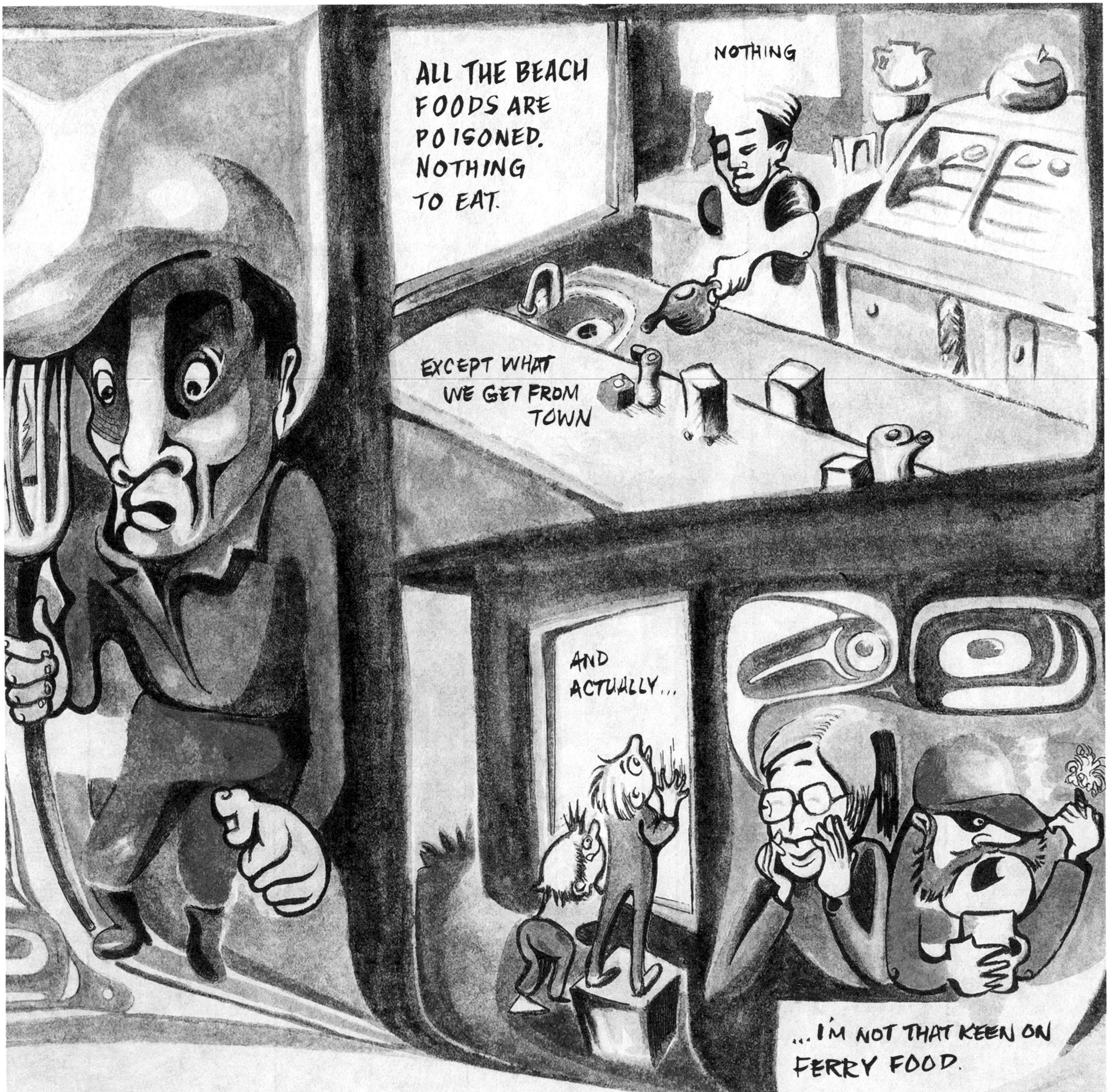
ALL THE BEACH FOODS ARE POISONED. NOTHING TO EAT.
NOTHING
EXCEPT WHAT WE GET FROM TOWN
AND ACTUALLY...
...I'M NOT THAT KEEN ON FERRY FOOD.

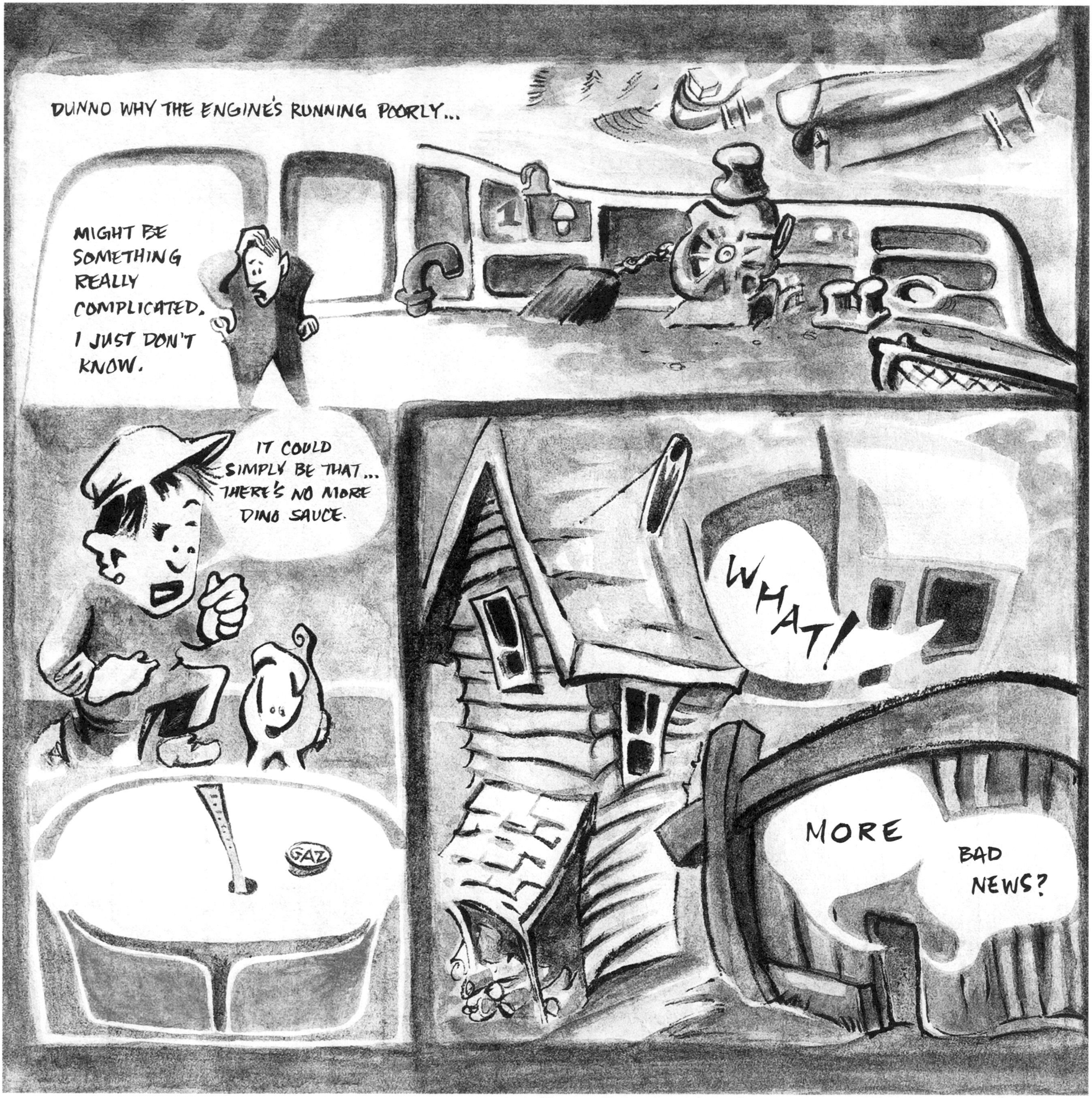
DUNNO WHY THE ENGINE'S RUNNING POORLY...
MIGHT BE SOMETHING REALLY COMPLICATED.
I JUST DON'T KNOW.
IT COULD SIMPLY BE THAT... THERE'S NO MORE DINO SAUCE.
GAZ
WHAT!
MORE
BAD NEWS?

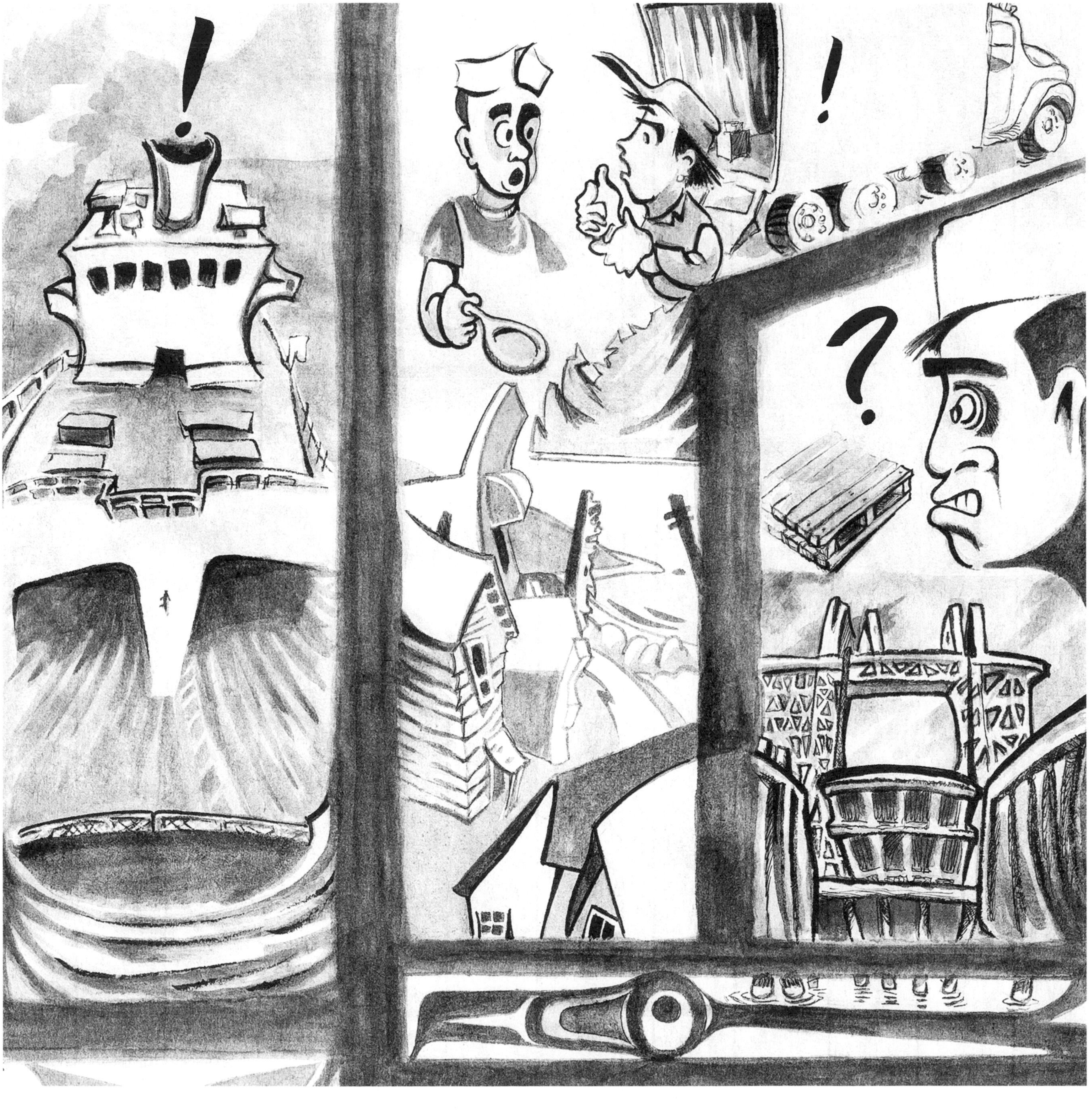

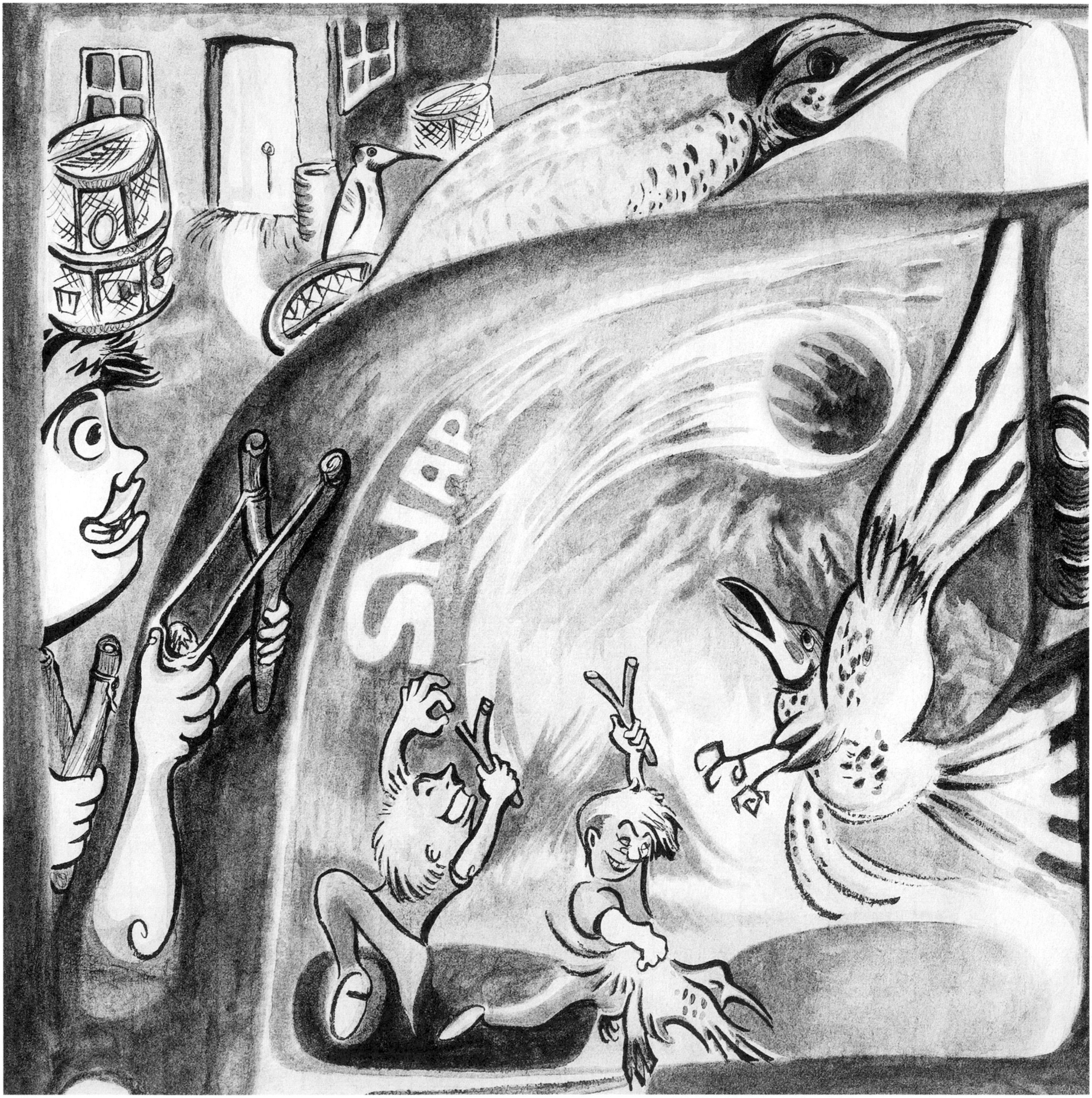
SNAP

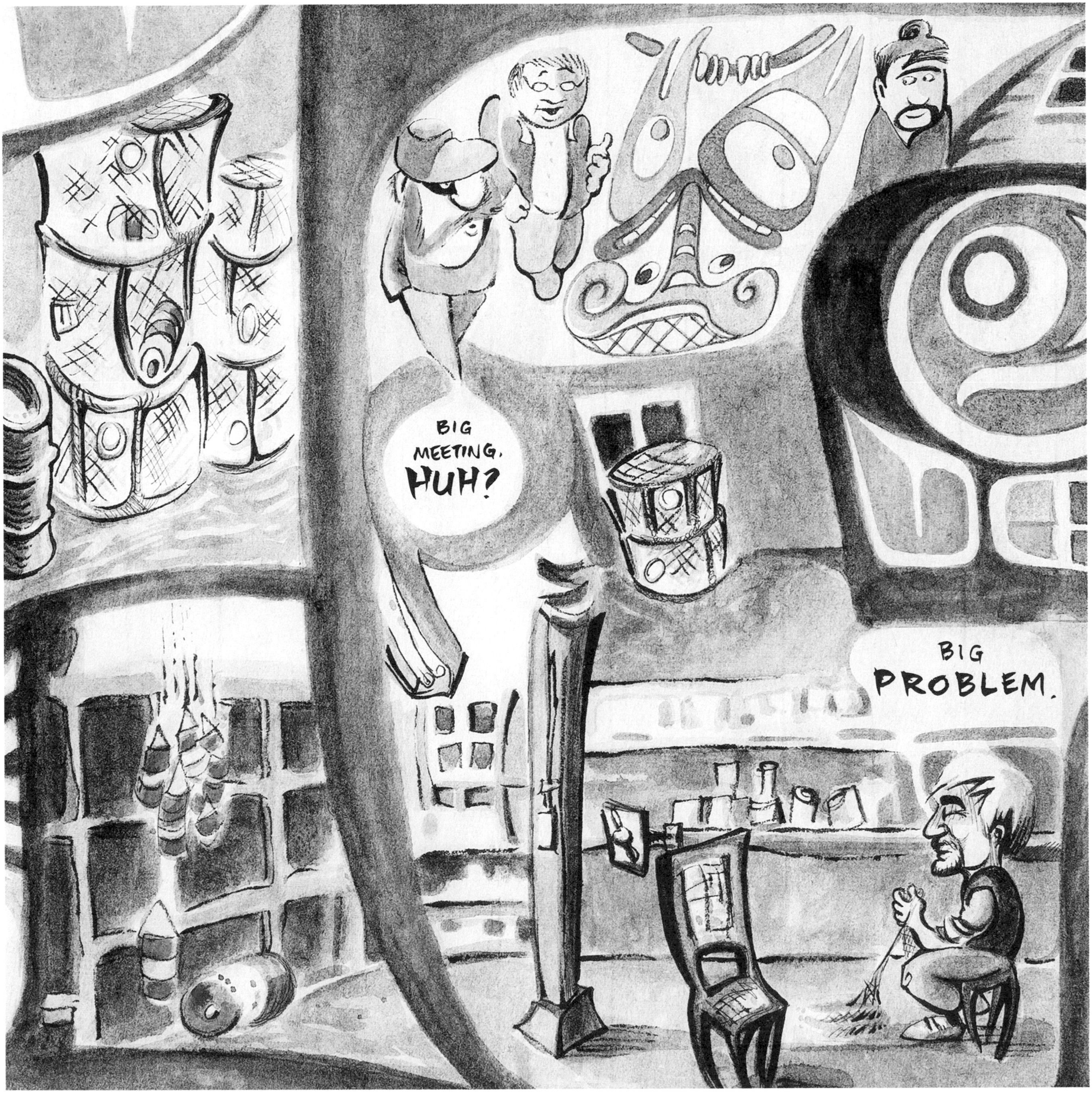
BIG MEETING, HUH?
BIG PROBLEM.

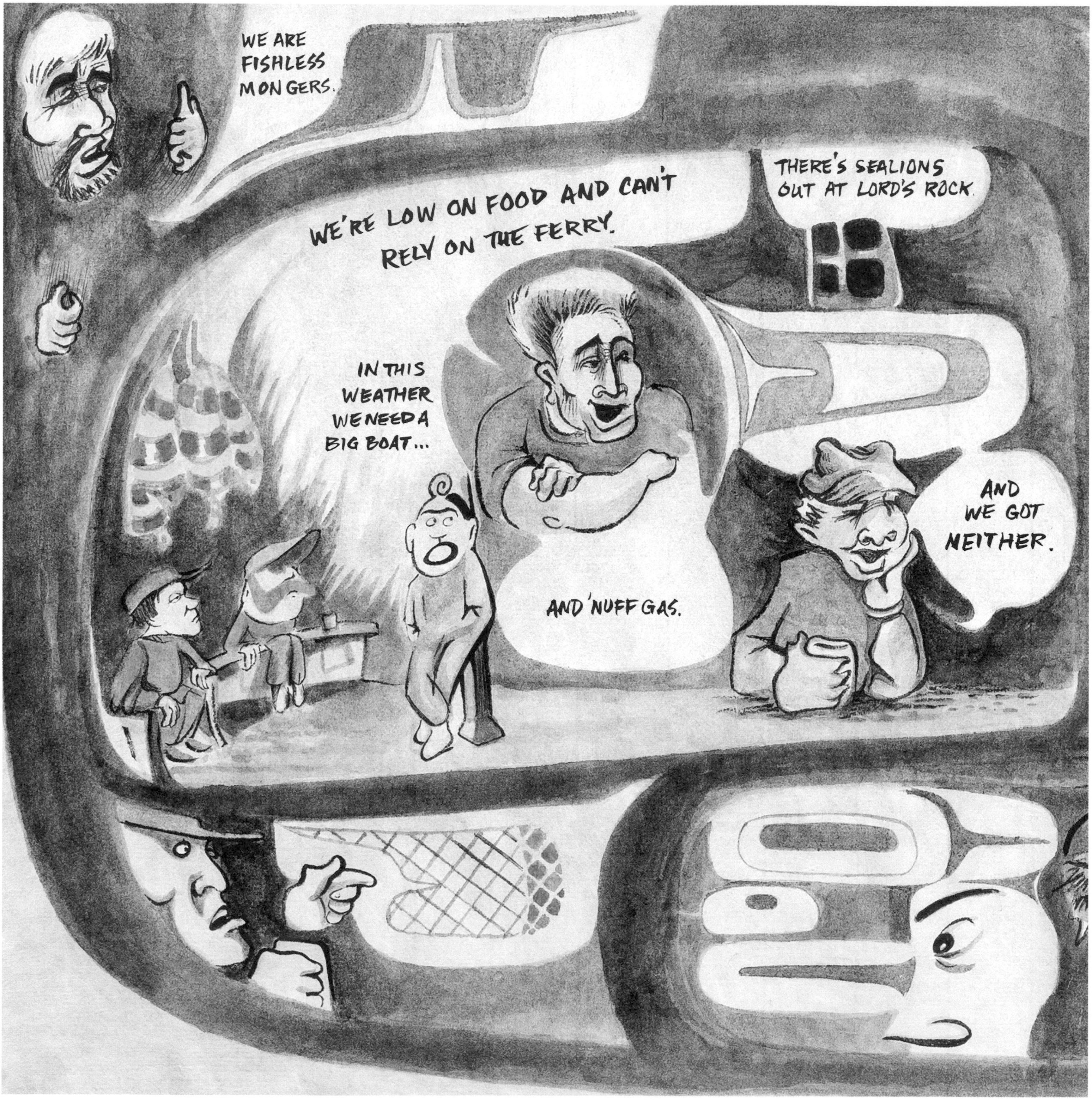
WE ARE FISHLESS MONGERS.
WE'RE LOW ON FOOD AND CAN'T RELY ON THE FERRY.
THERE'S SEALIONS OUT AT LORD'S ROCK.
IN THIS WEATHER WE NEED A BIG BOAT...
AND 'NUFF GAS.
AND WE GOT NEITHER.

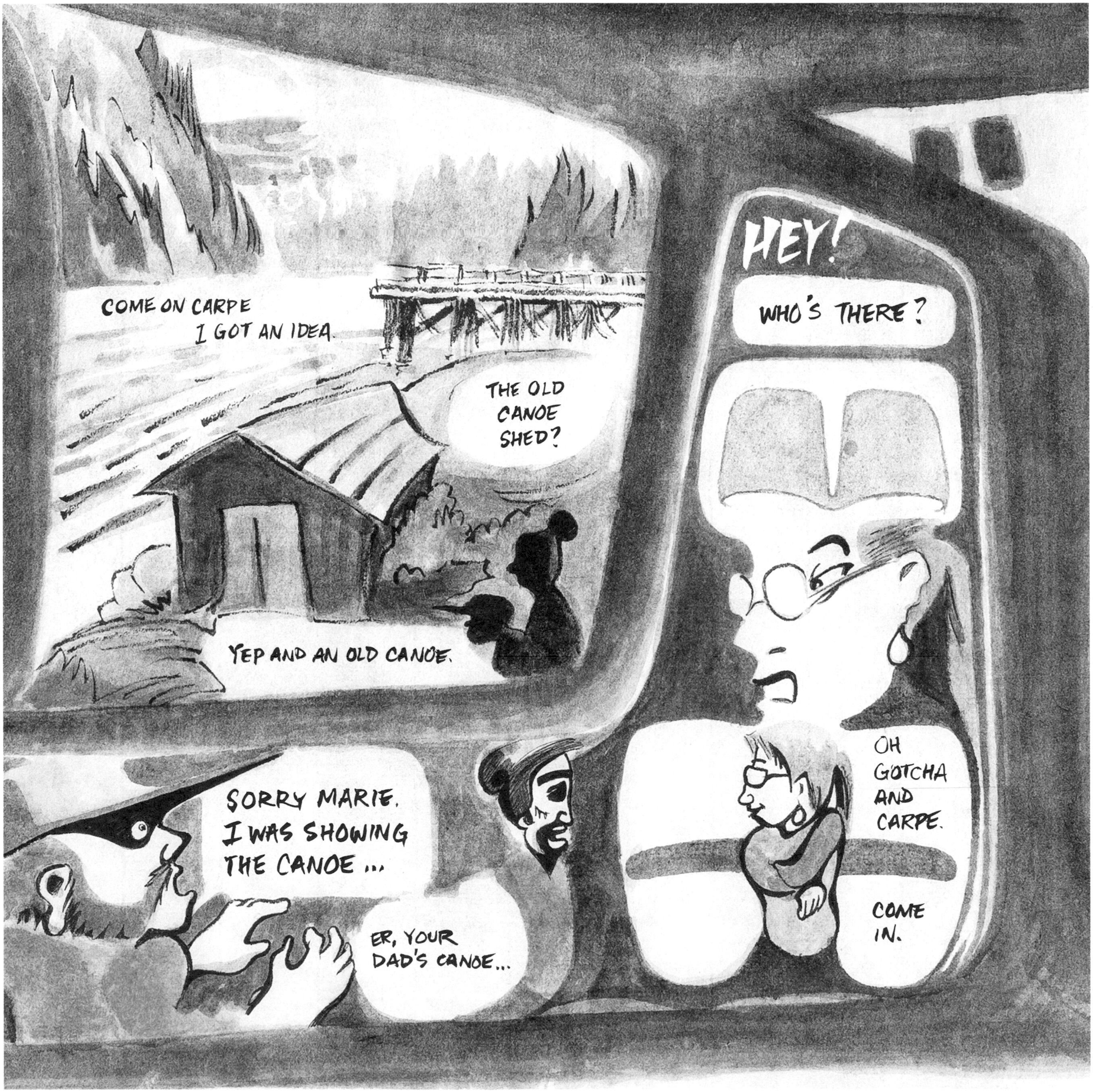
COME ON CARPE I GOT AN IDEA.
THE OLD CANOE SHED?
YEP AND AN OLD CANOE.
HEY!
WHO'S THERE?
SORRY MARIE. I WAS SHOWING THE CANOE ...
ER, YOUR DAD'S CANOE...
OH GOTCHA AND CARPE.
COME IN.

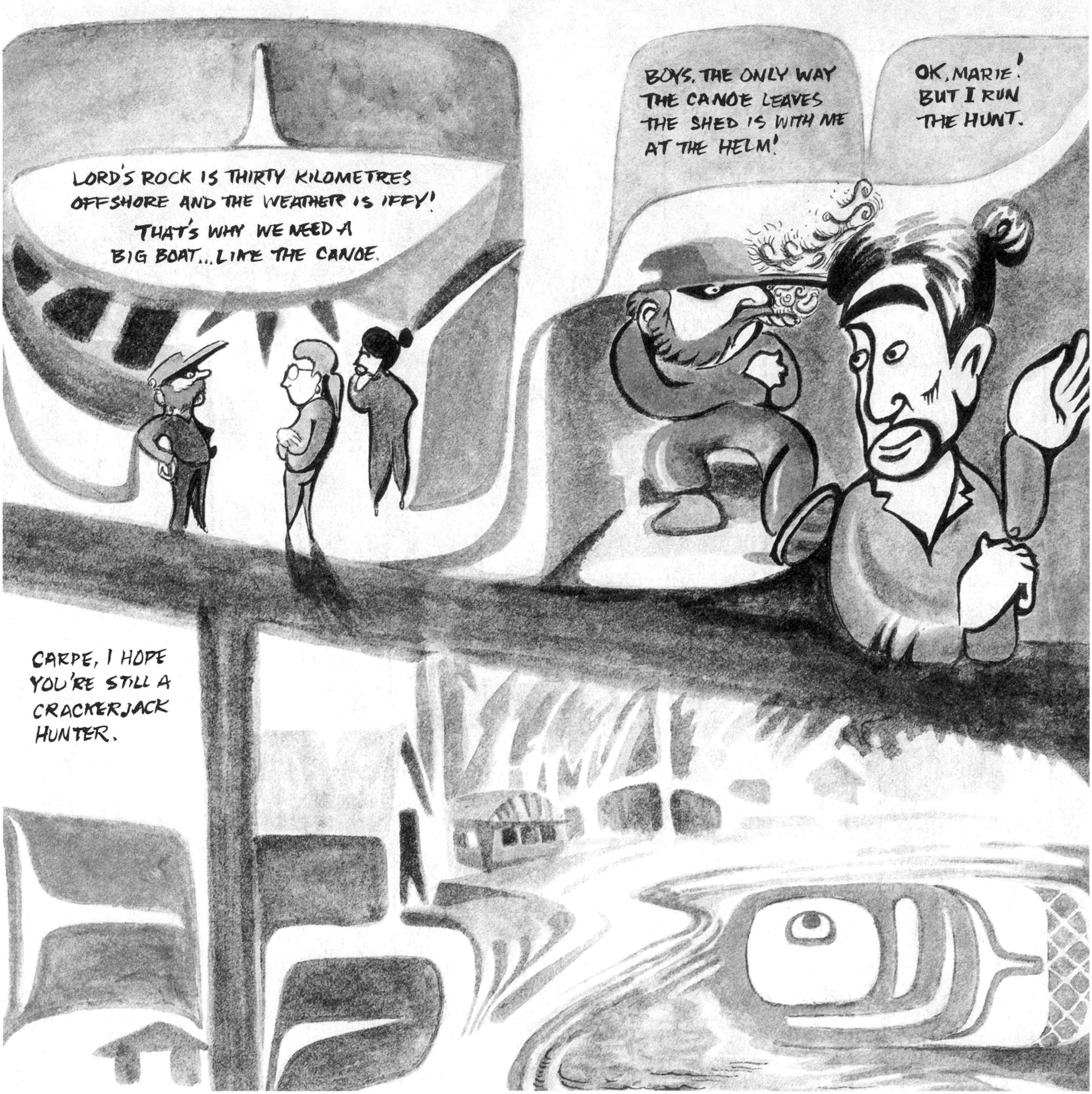
LORD'S ROCK IS THIRTY KILOMETRES OFFSHORE AND THE WEATHER IS IFFY! THAT'S WHY WE NEED A BIG BOAT... LIKE THE CANOE.
BOYS, THE ONLY WAY THE CANOE LEAVES THE SHED IS WITH ME AT THE HELM!
OK, MARIE! BUT I RUN THE HUNT.
CARPE, I HOPE YOU'RE STILL A CRACKERJACK HUNTER.

THE PADDLES LOOK IN GOOD SHAPE.

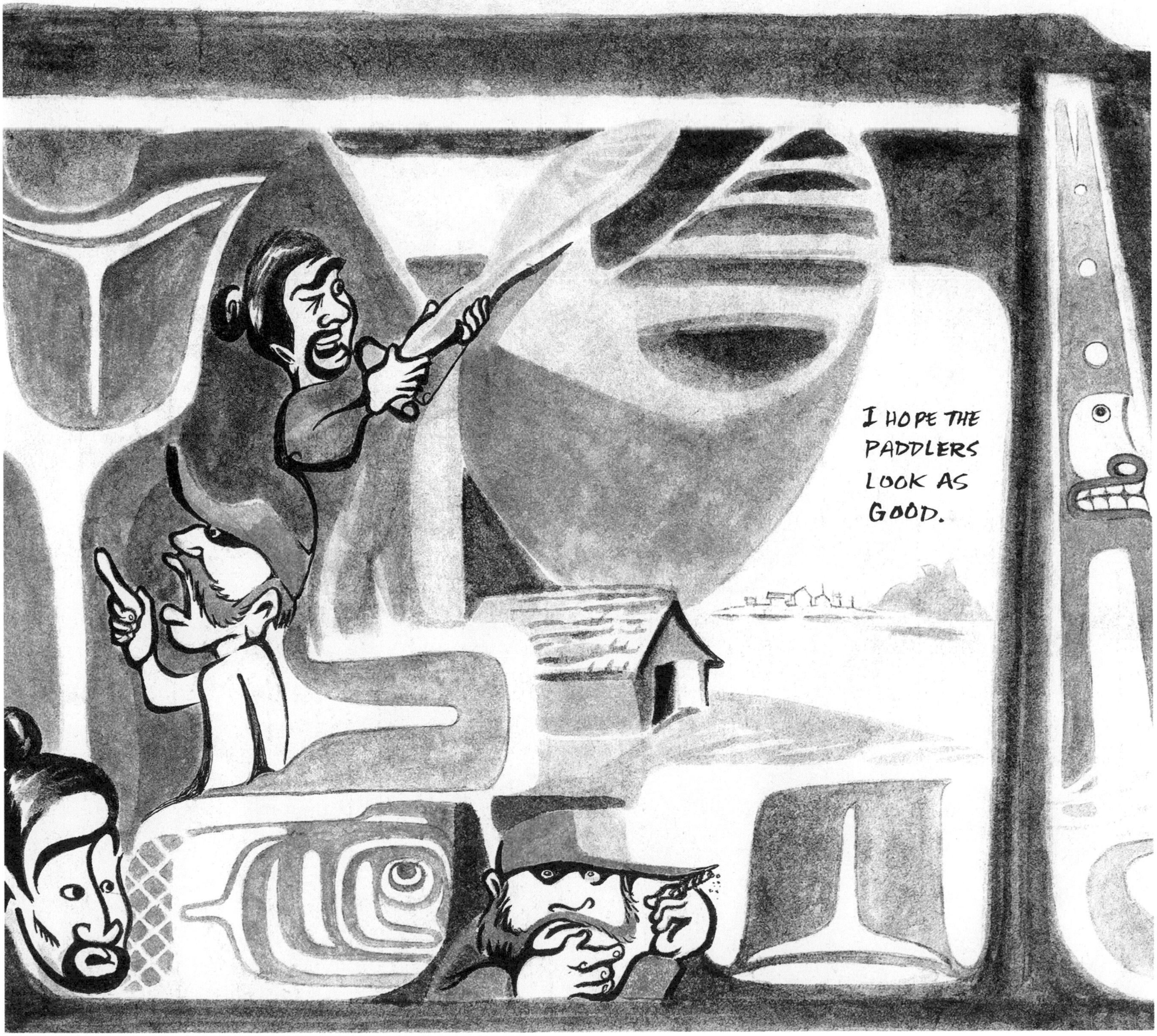
I HOPE THE PADDLERS LOOK AS GOOD.

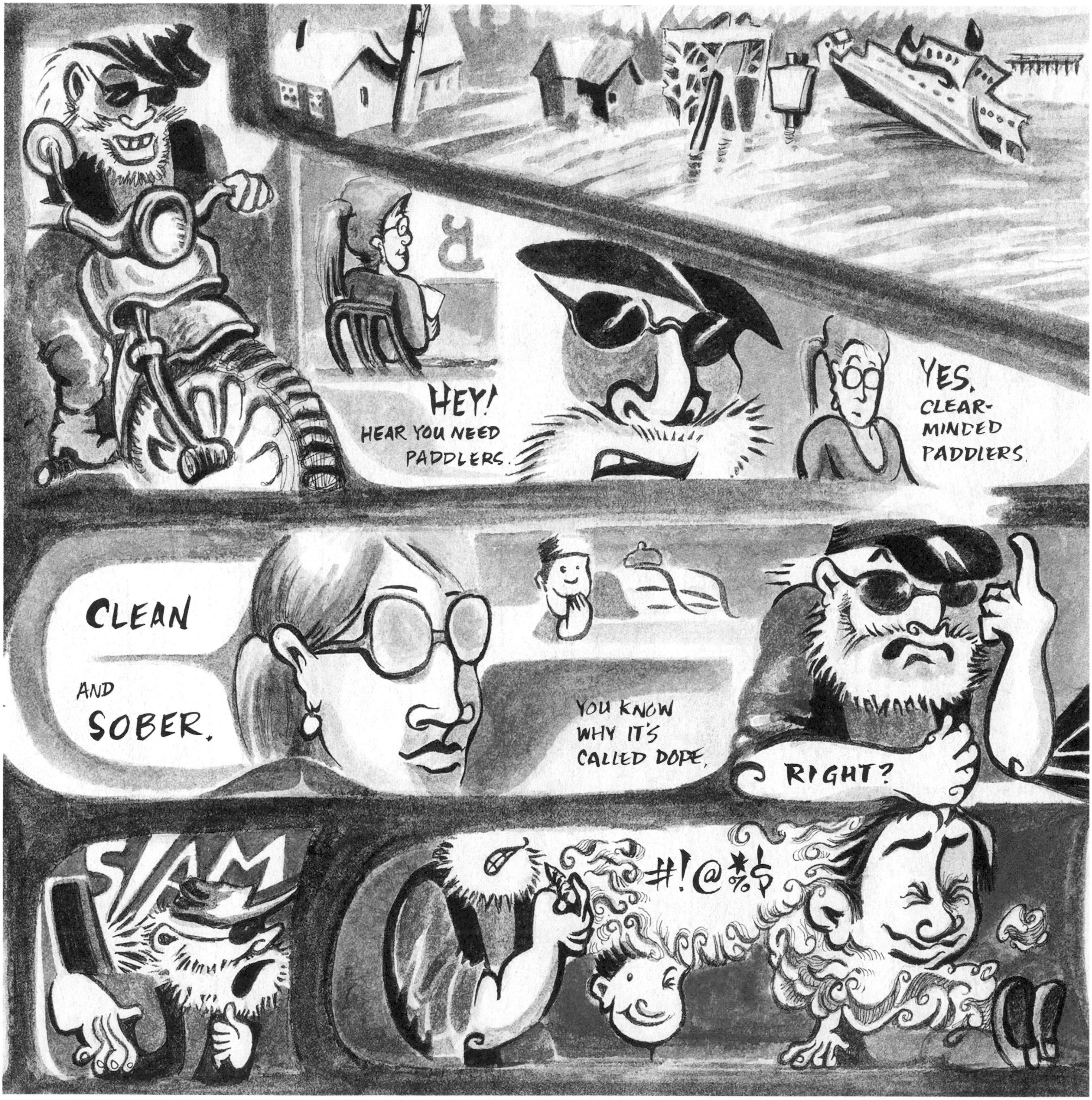
HEY!
HEAR YOU NEED PADDLERS.
YES. CLEAR-MINDED PADDLERS.
CLEAN
AND
SOBER.
YOU KNOW WHY IT'S CALLED DOPE,
RIGHT?
SLAM
#!@*%$

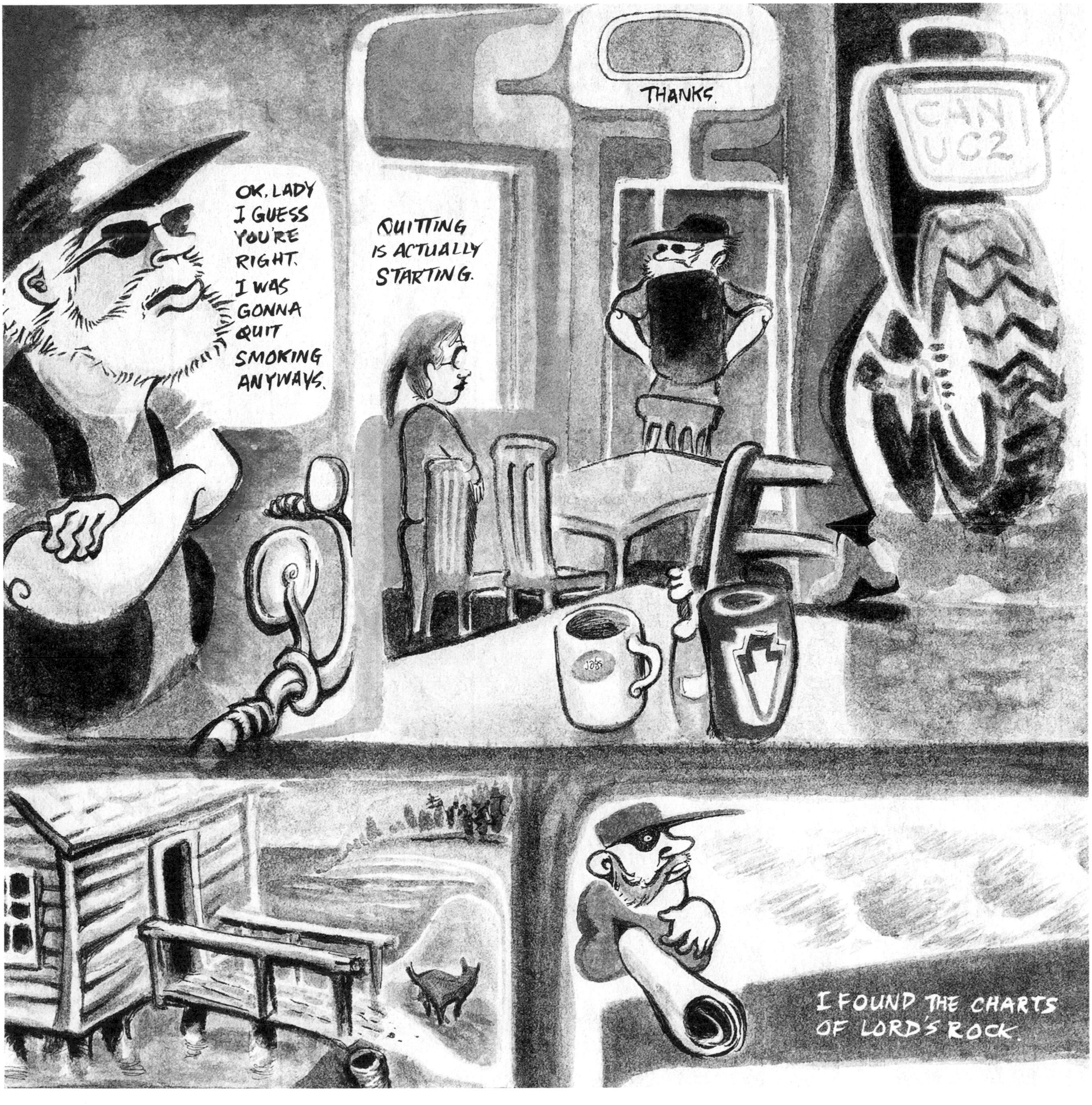
OK, LADY I GUESS YOU'RE RIGHT. I WAS GONNA QUIT SMOKING ANYWAYS.
QUITTING IS ACTUALLY STARTING.
THANKS.
CAN UC2
I FOUND THE CHARTS OF LORD'S ROCK.

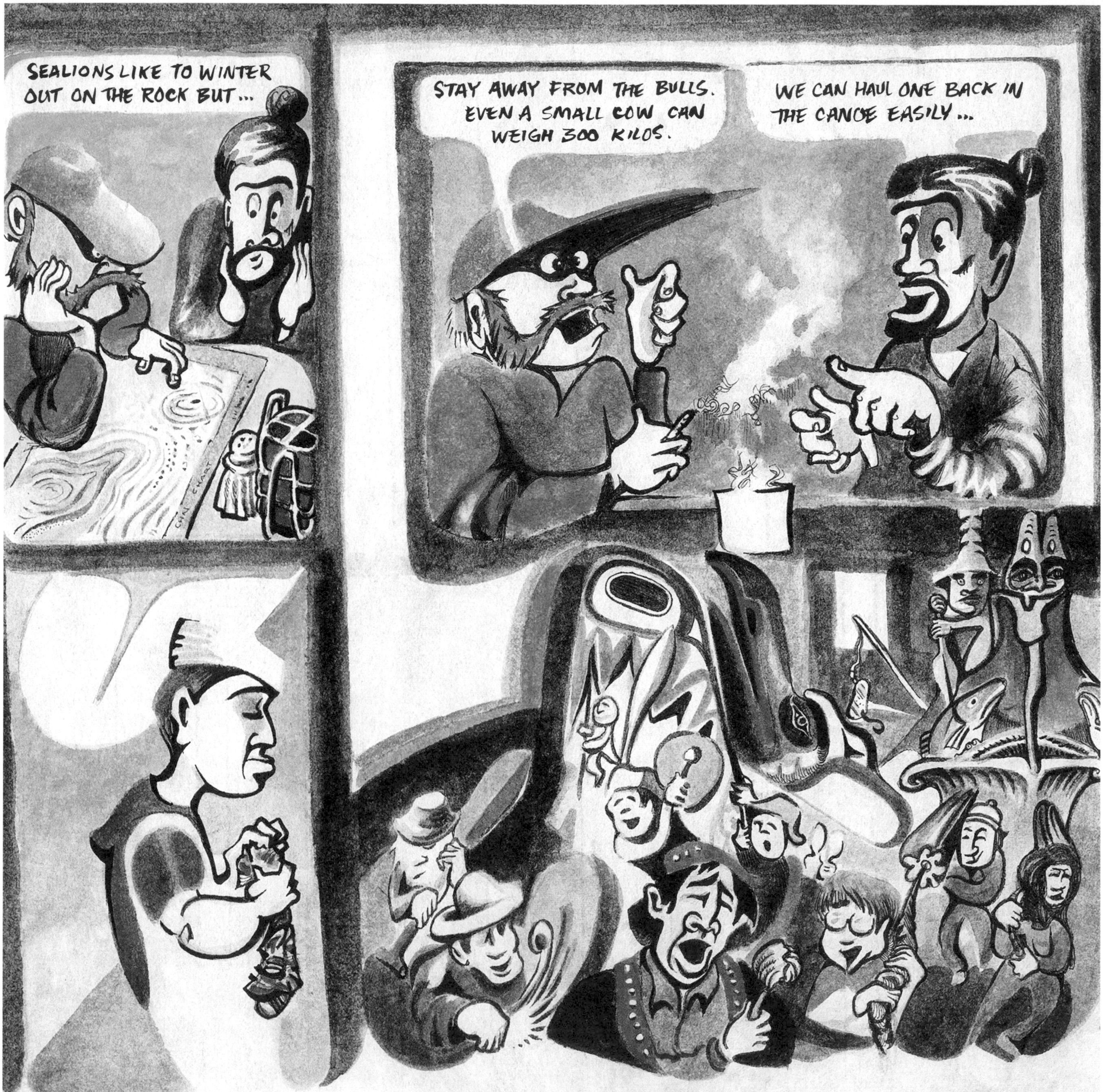
SEALIONS LIKE TO WINTER OUT ON THE ROCK BUT...
STAY AWAY FROM THE BULLS. EVEN A SMALL COW CAN WEIGH 300 KILOS.
WE CAN HAUL ONE BACK IN THE CANOE EASILY...

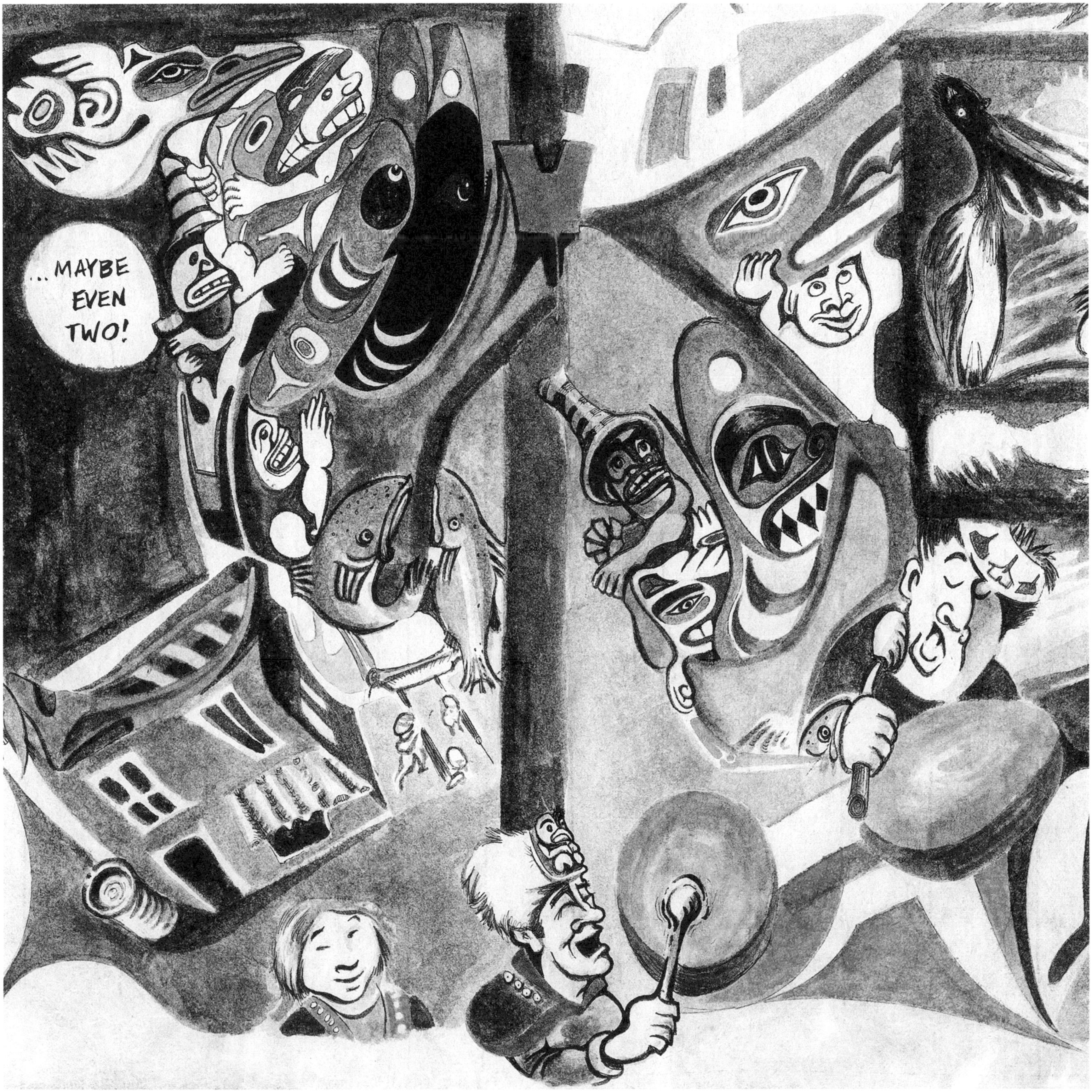
...MAYBE EVEN TWO!

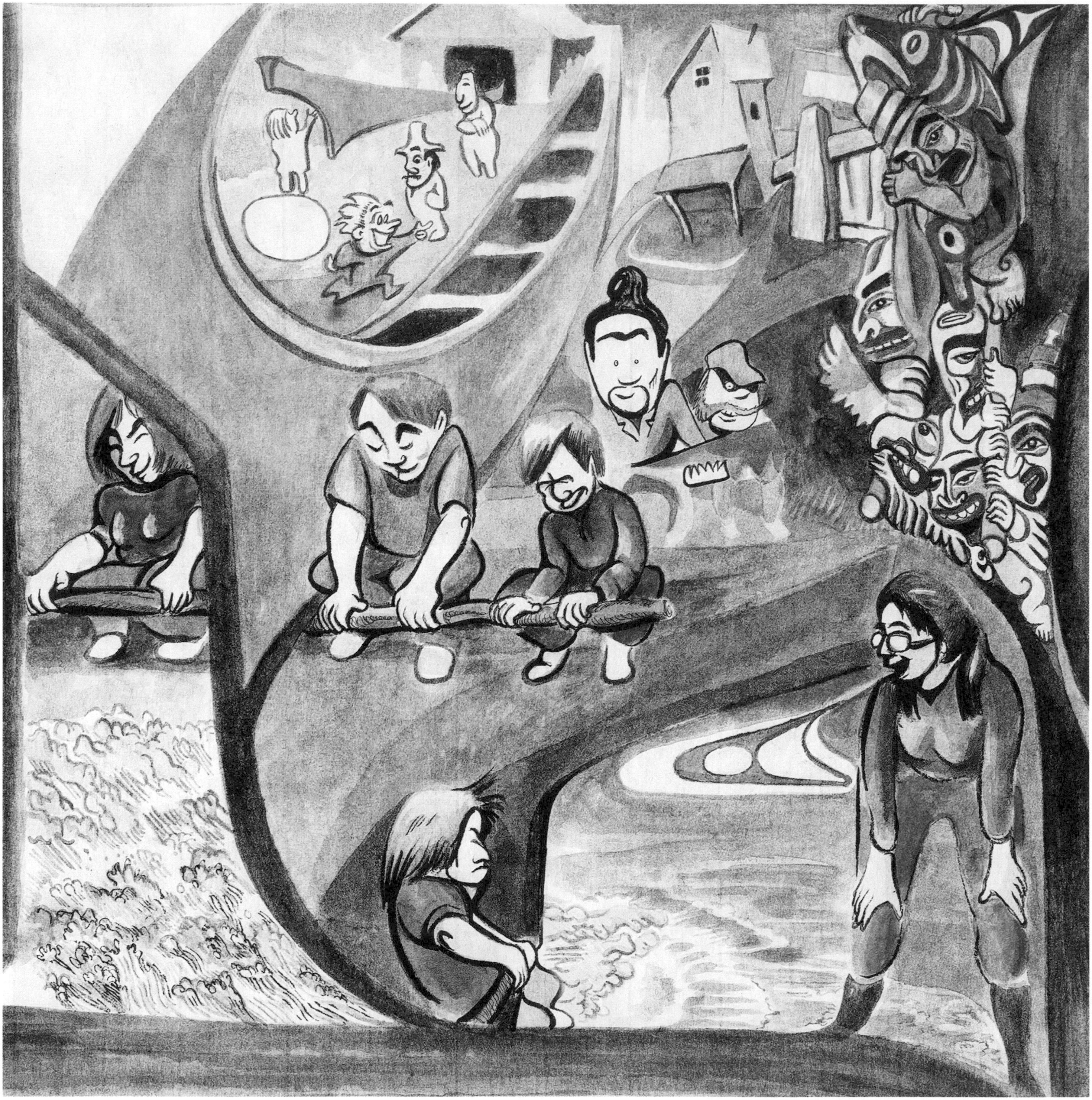

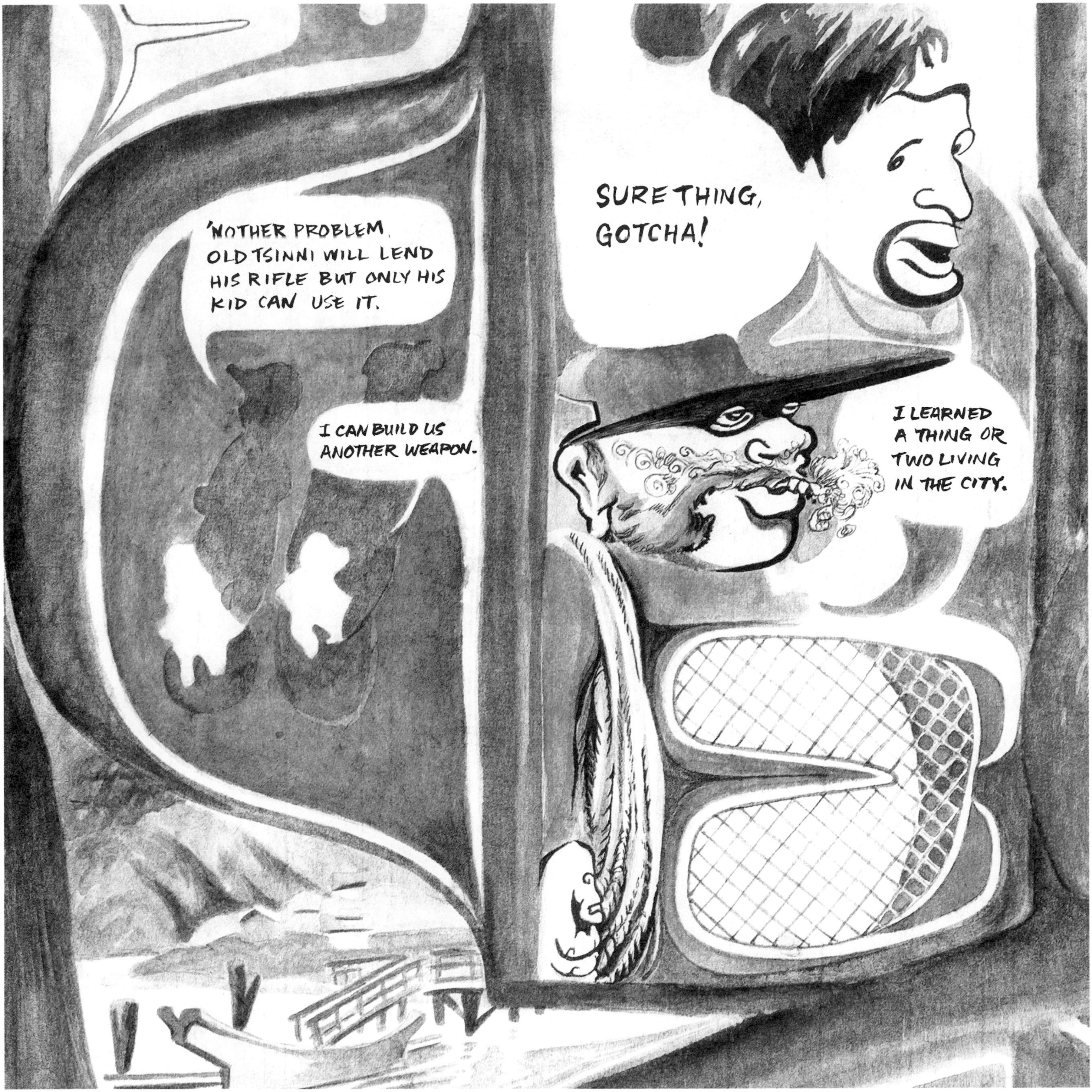
'NOTHER PROBLEM. OLD TSINNI WILL LEND HIS RIFLE BUT ONLY HIS KID CAN USE IT.
SURE THING, GOTCHA!
I CAN BUILD US ANOTHER WEAPON.
I LEARNED A THING OR TWO LIVING IN THE CITY.

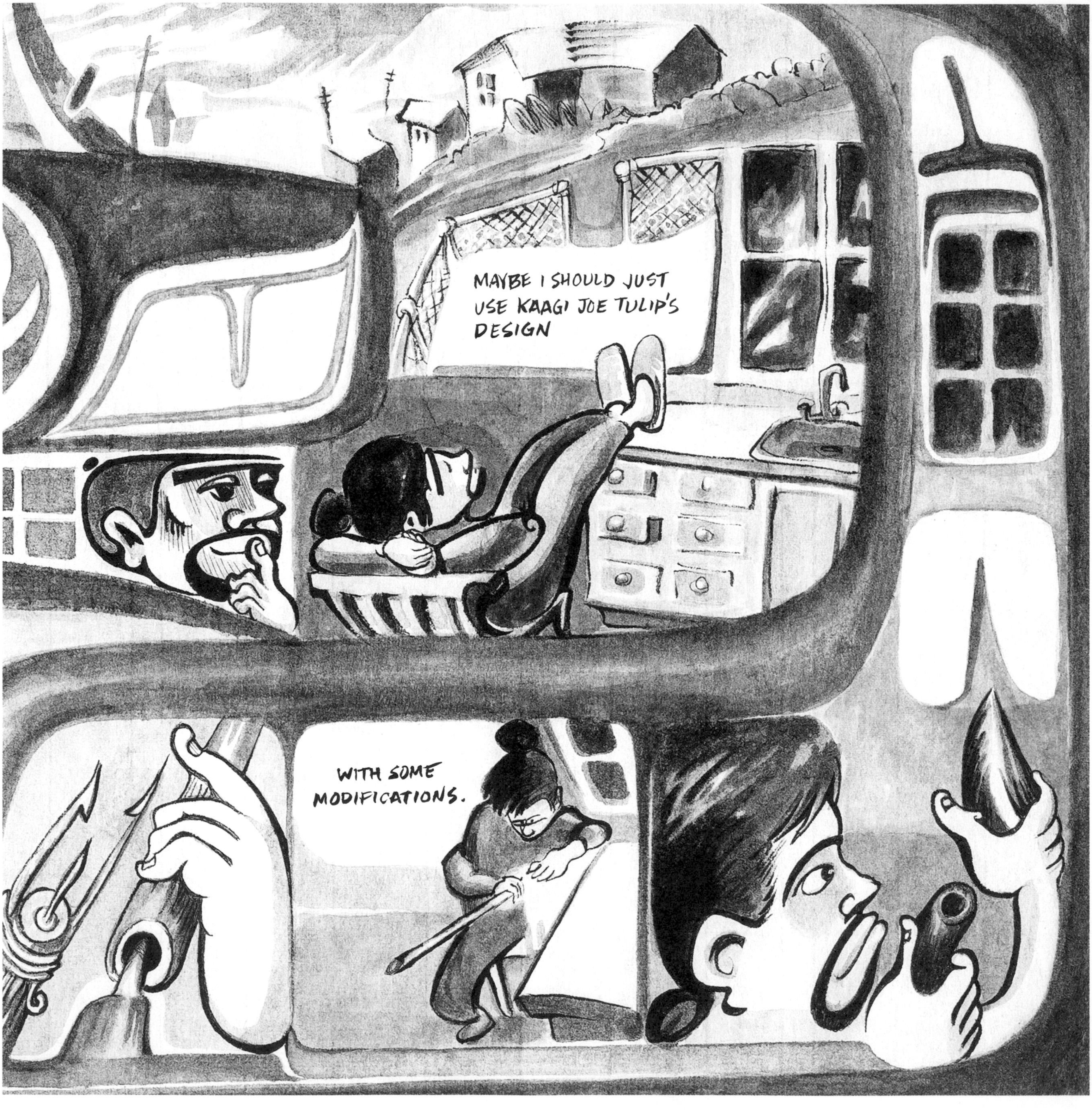
MAYBE I SHOULD JUST USE KAAGI JOE TULIP'S DESIGN
WITH SOME MODIFICATIONS.

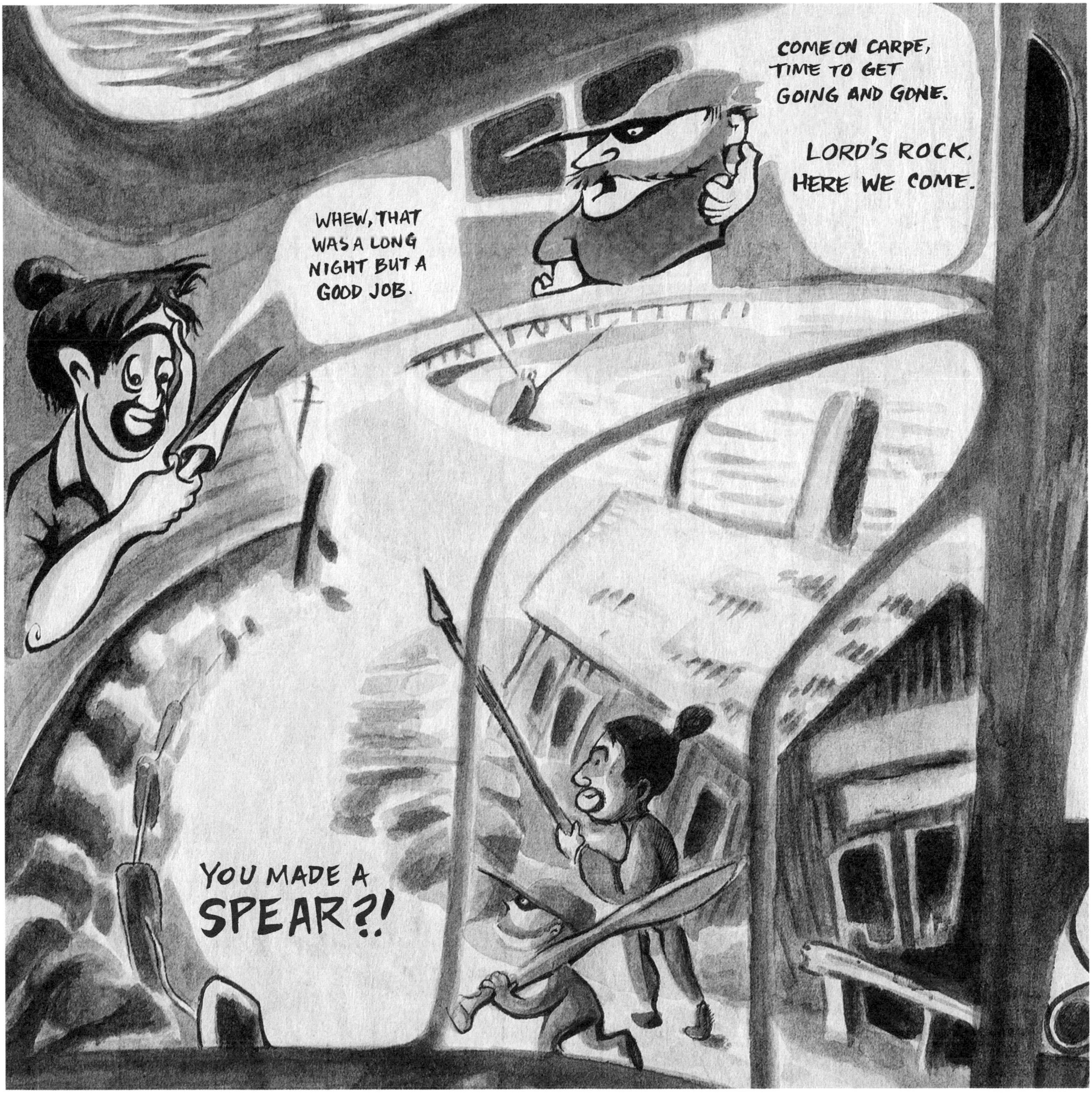
COME ON CARPE, TIME TO GET GOING AND GONE.
LORD'S ROCK. HERE WE COME.
WHEW, THAT WAS A LONG NIGHT BUT A GOOD JOB.
YOU MADE A SPEAR?!

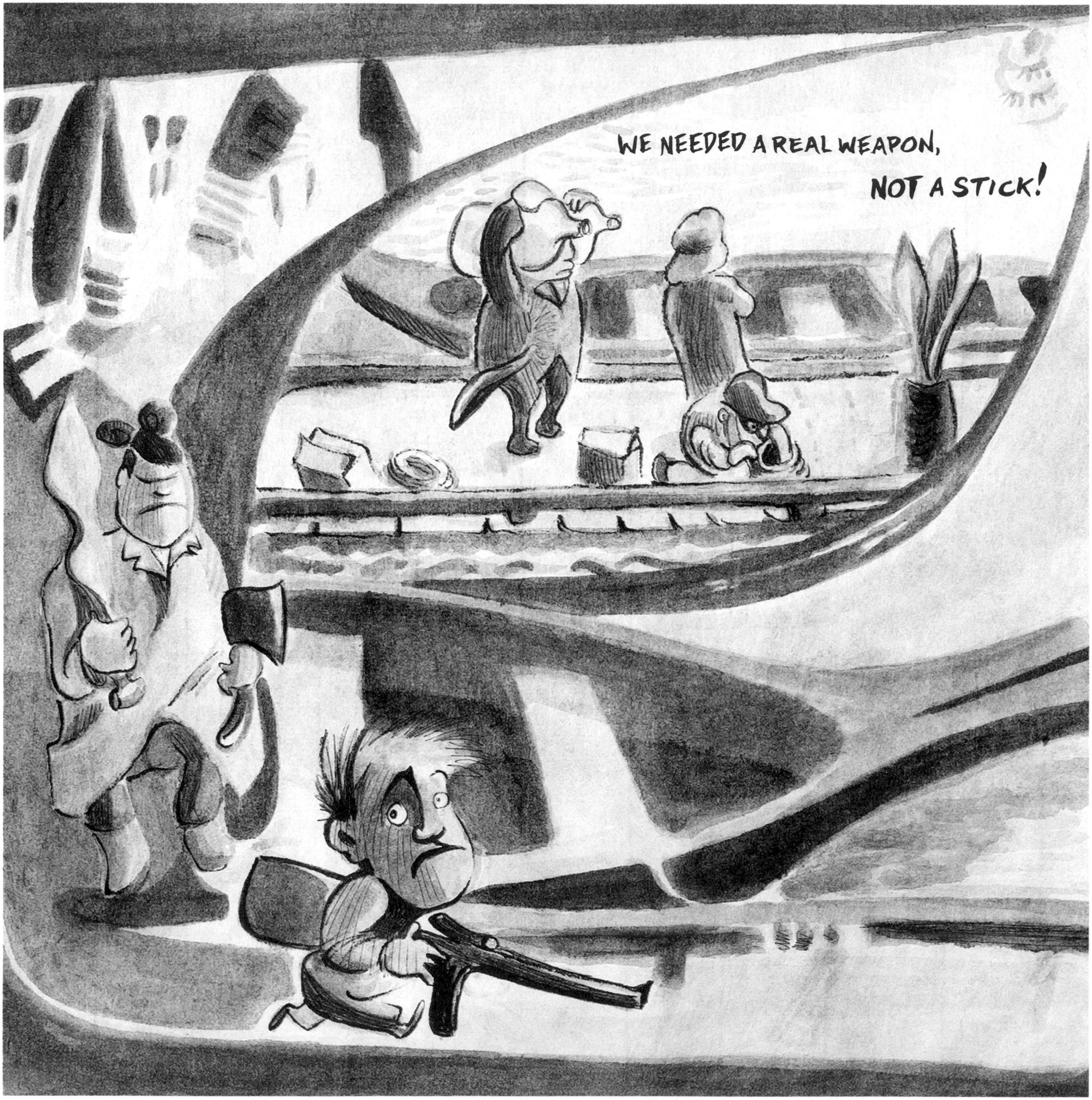
WE NEEDED A REAL WEAPON,
NOT A STICK!

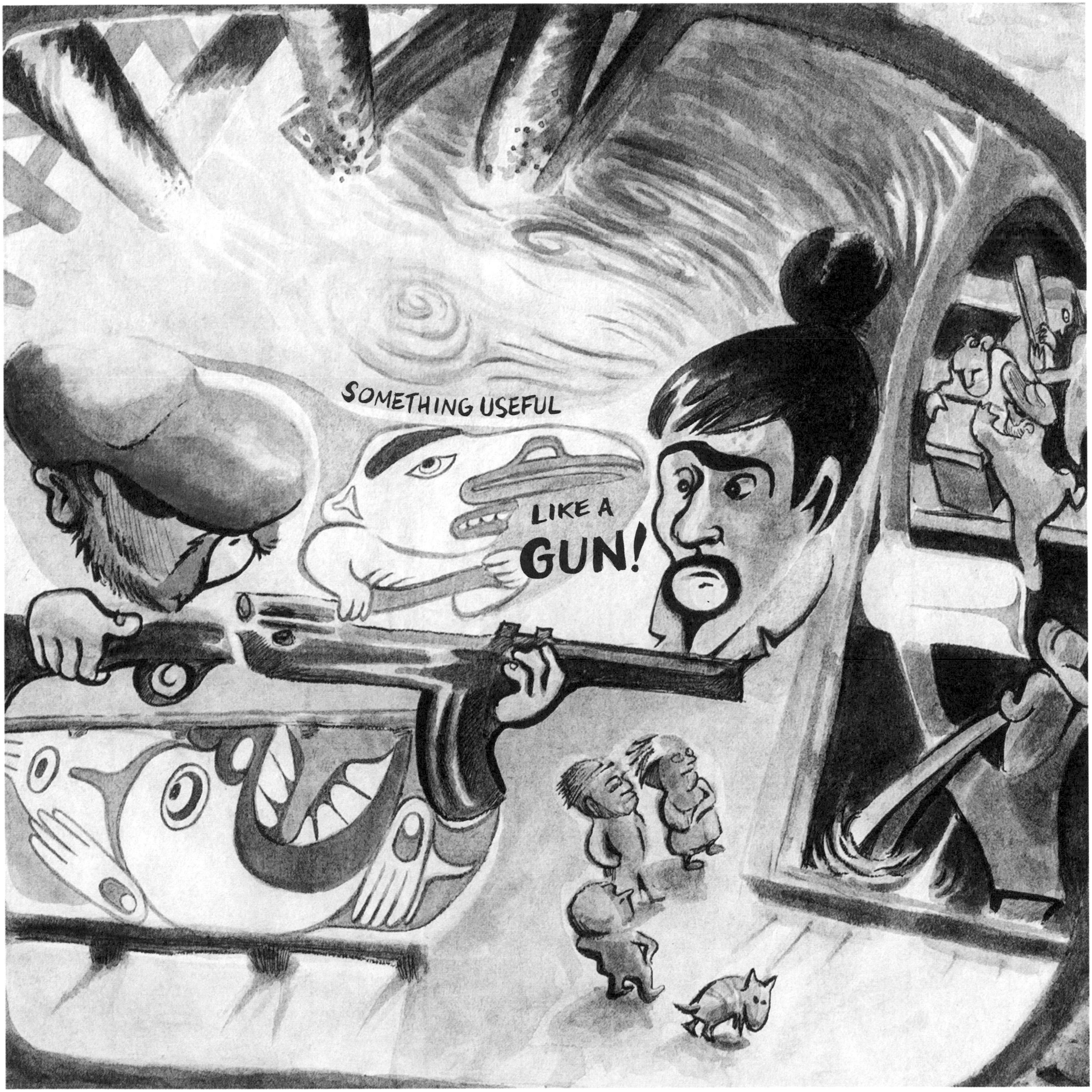
SOMETHING USEFUL
LIKE A
GUN!

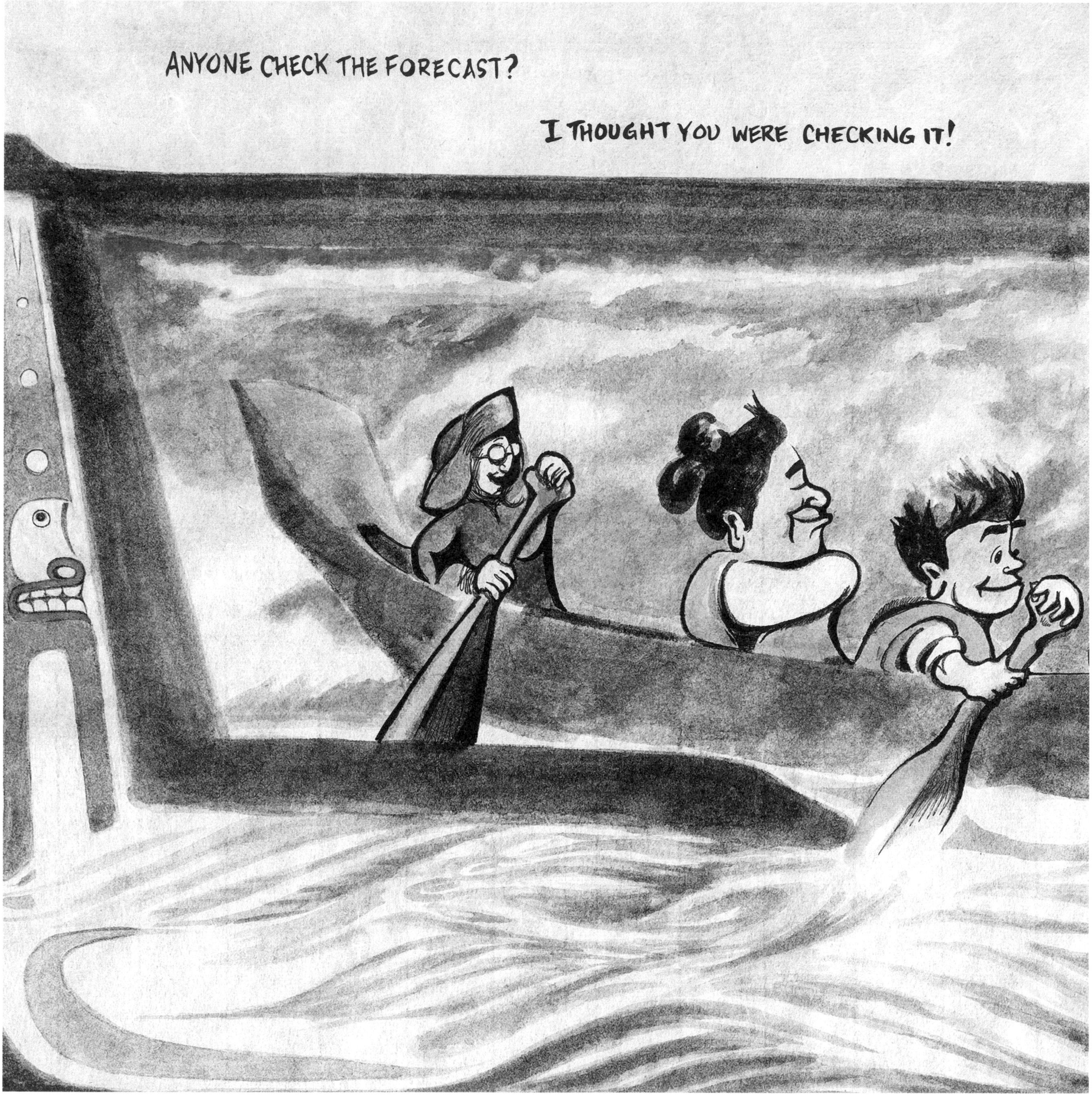
ANYONE CHECK THE FORECAST?
I THOUGHT YOU WERE CHECKING IT!

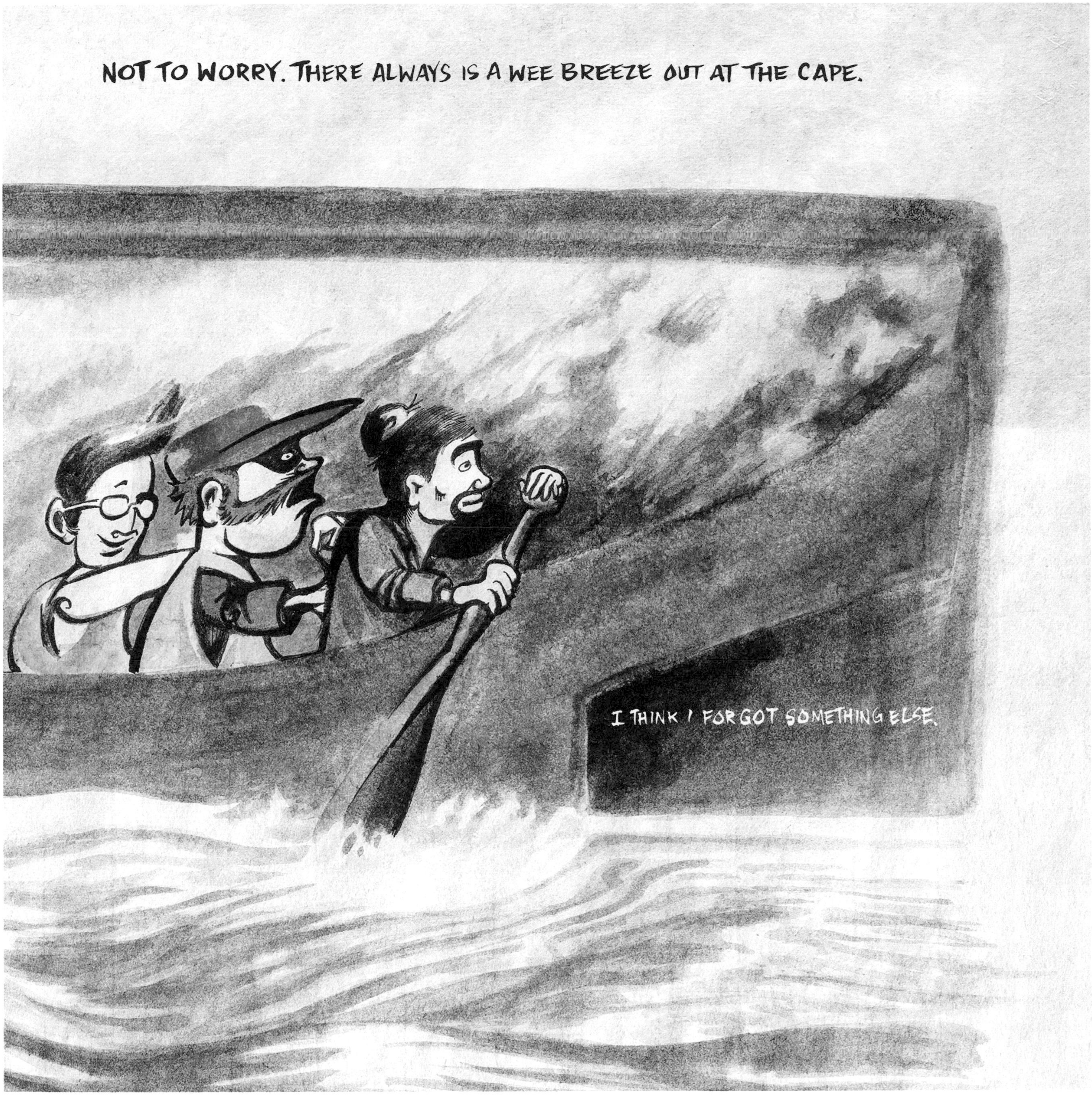
NOT TO WORRY. THERE ALWAYS IS A WEE BREEZE OUT AT THE CAPE.
I THINK I FORGOT SOMETHING ELSE.

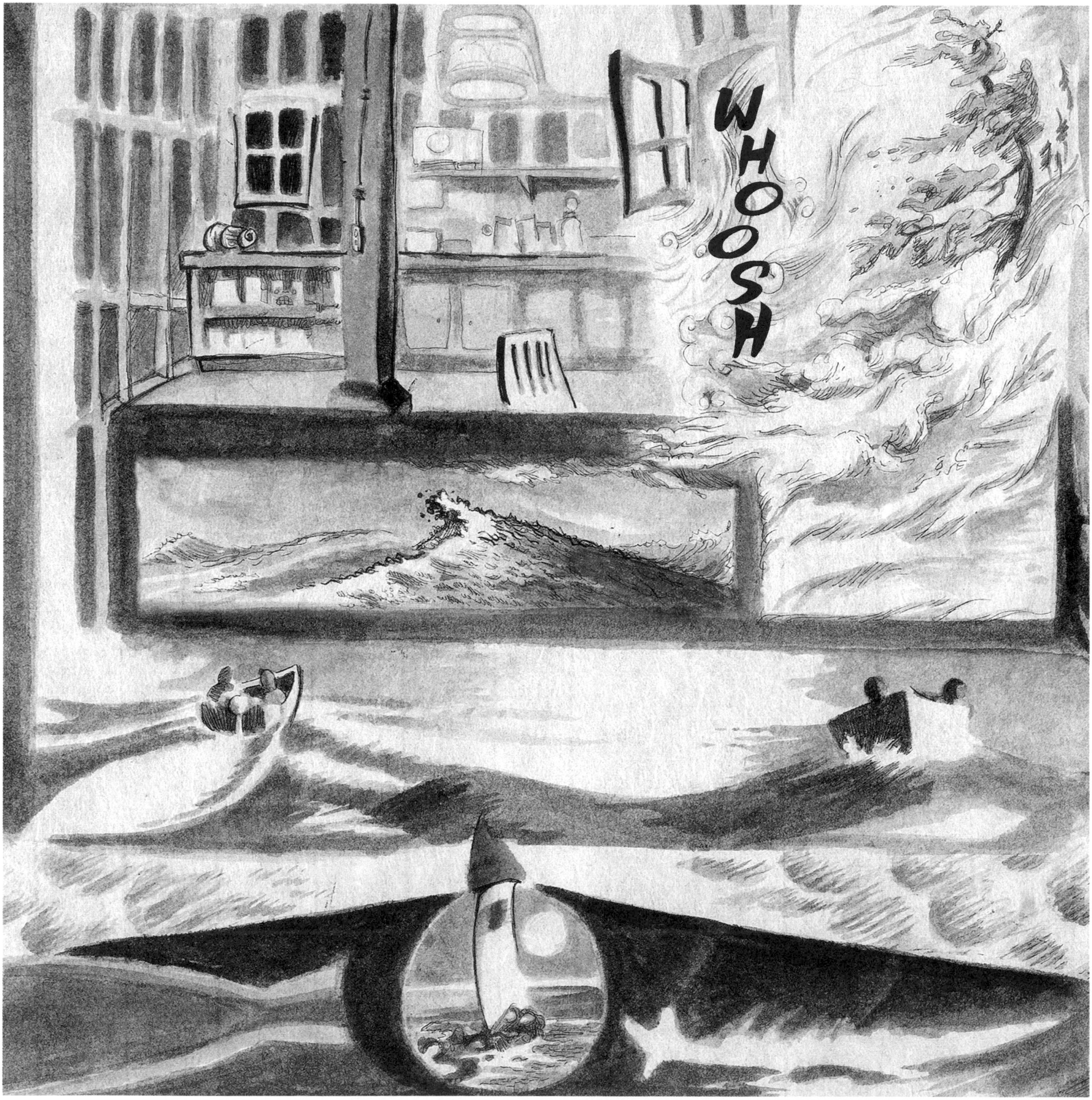
WHOOSH

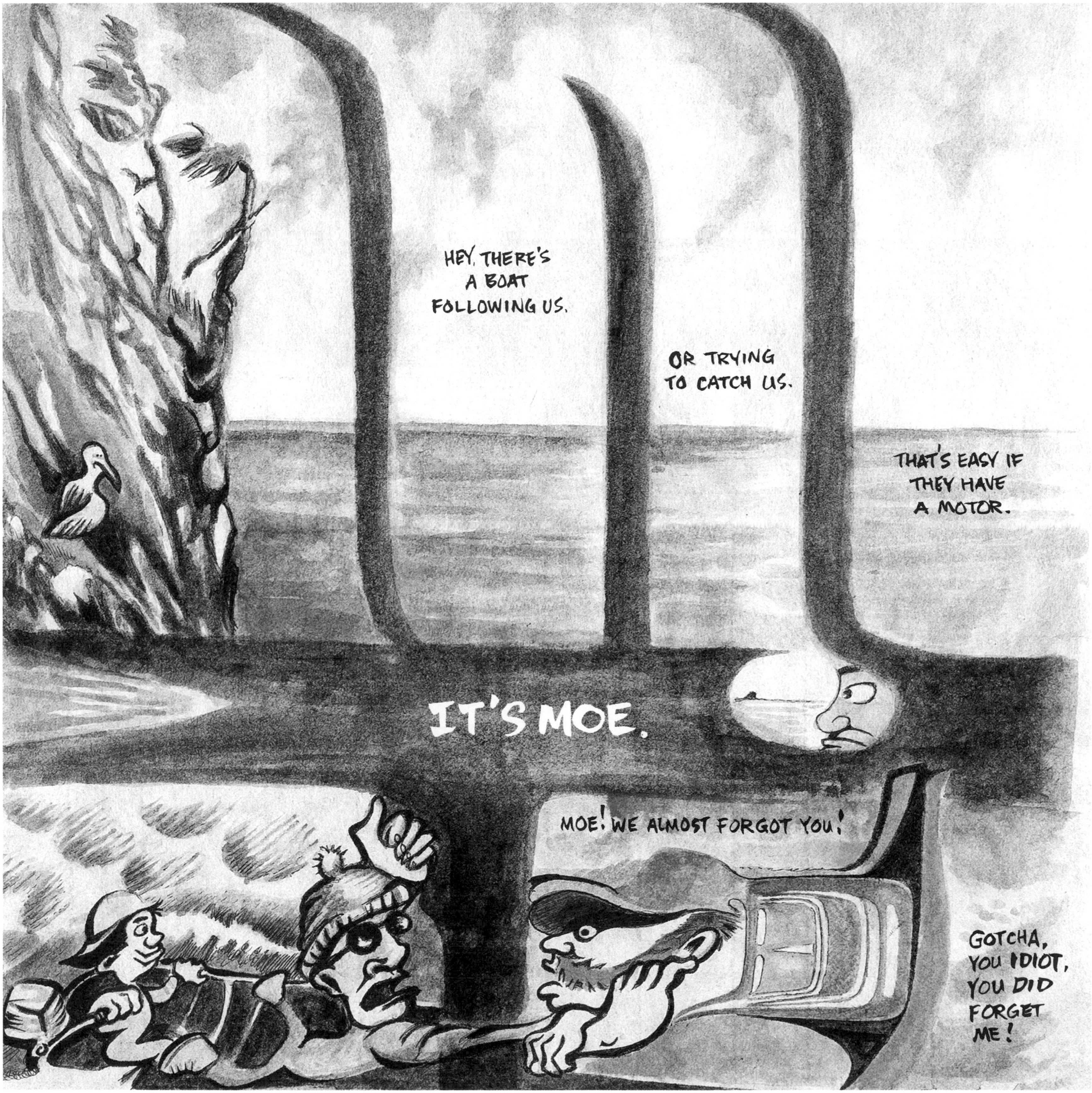
HEY, THERE'S A BOAT FOLLOWING US.
OR TRYING TO CATCH US.
THAT'S EASY IF THEY HAVE A MOTOR.
IT'S MOE.
MOE! WE ALMOST FORGOT YOU!
GOTCHA, YOU IDIOT, YOU DID FORGET ME!

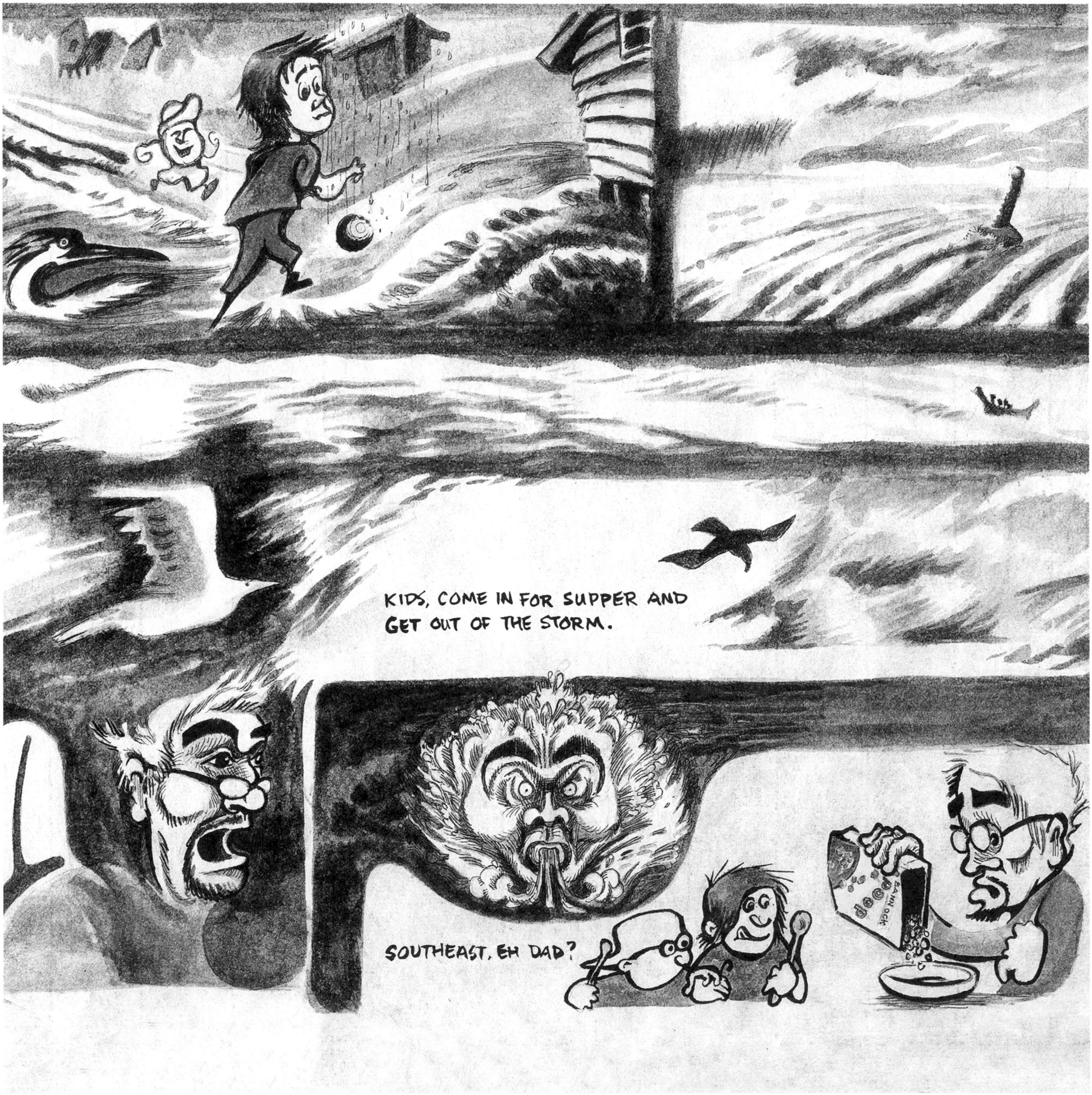
KIDS, COME IN FOR SUPPER AND GET OUT OF THE STORM.
SOUTHEAST, EH DAD?

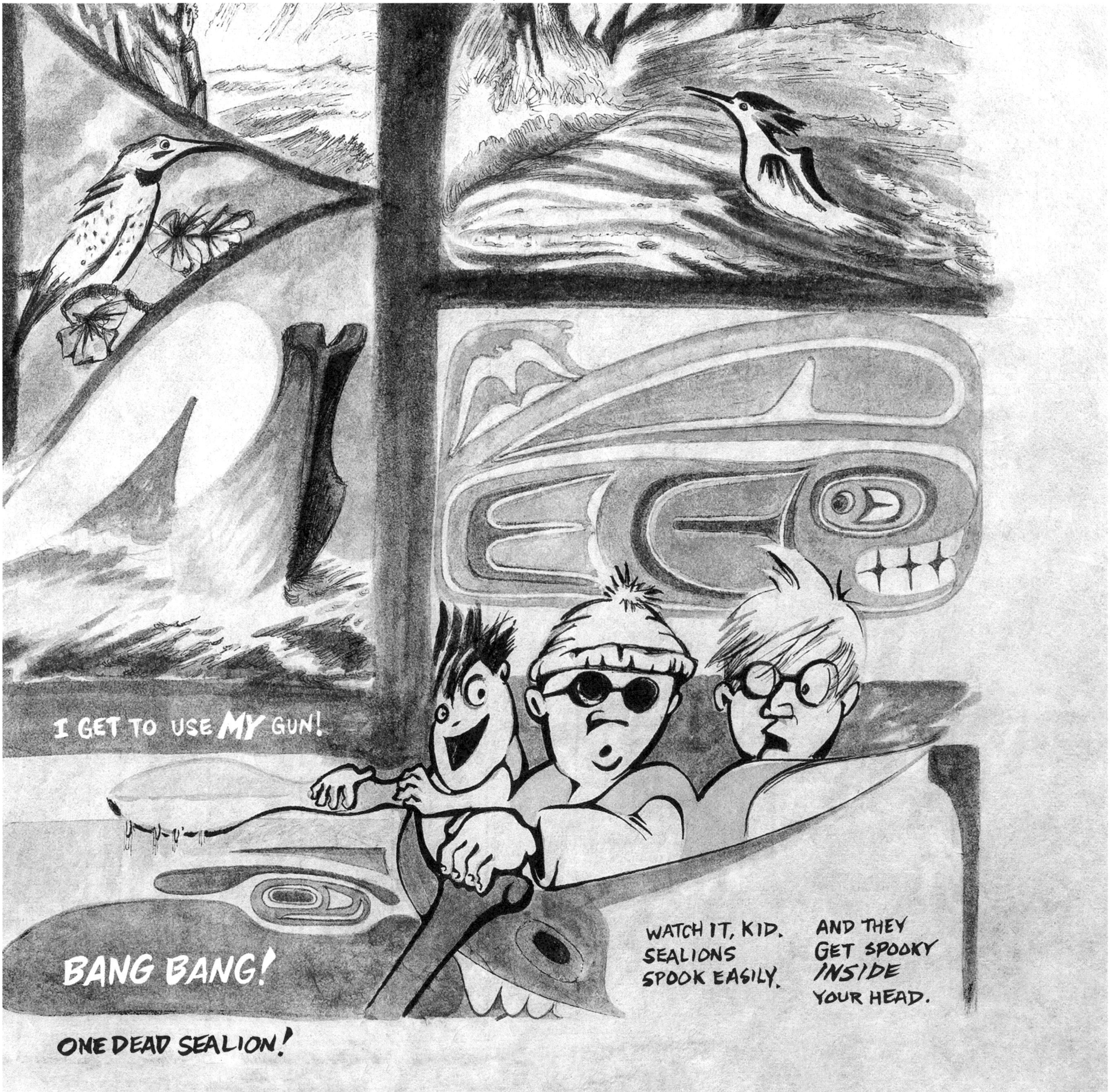
I GET TO USE MY GUN!
BANG BANG!
ONE DEAD SEALION!
WATCH IT, KID. SEALIONS SPOOK EASILY.
AND THEY GET SPOOKY INSIDE YOUR HEAD.

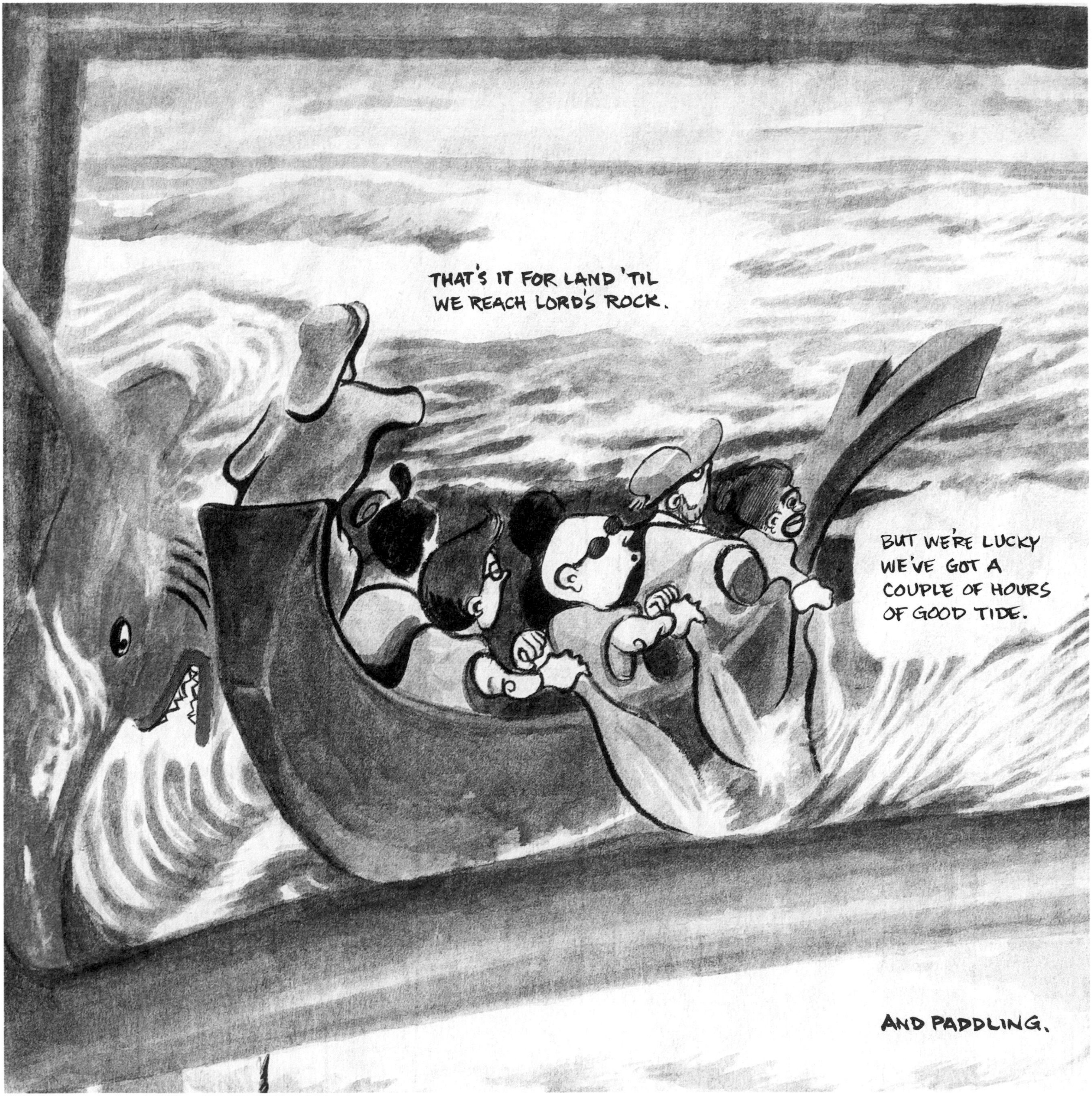
THAT'S IT FOR LAND 'TIL WE REACH LORD'S ROCK.
BUT WE'RE LUCKY WE'VE GOT A COUPLE OF HOURS OF GOOD TIDE.
AND PADDLING.

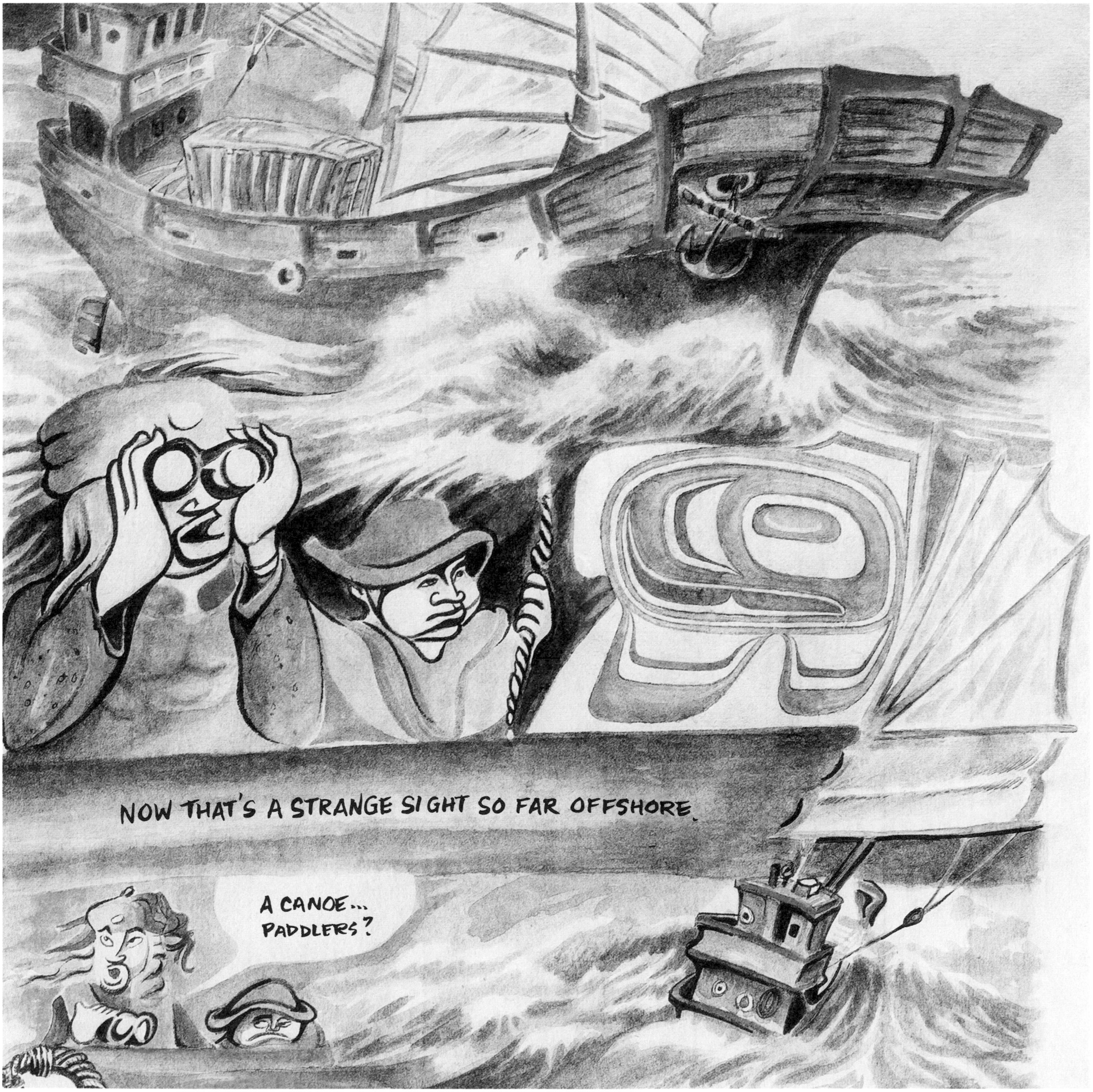
NOW THAT'S A STRANGE SIGHT SO FAR OFFSHORE.
A CANOE... PADDLERS?

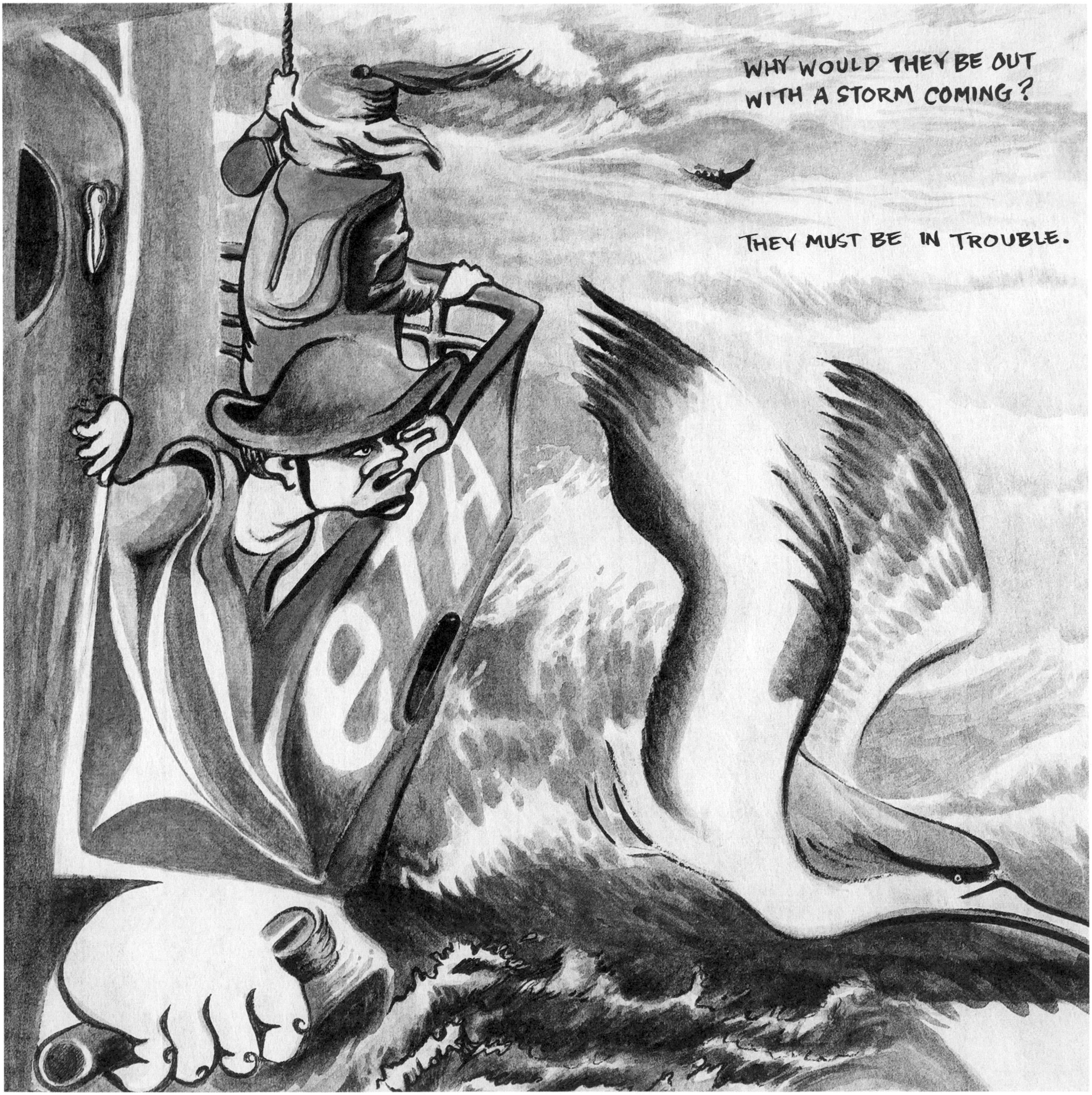
WHY WOULD THEY BE OUT WITH A STORM COMING?
THEY MUST BE IN TROUBLE.

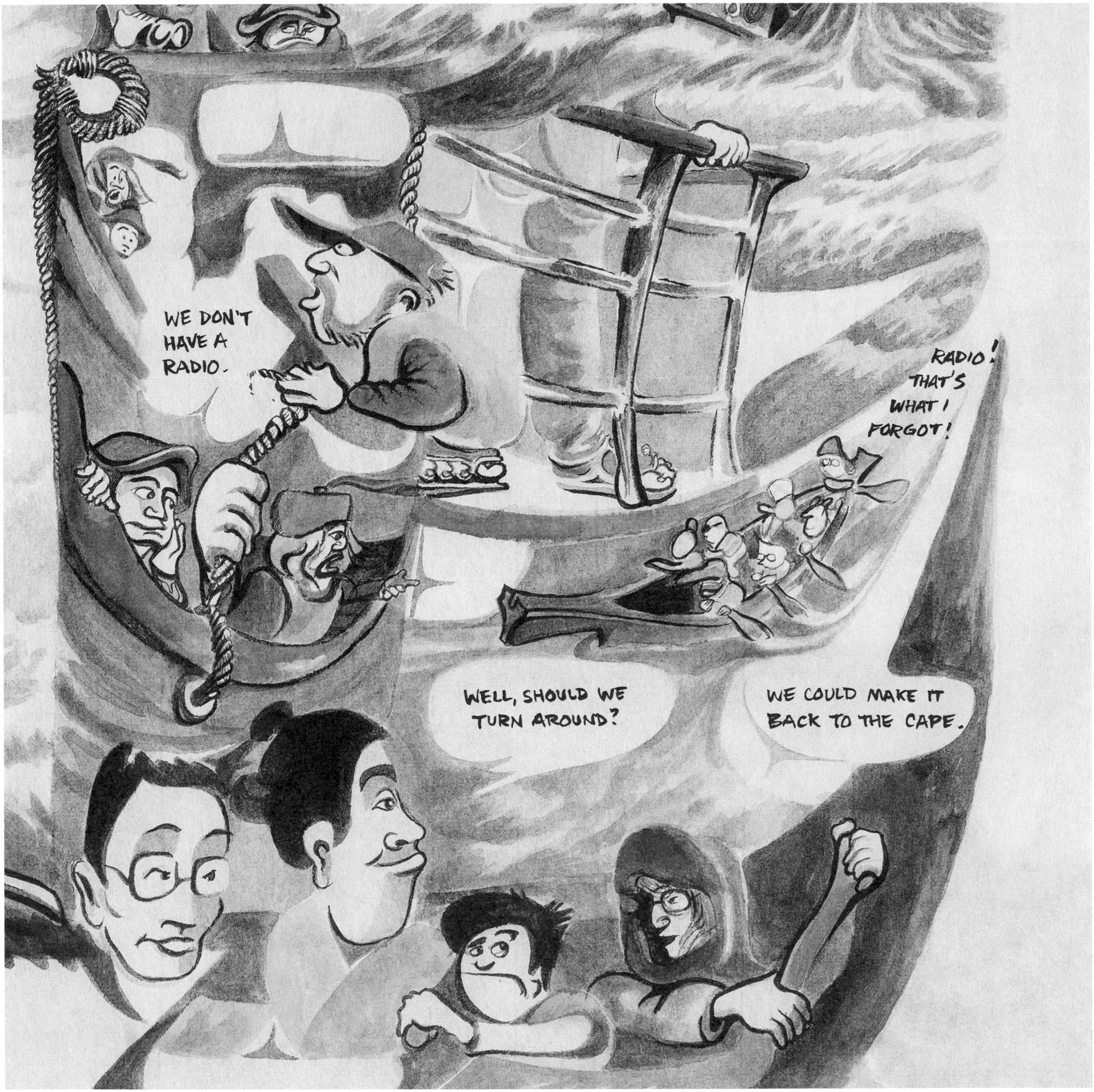
WE DON'T HAVE A RADIO.
RADIO! THAT'S WHAT I FORGOT!
WELL, SHOULD WE TURN AROUND?
WE COULD MAKE IT BACK TO THE CAPE.

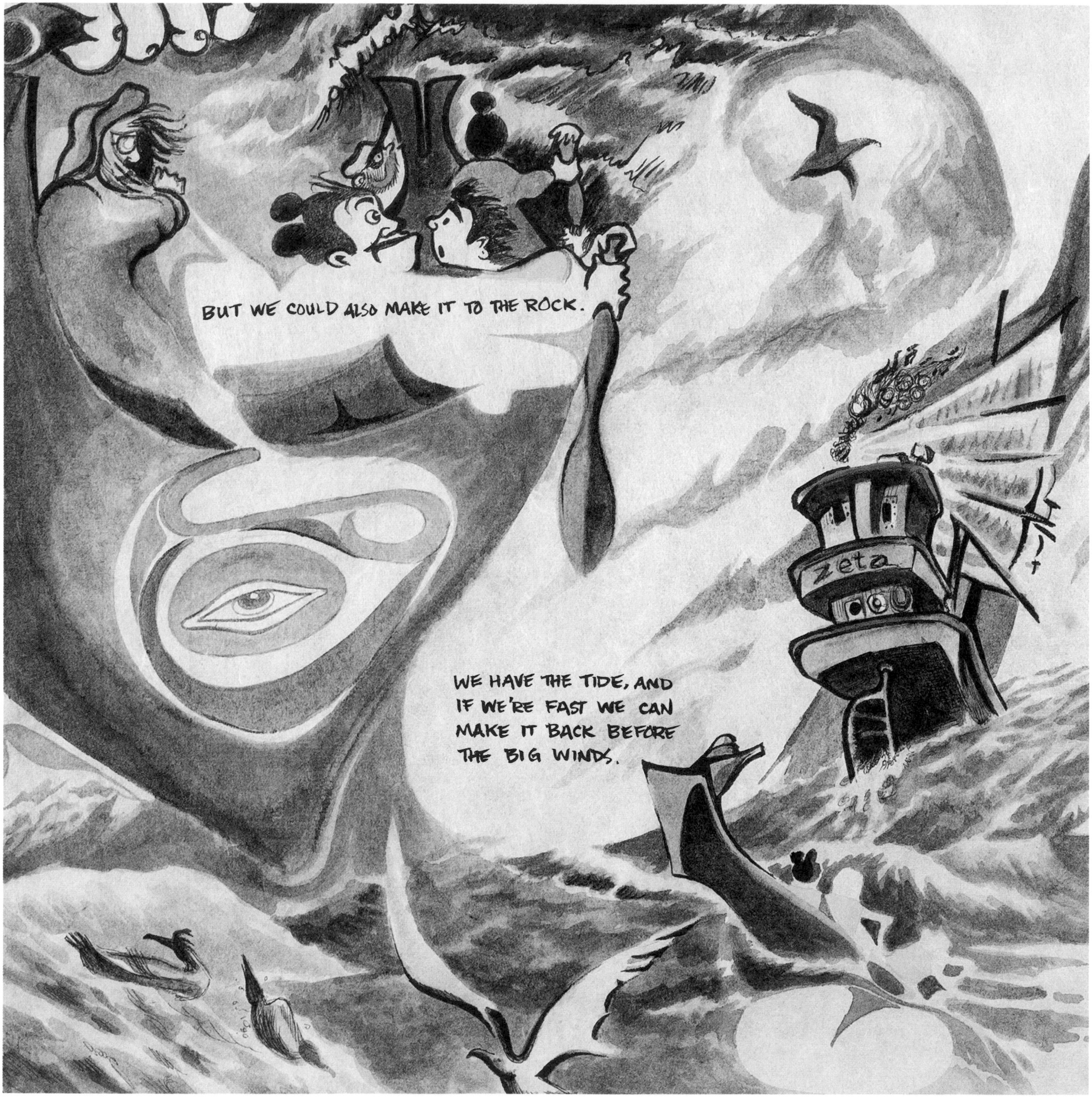
BUT WE COULD ALSO MAKE IT TO THE ROCK.
WE HAVE THE TIDE, AND IF WE'RE FAST WE CAN MAKE IT BACK BEFORE THE BIG WINDS.
zeta

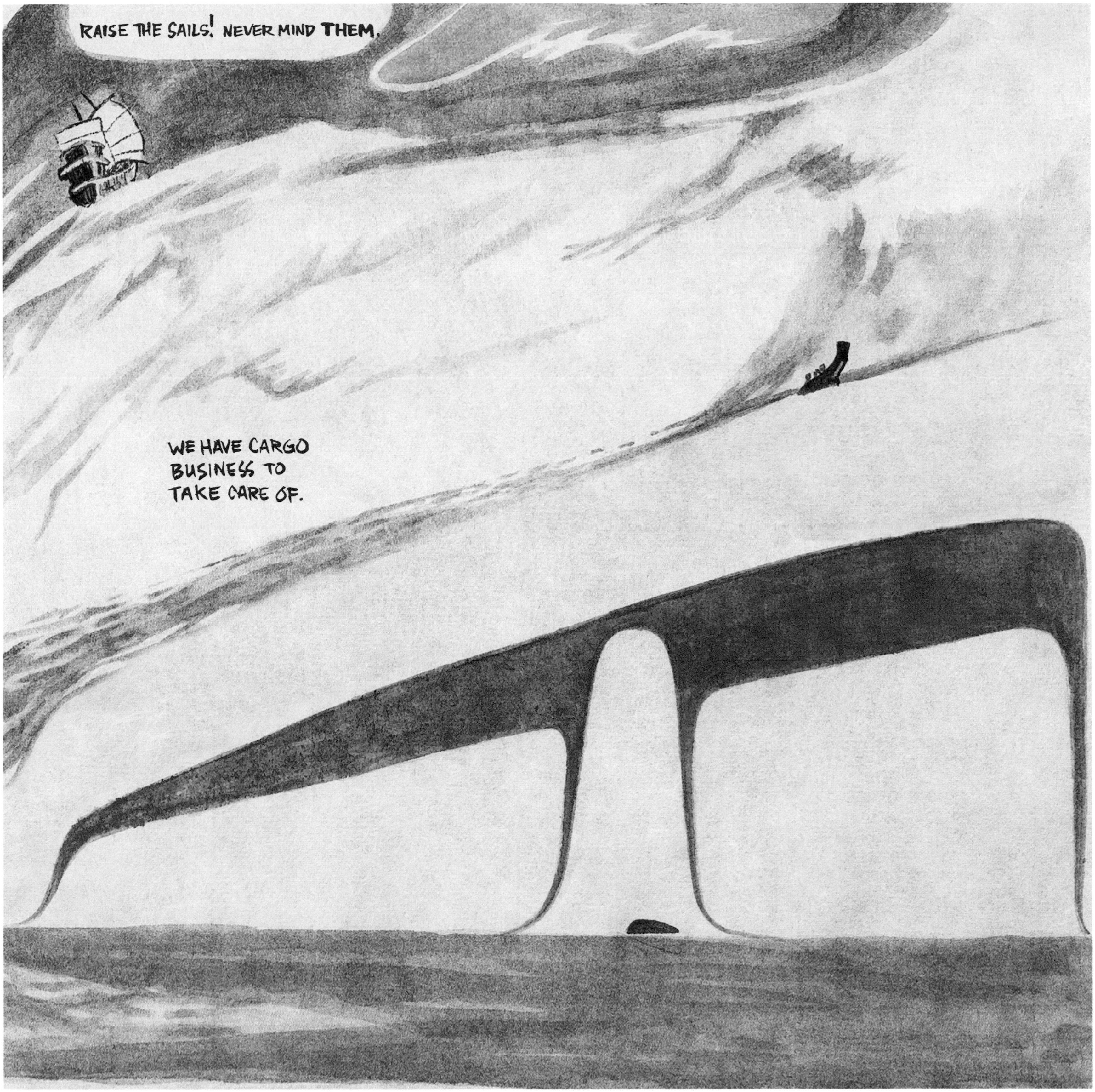
RAISE THE SAILS! NEVER MIND THEM.
WE HAVE CARGO BUSINESS TO TAKE CARE OF.

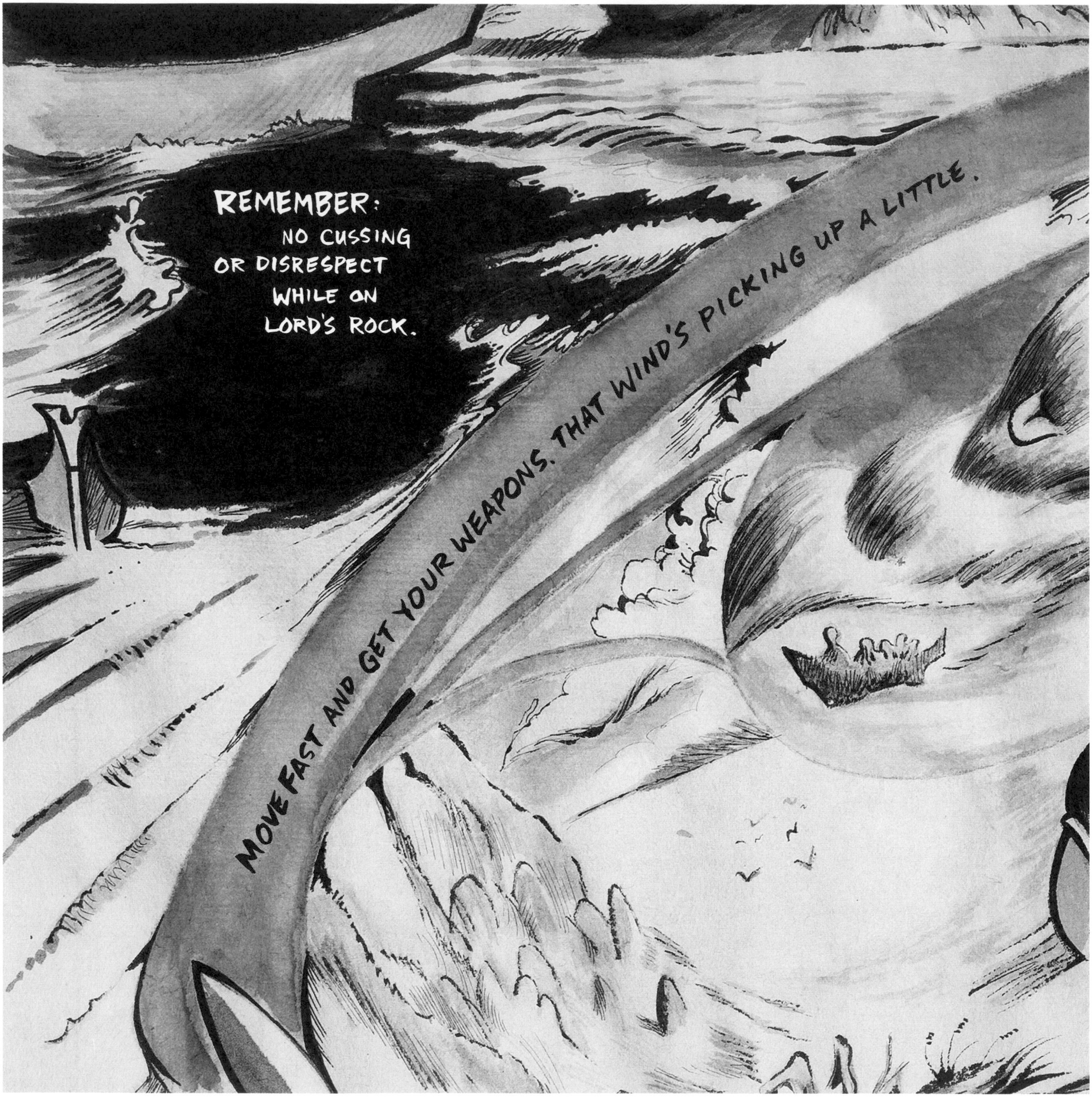

REMEMBER:
NO CUSSING
OR DISRESPECT
WHILE ON
LORD'S ROCK.
MOVE FAST AND GET YOUR WEAPONS. THAT WIND'S PICKING UP A LITTLE.

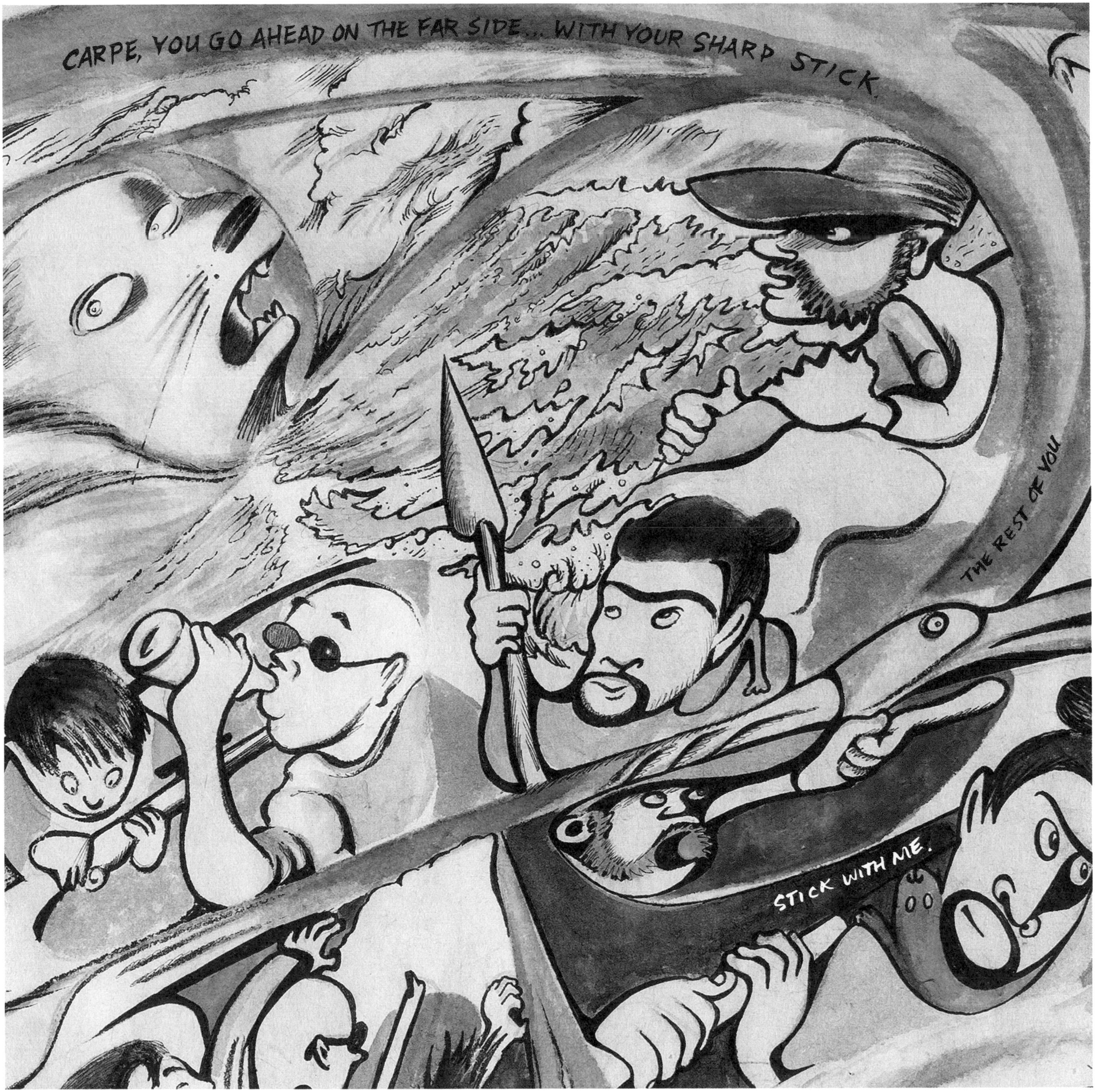
CARPE, YOU GO AHEAD ON THE FAR SIDE... WITH YOUR SHARP STICK.
THE REST OF YOU
STICK WITH ME.

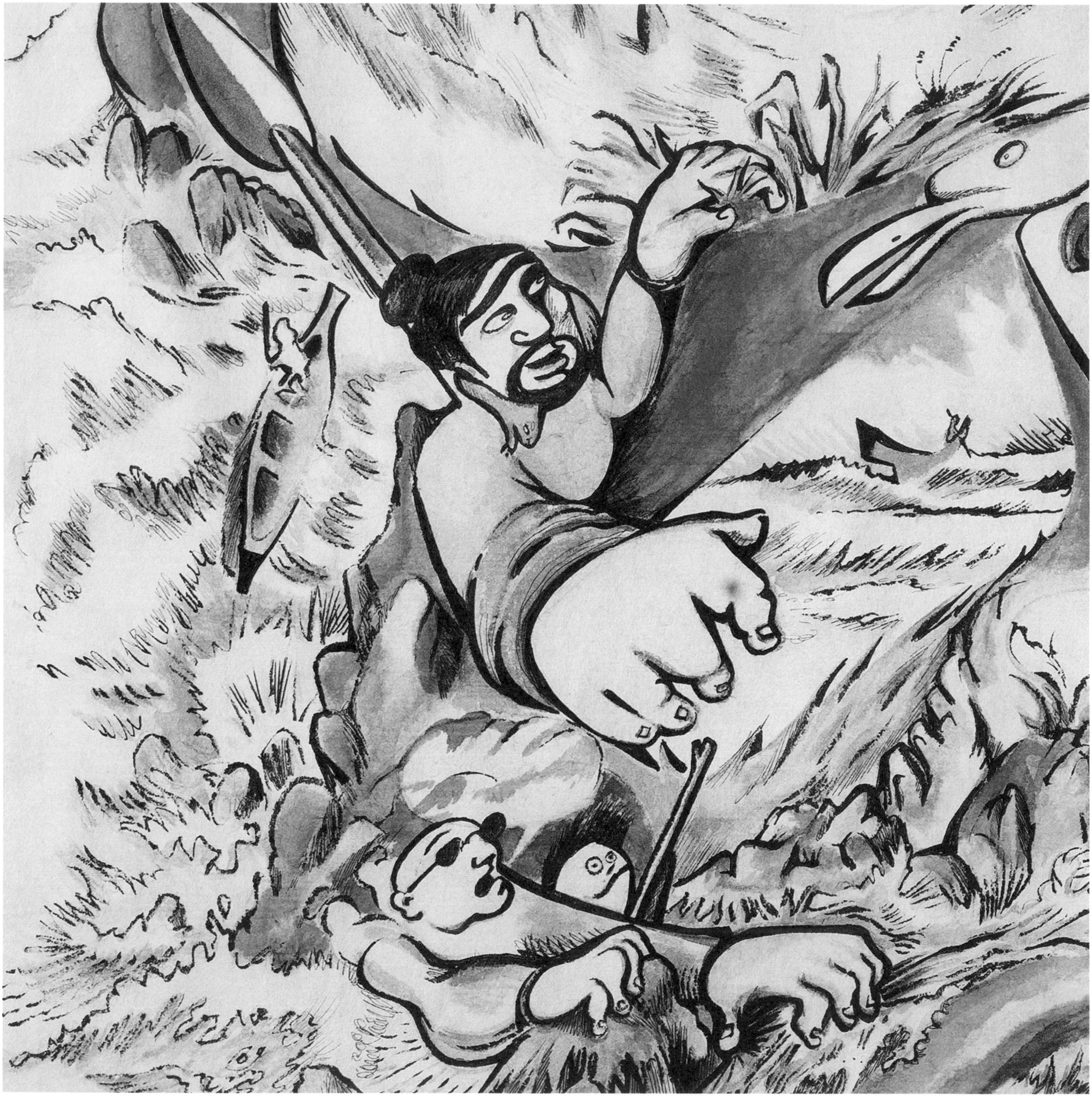

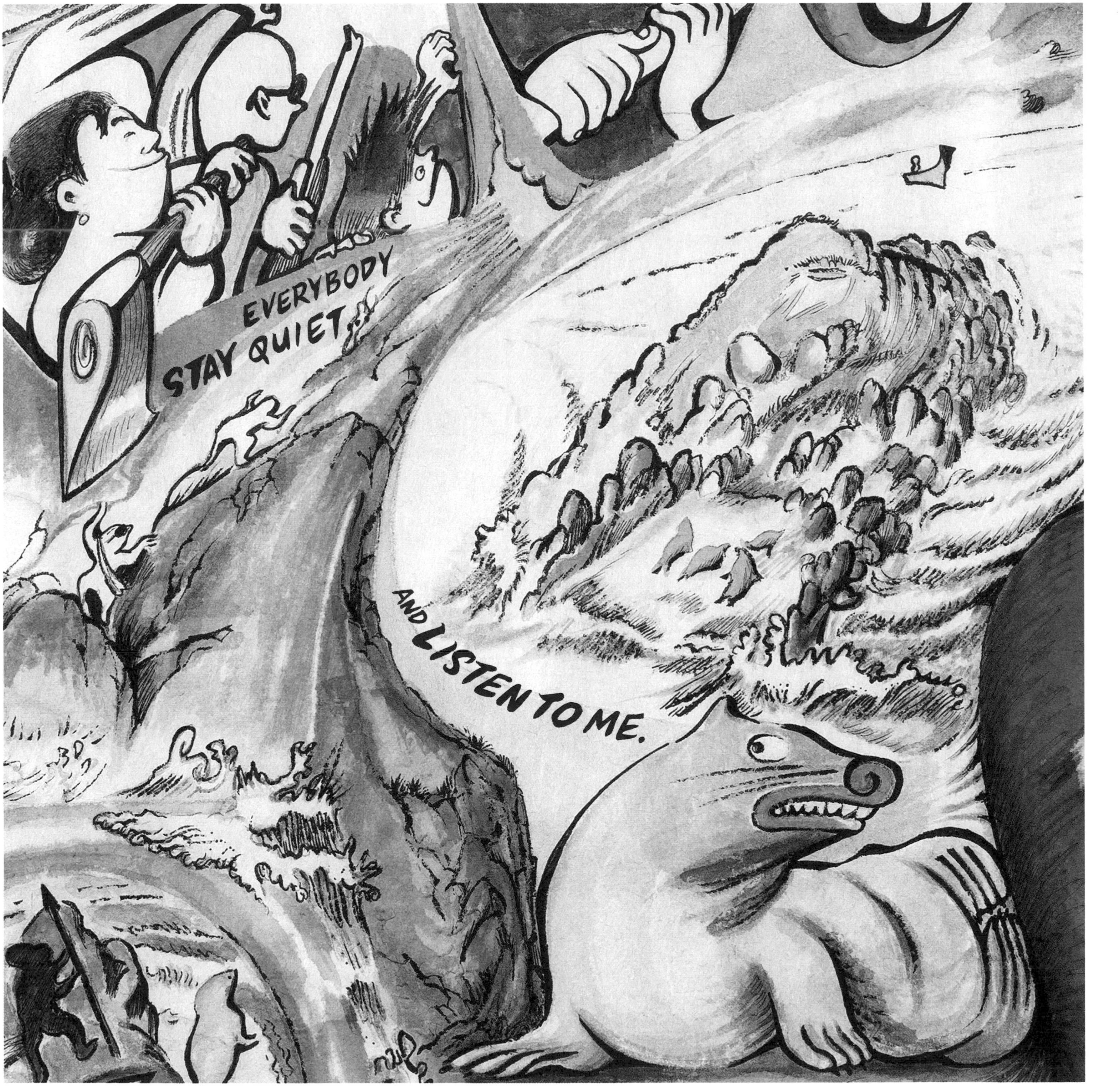

EVERYBODY
STAY QUIET
AND LISTEN TO ME.

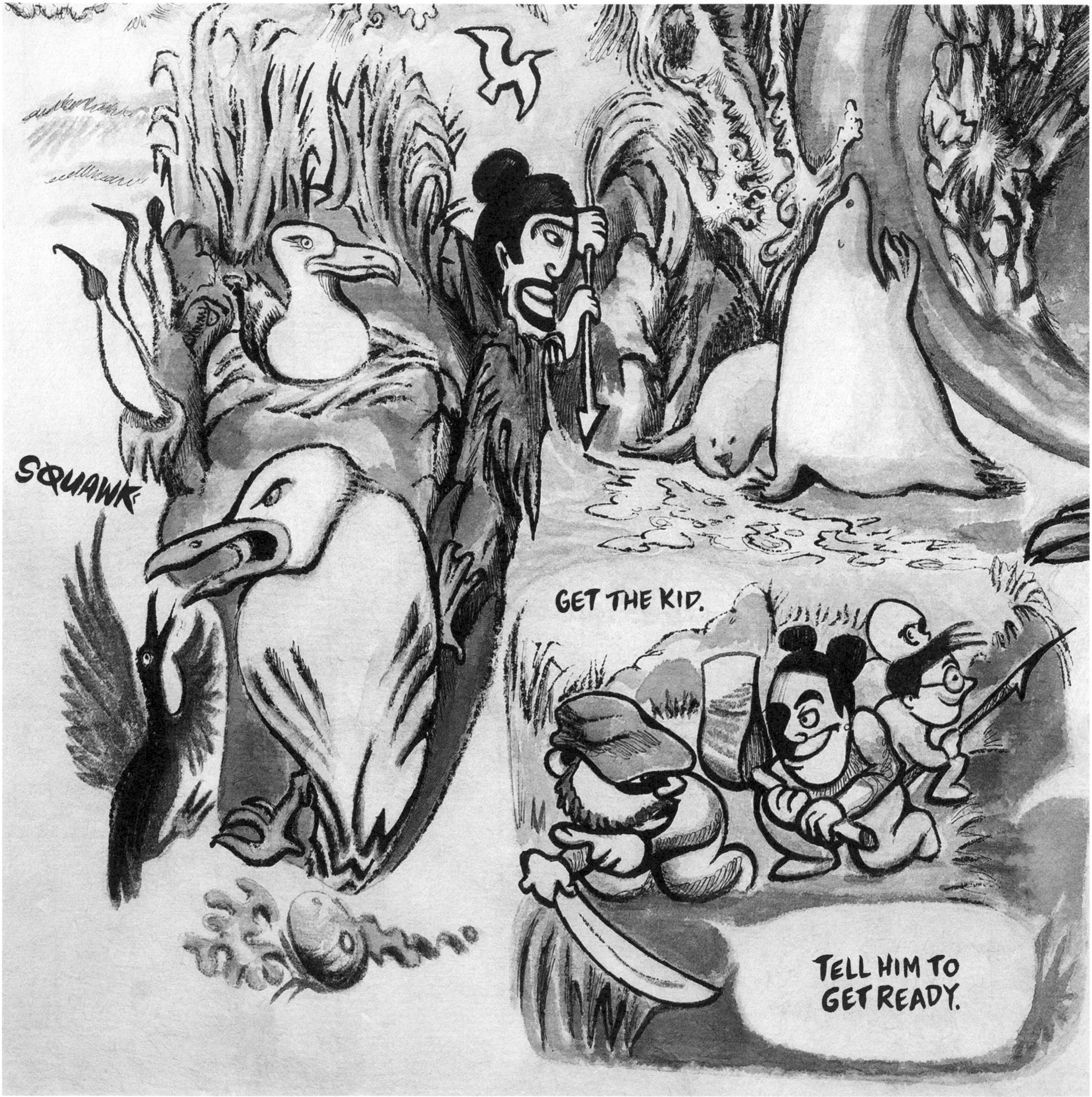
SQUAWK
GET THE KID.
TELL HIM TO GET READY.

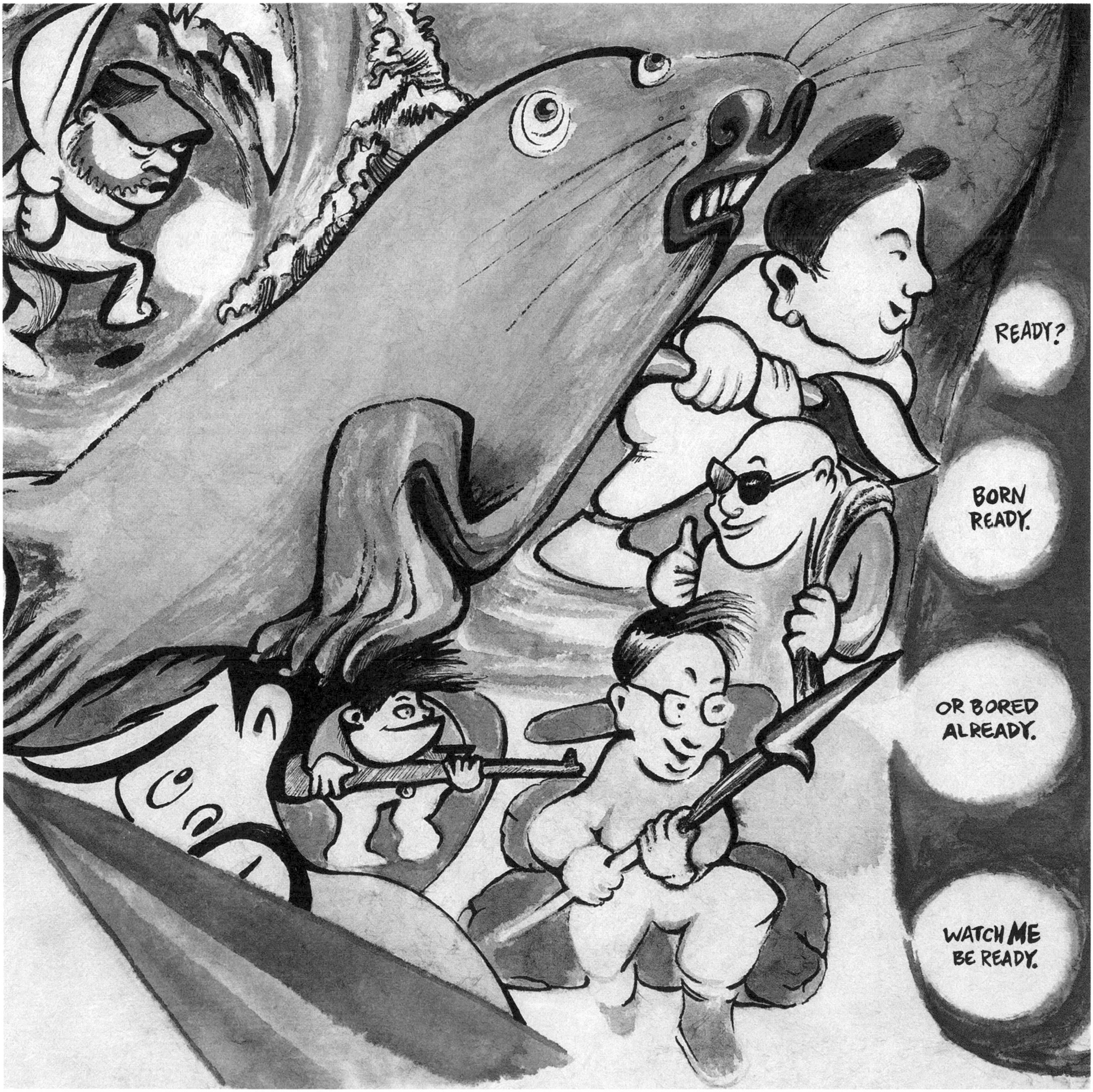
READY?
BORN READY.
OR BORED ALREADY.
WATCH ME BE READY.

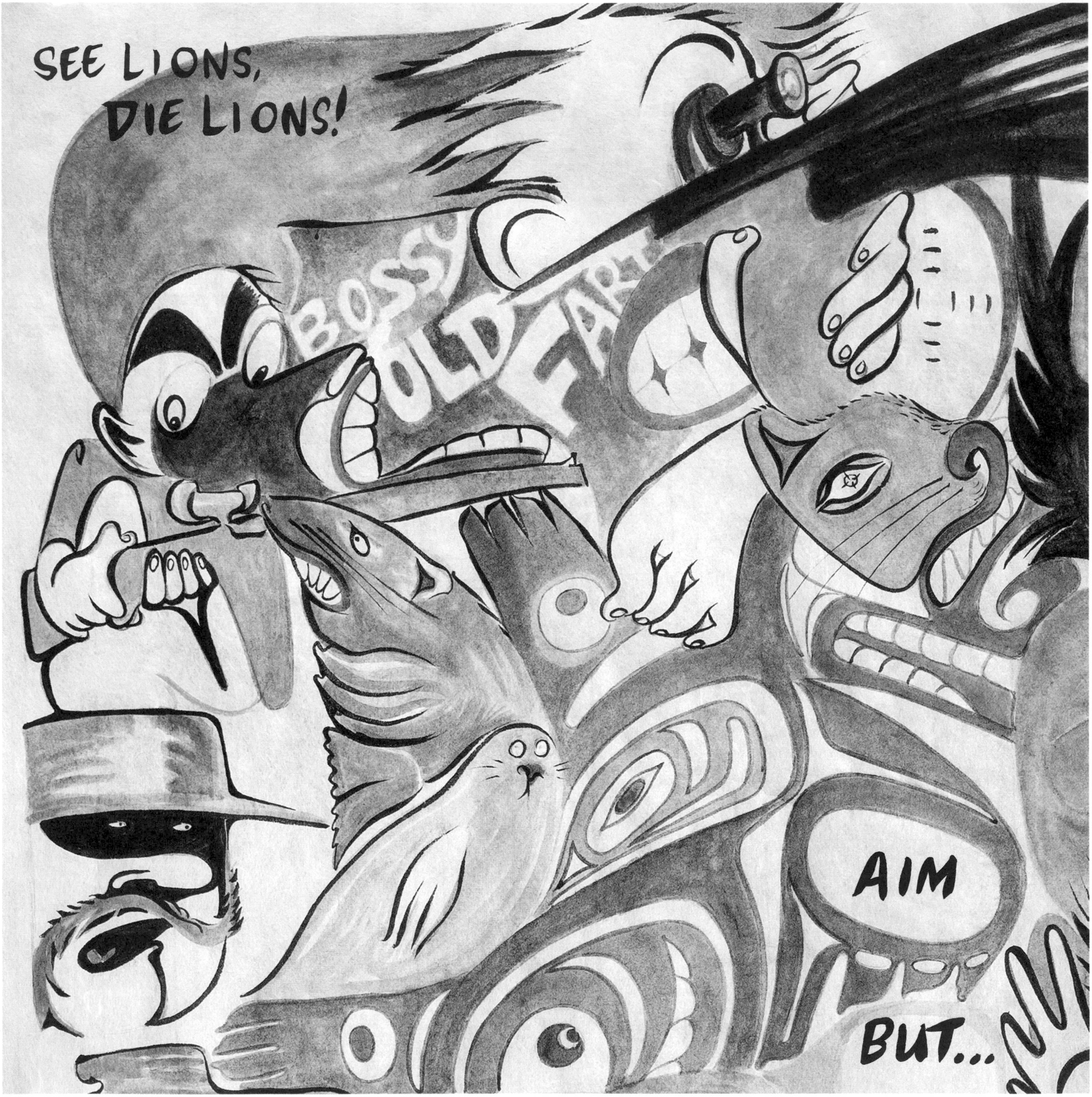
SEE LIONS,
DIE LIONS!
BOSSY
OLD
FART
AIM
BUT...

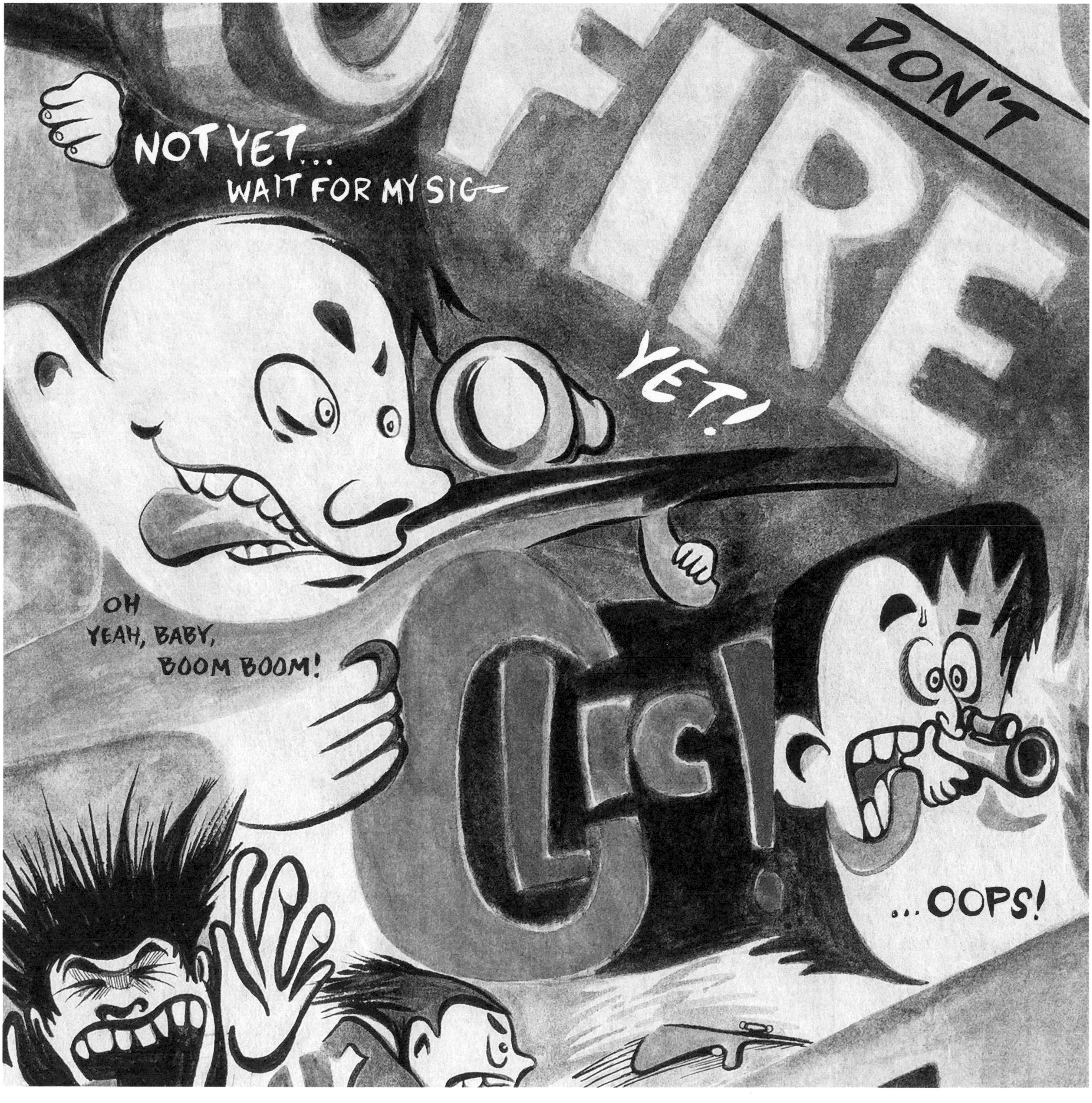

DON'T
FIRE
NOT YET...
WAIT FOR MY SIG—
YET!
OH YEAH, BABY, BOOM BOOM!
CLIC!
...OOPS!

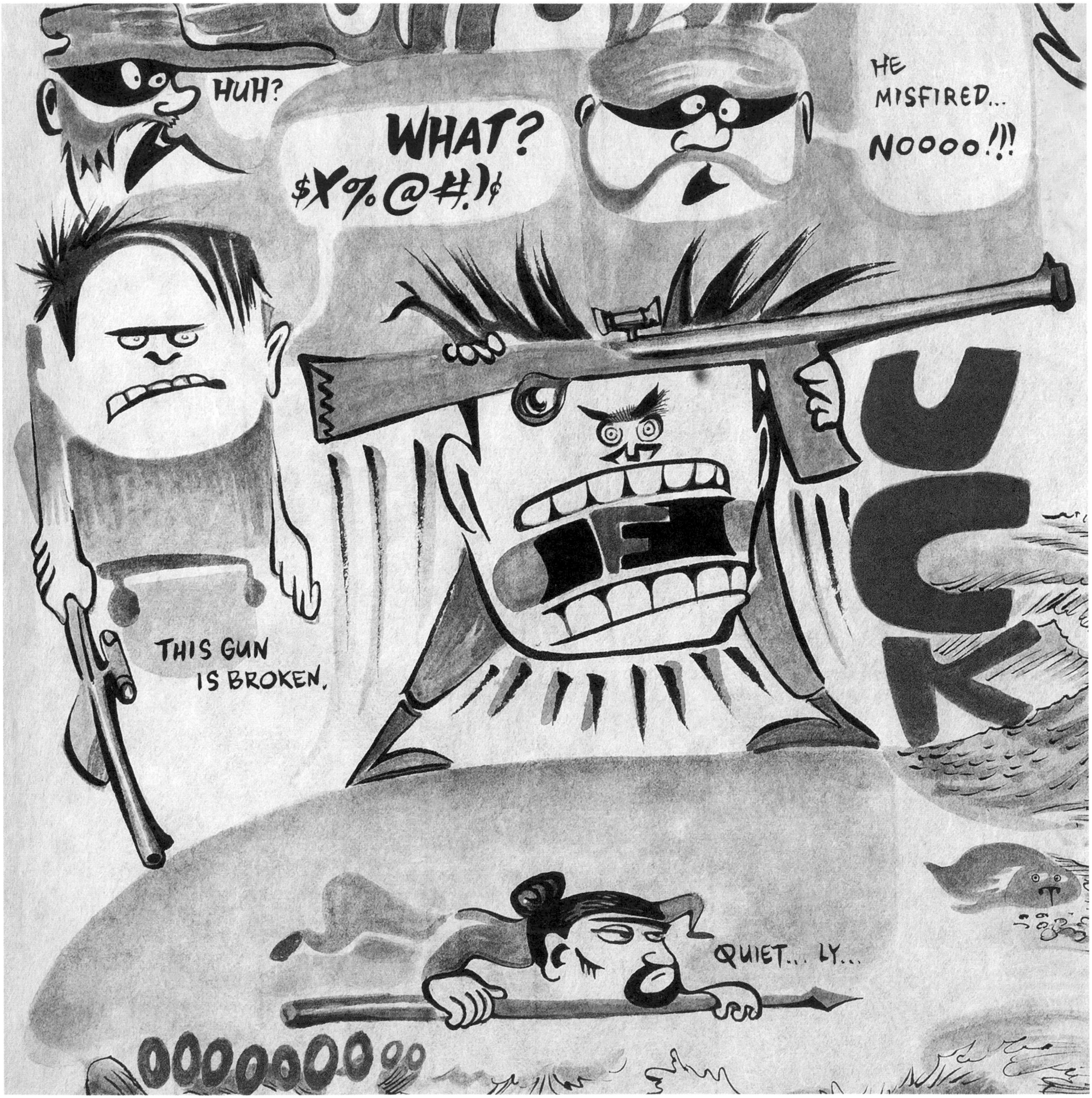
HUH?
WHAT?
$X%@#!¢
HE
MISFIRED...
NOOOO!!!
THIS GUN
IS BROKEN.
F
UCK
QUIET... LY...
OOOOOOOOoo

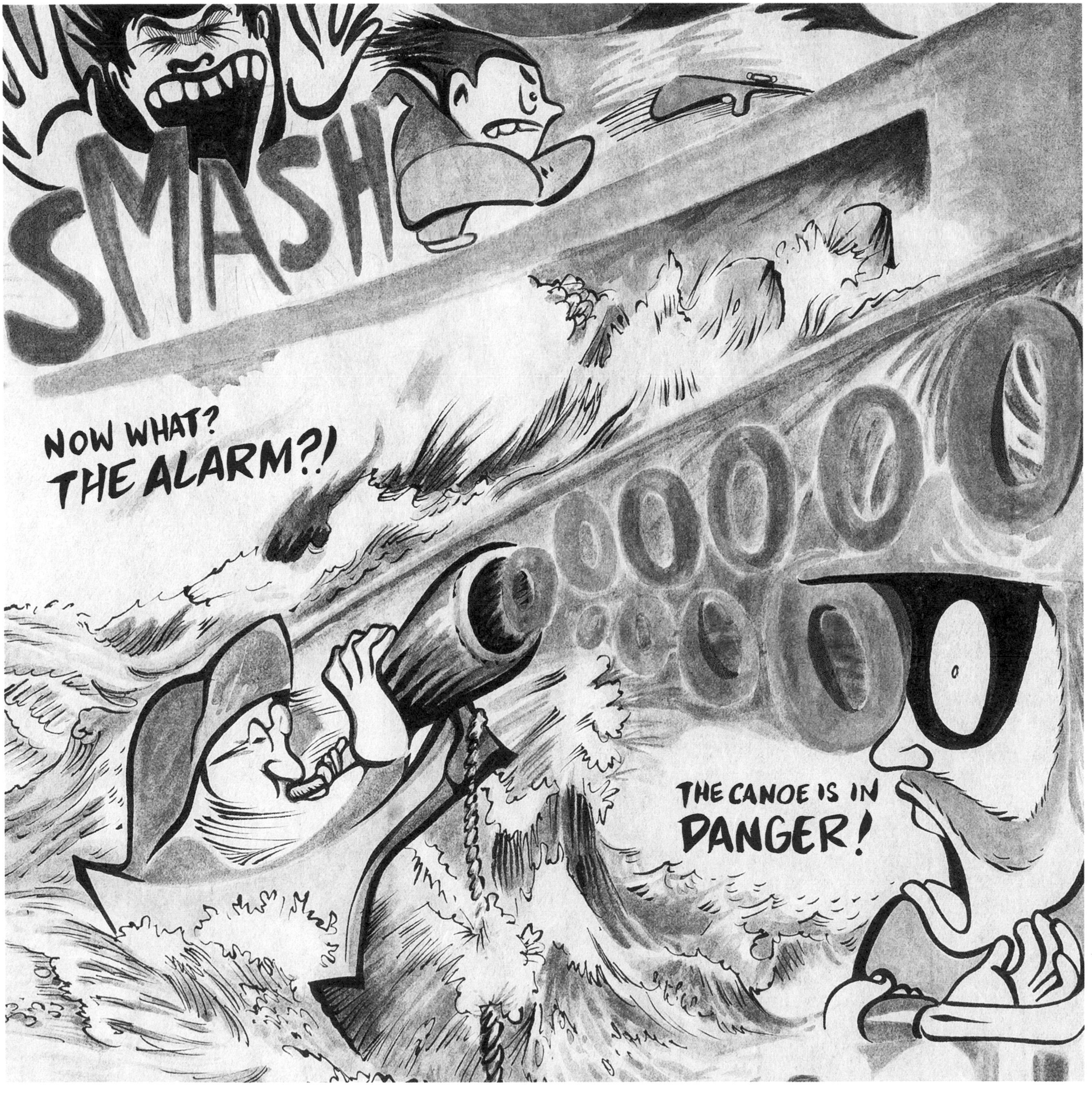
SMASH
NOW WHAT? THE ALARM?!
THE CANOE IS IN DANGER!

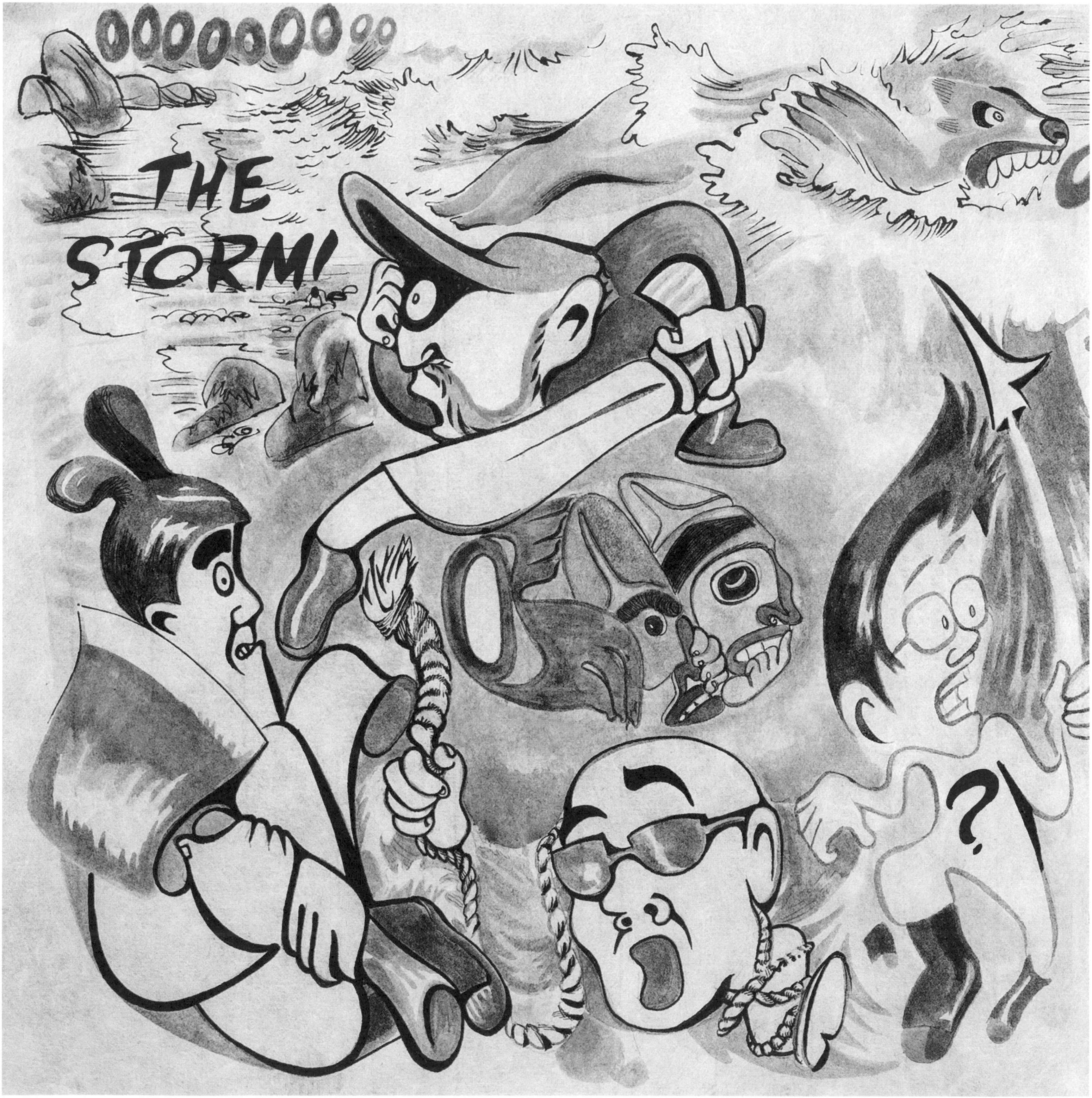
OOOOOOOOoo
THE STORM!
?

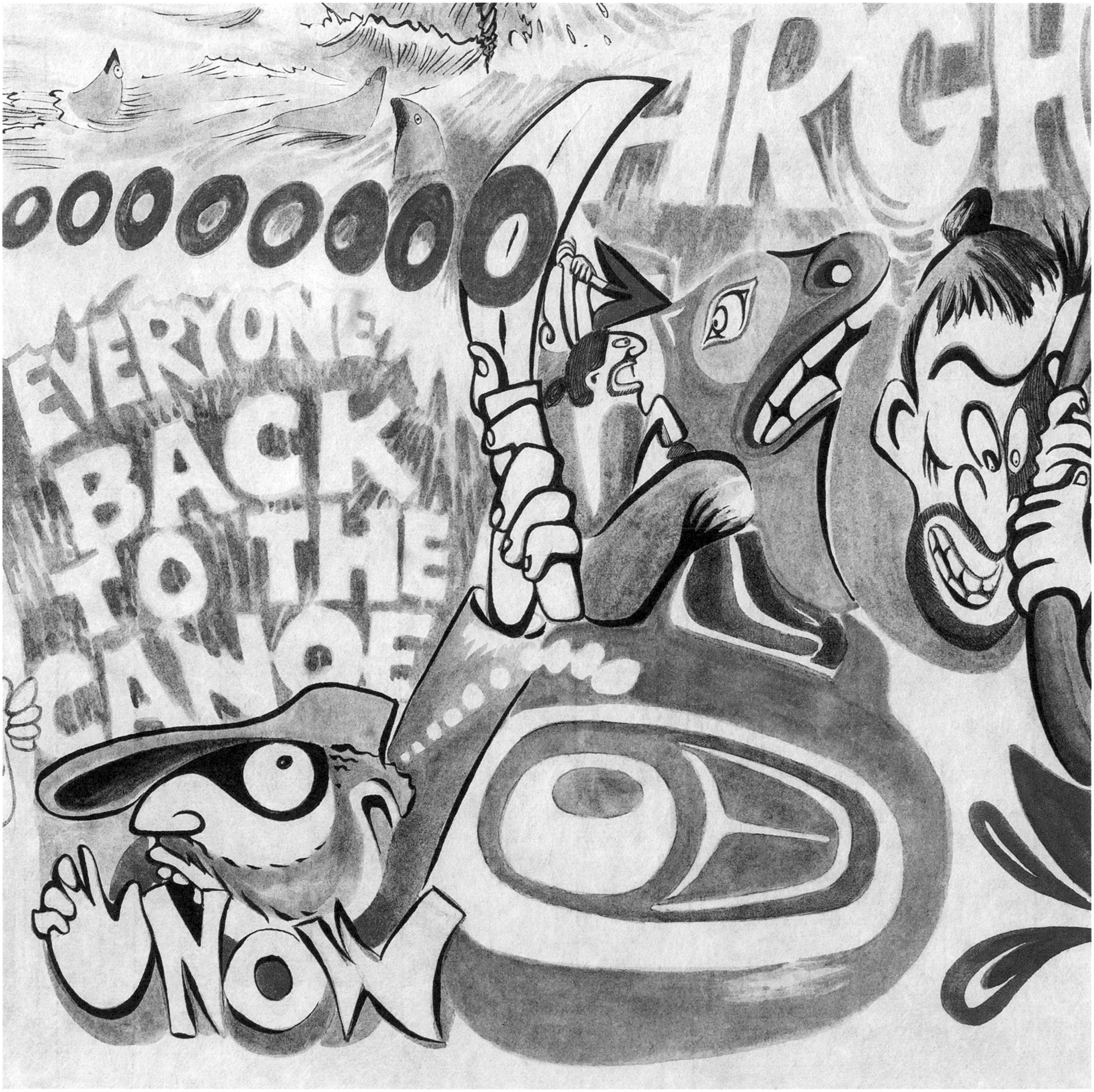

OOOOOOOOO
ARGH
EVERYONE BACK TO THE CANOE
NOW

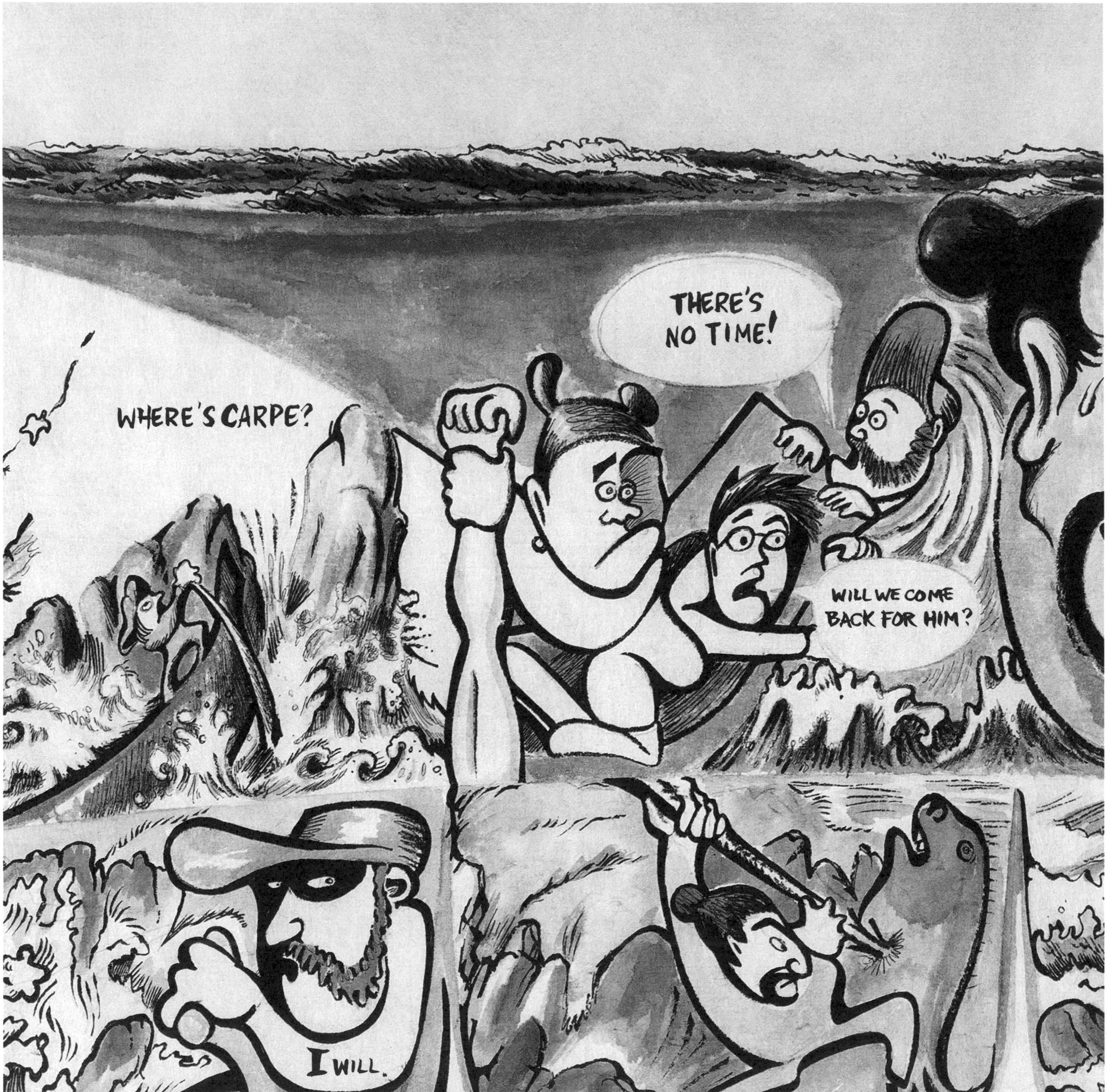
WHERE'S CARPE?
THERE'S NO TIME!
WILL WE COME BACK FOR HIM?
I WILL.

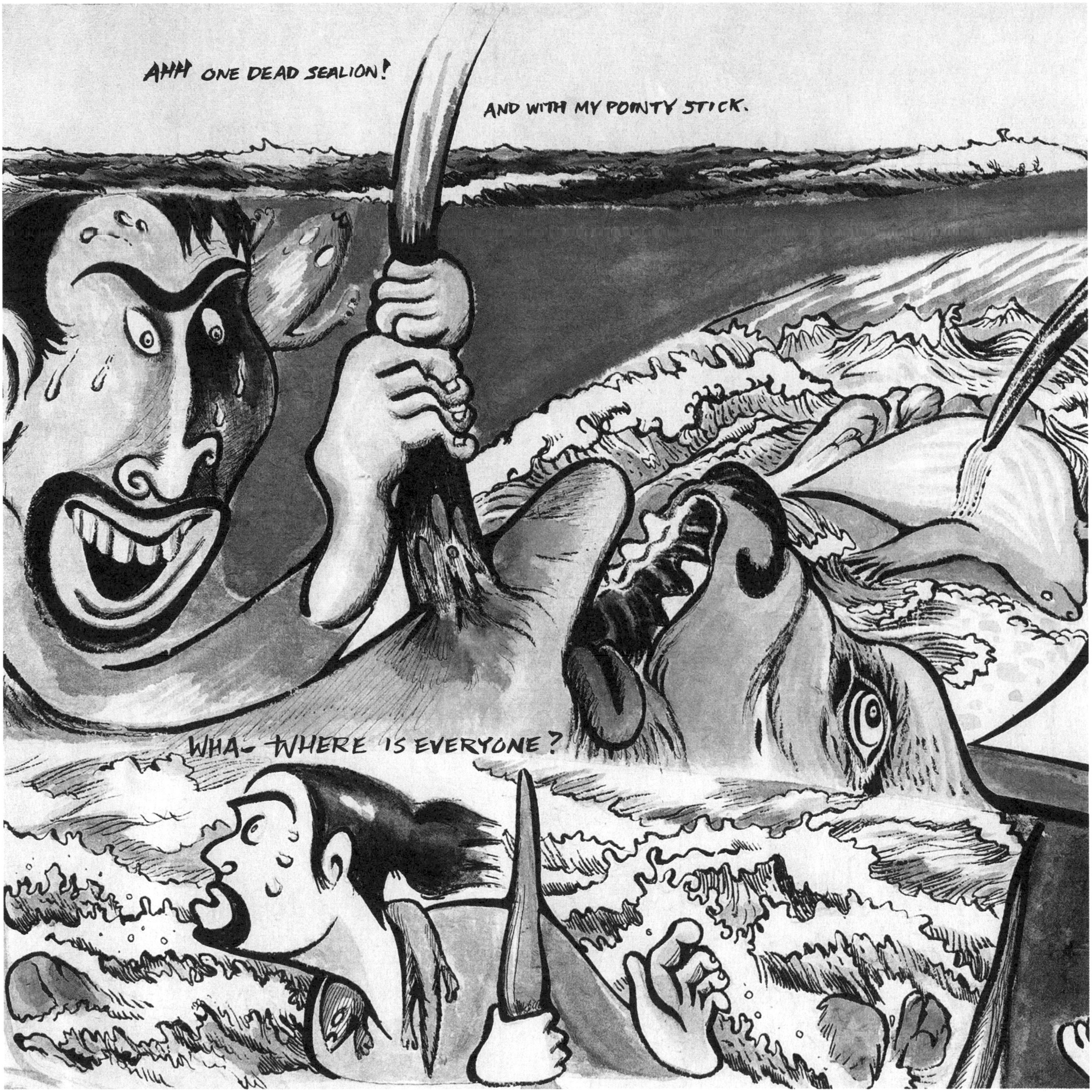
AHH ONE DEAD SEALION!
AND WITH MY POINTY STICK.
WHA- WHERE IS EVERYONE?

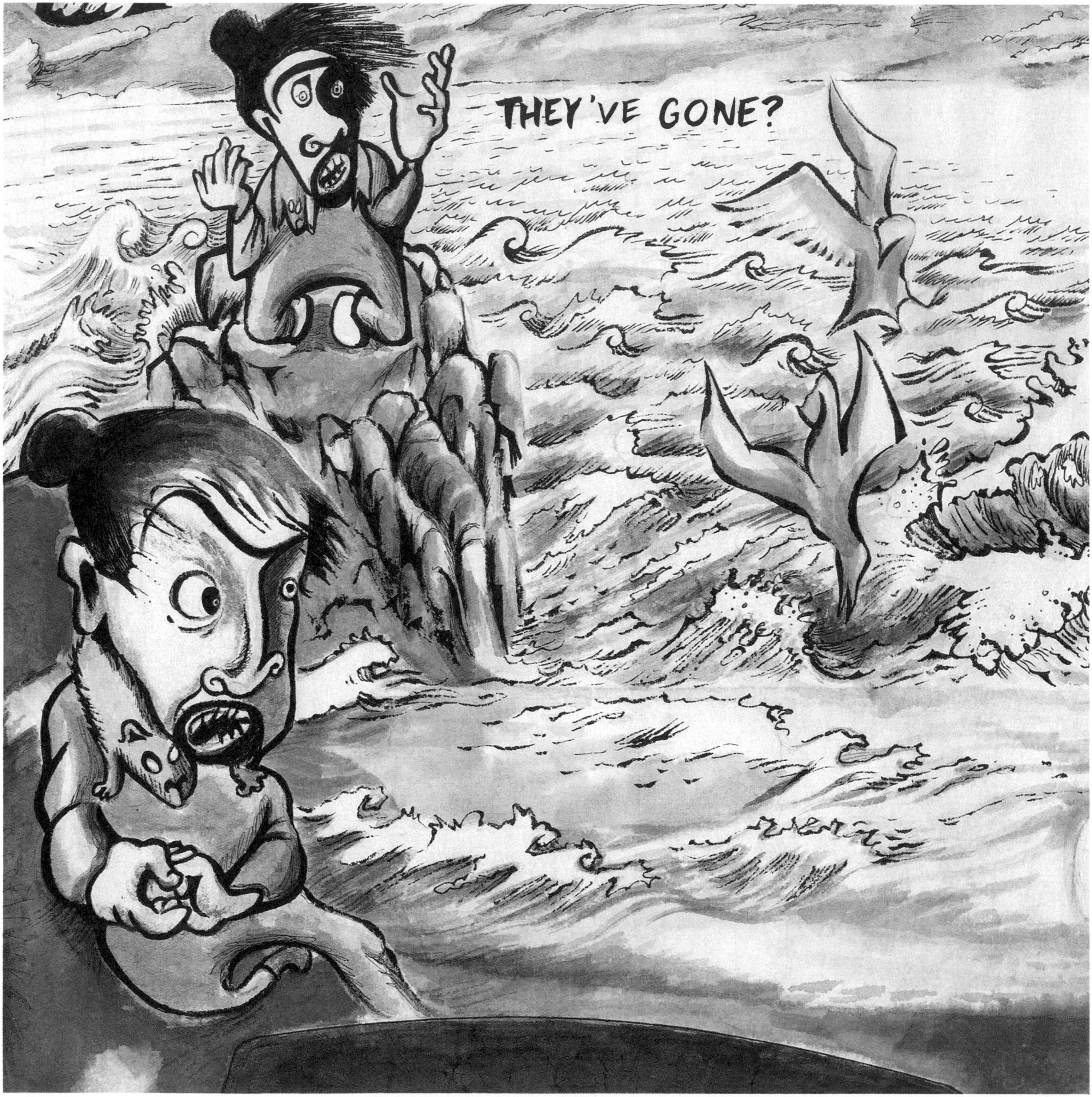
THEY'VE GONE?

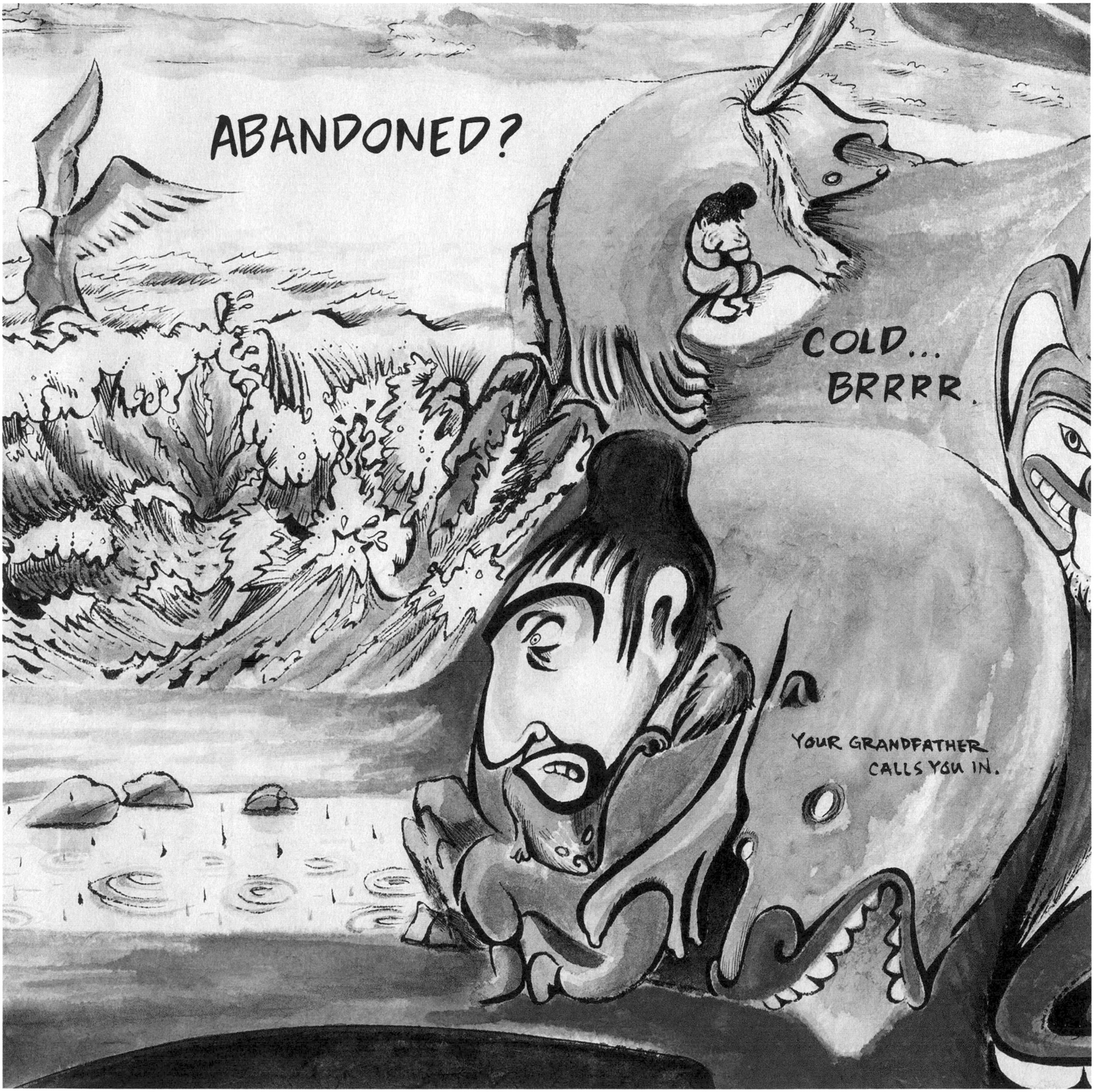
ABANDONED?
COLD... BRRRR.
YOUR GRANDFATHER CALLS YOU IN.

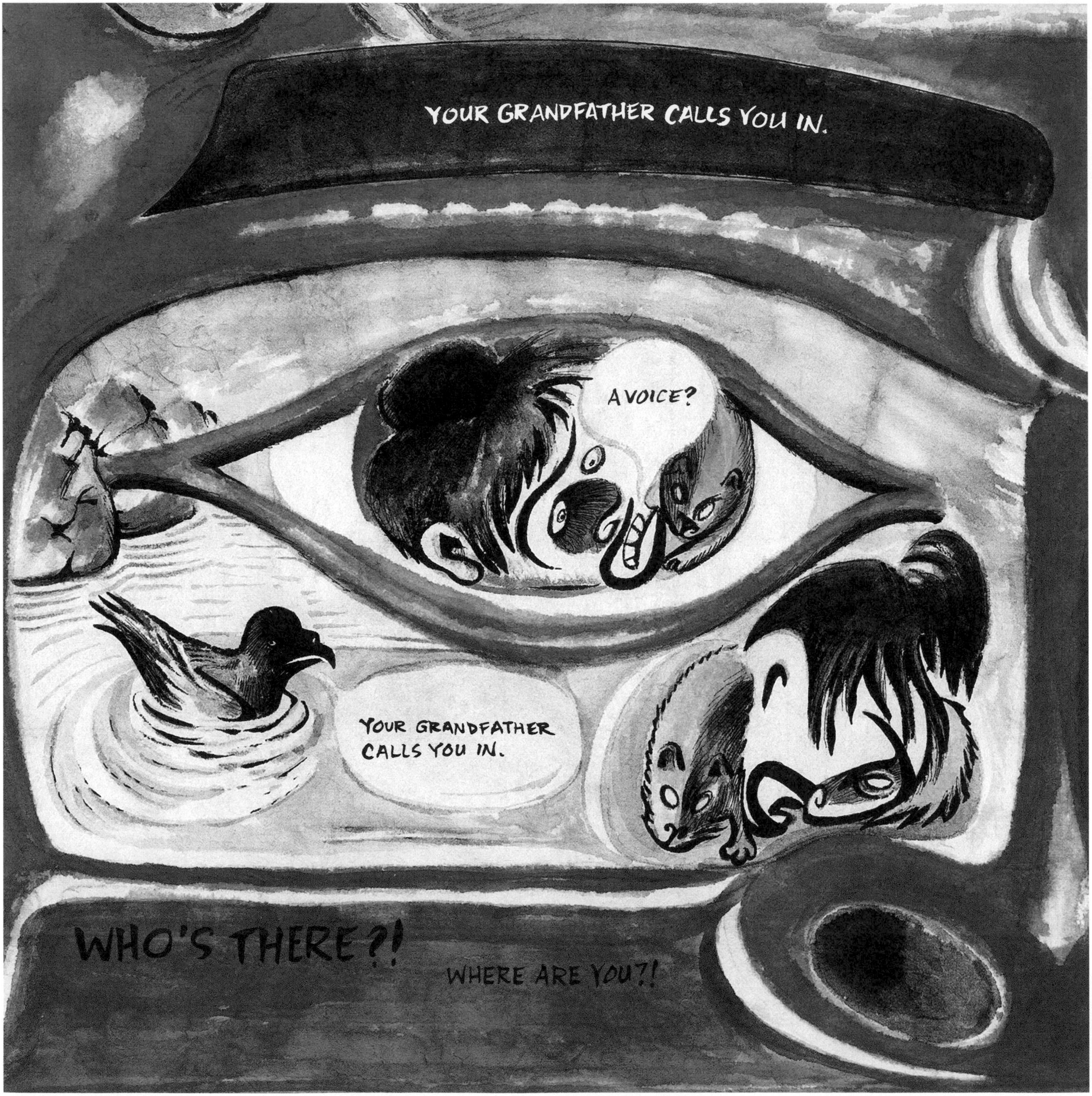
YOUR GRANDFATHER CALLS YOU IN.
A VOICE?
YOUR GRANDFATHER CALLS YOU IN.
WHO'S THERE?!
WHERE ARE YOU?!

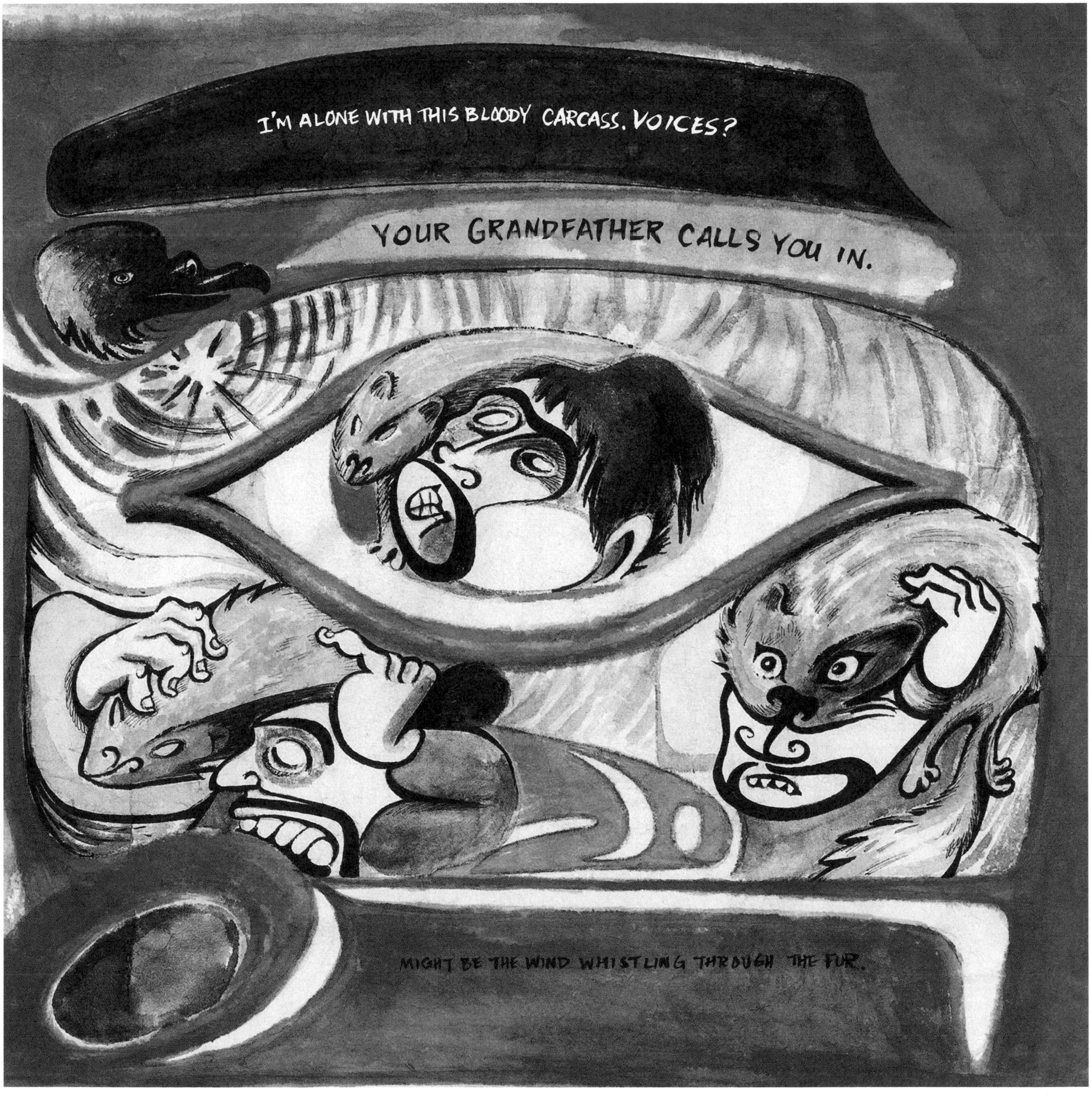
I'M ALONE WITH THIS BLOODY CARCASS. VOICES?
YOUR GRANDFATHER CALLS YOU IN.
MIGHT BE THE WIND WHISTLING THROUGH THE FUR.

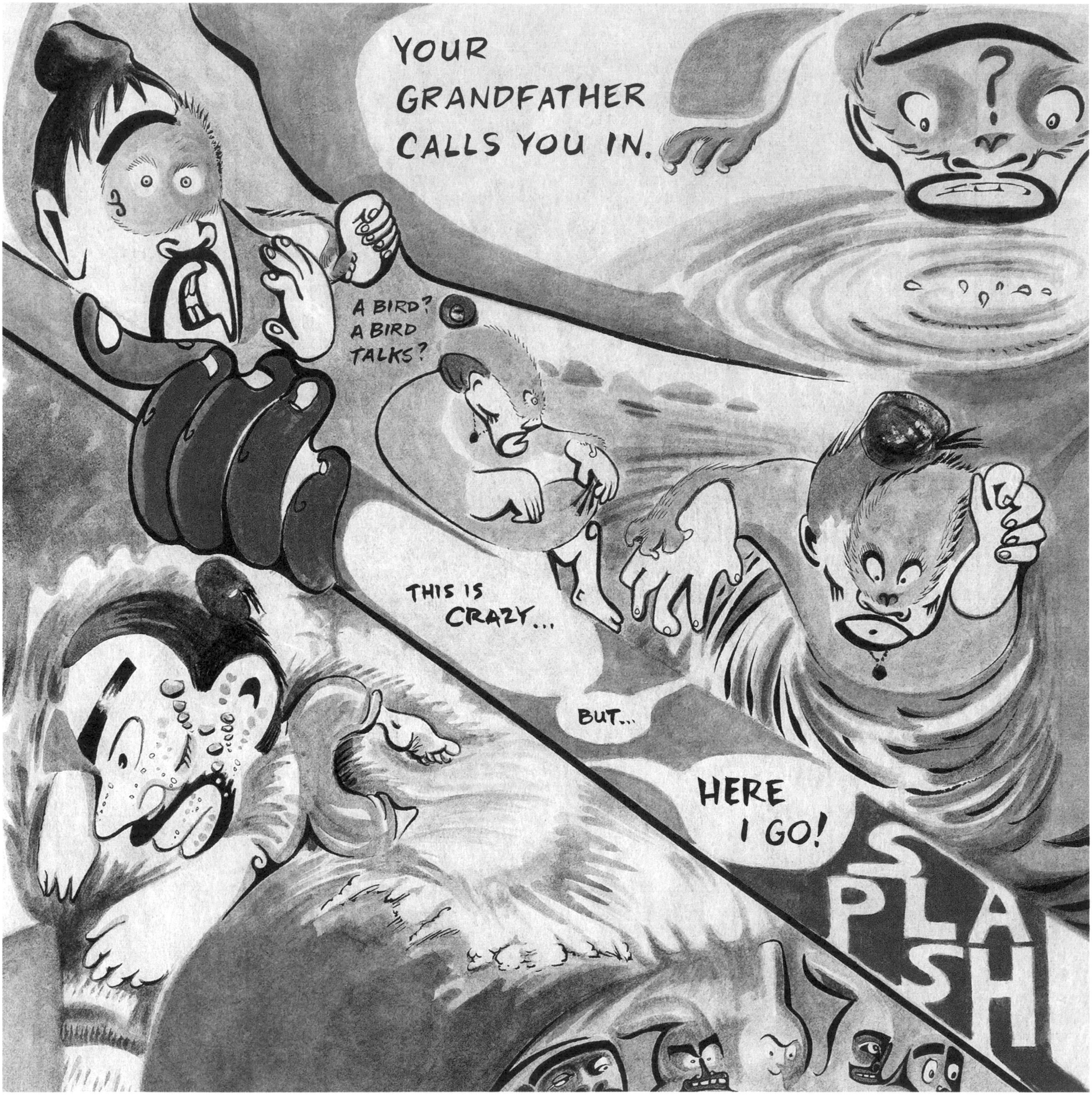
YOUR GRANDFATHER CALLS YOU IN.
A BIRD? A BIRD TALKS?
THIS IS CRAZY...
BUT...
HERE I GO!
SPLASH

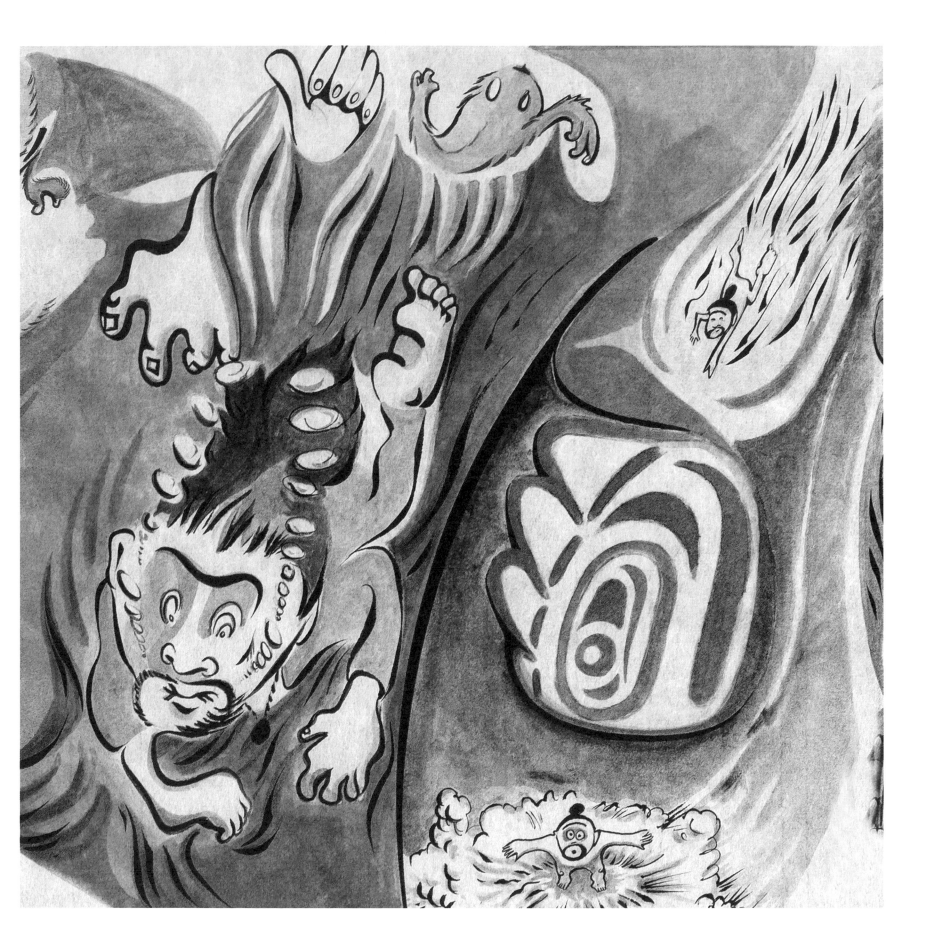

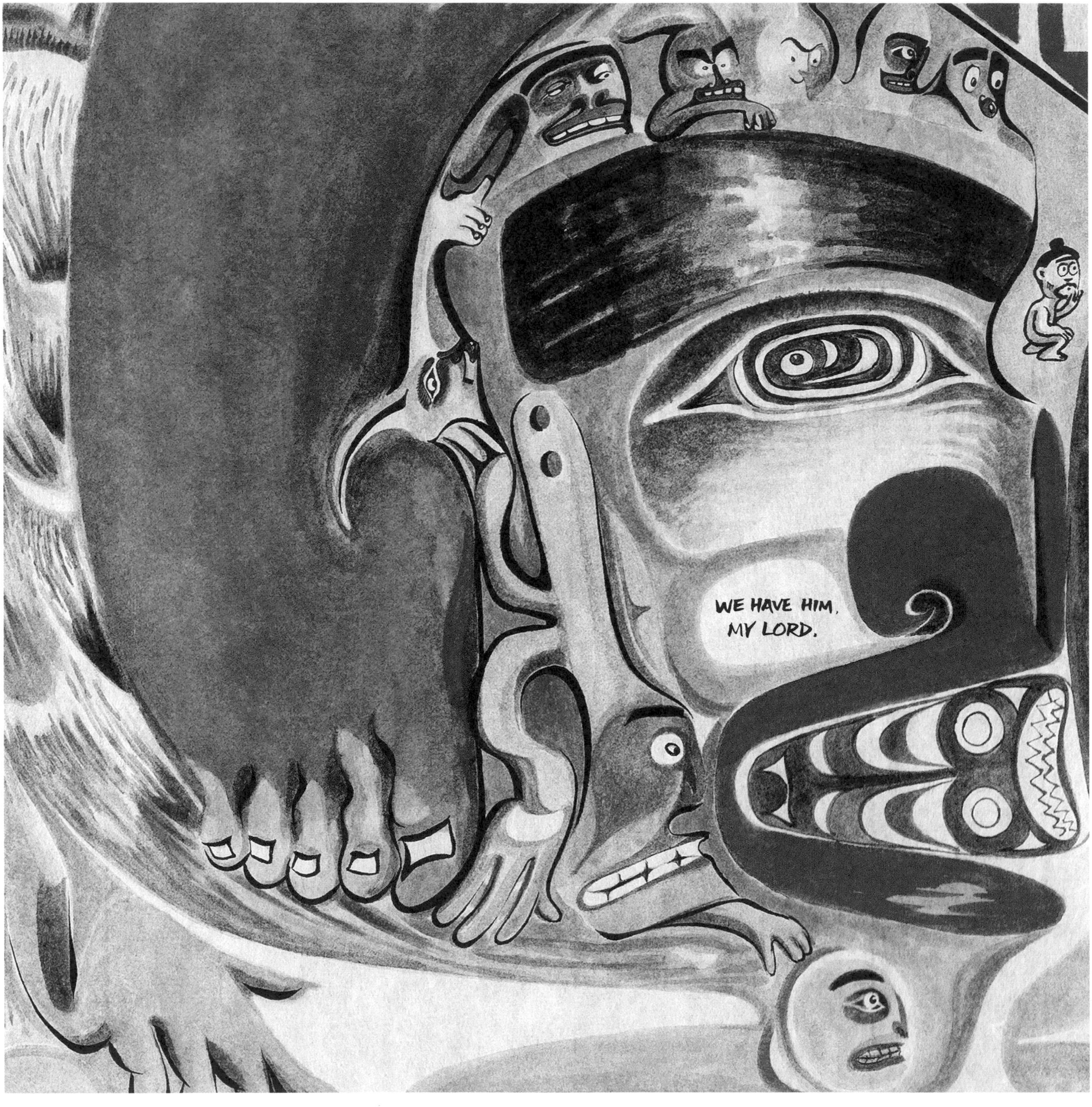
WE HAVE HIM,
MY LORD.

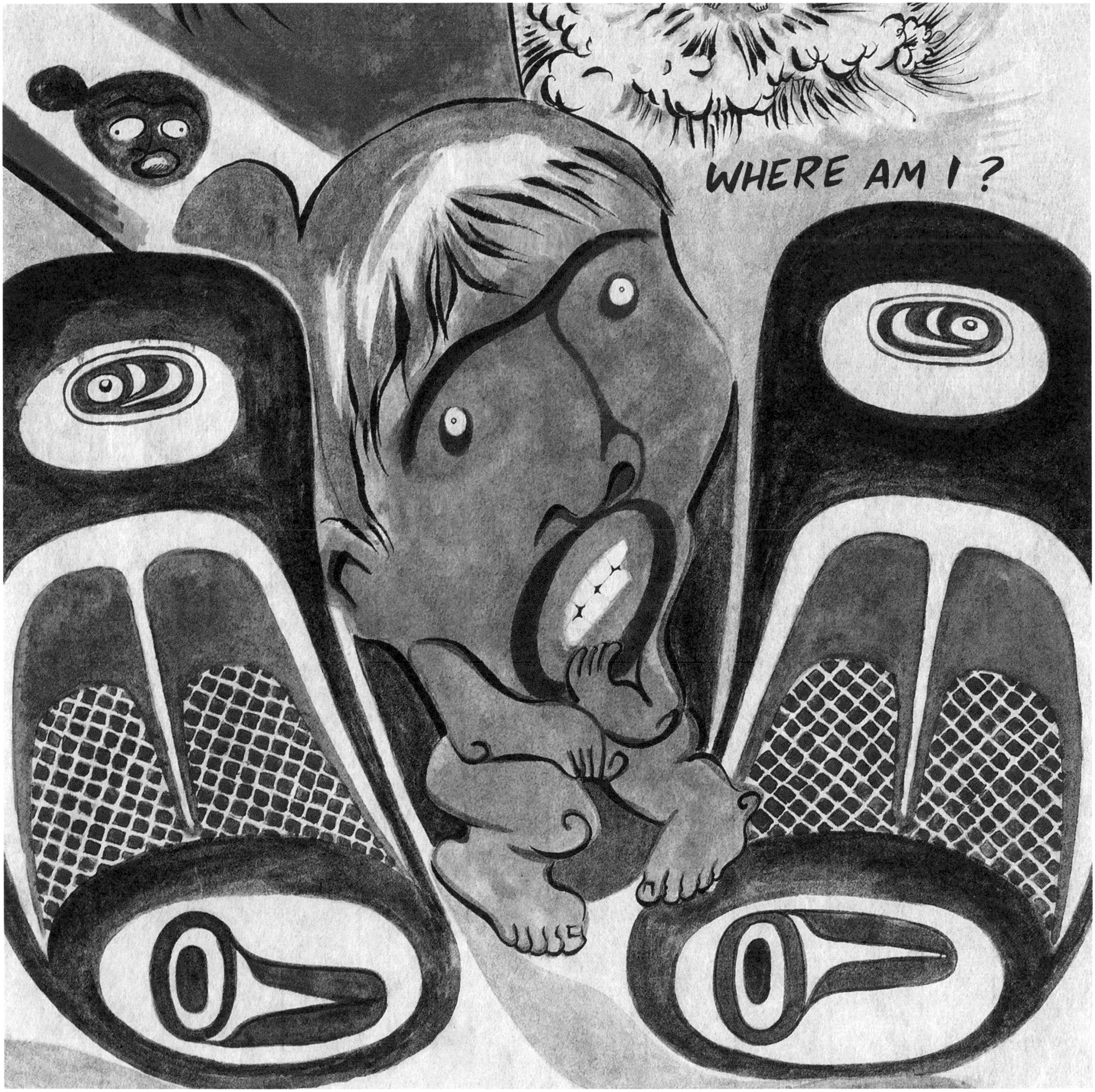
WHERE AM I ?

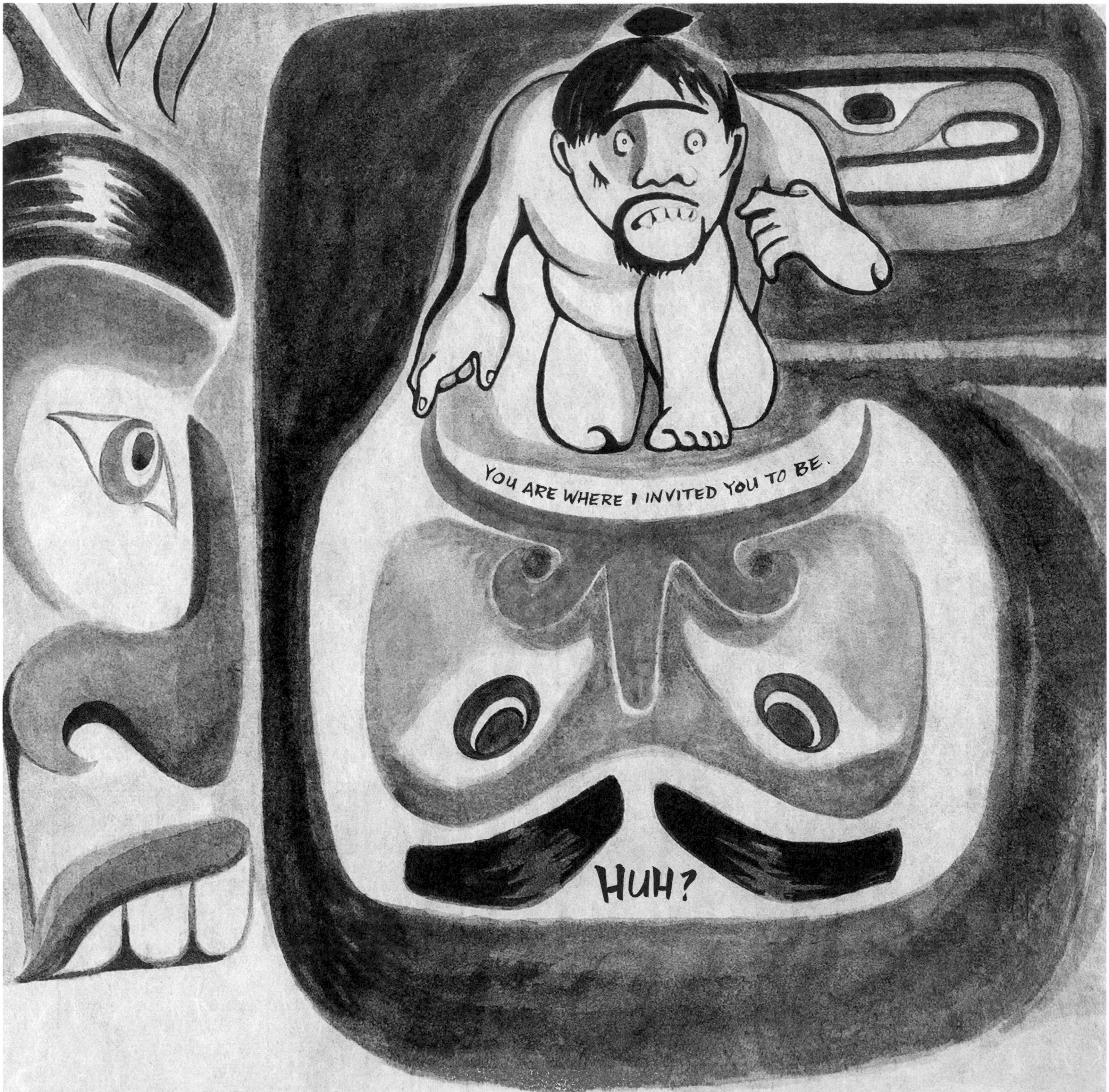
YOU ARE WHERE I INVITED YOU TO BE.
HUH?

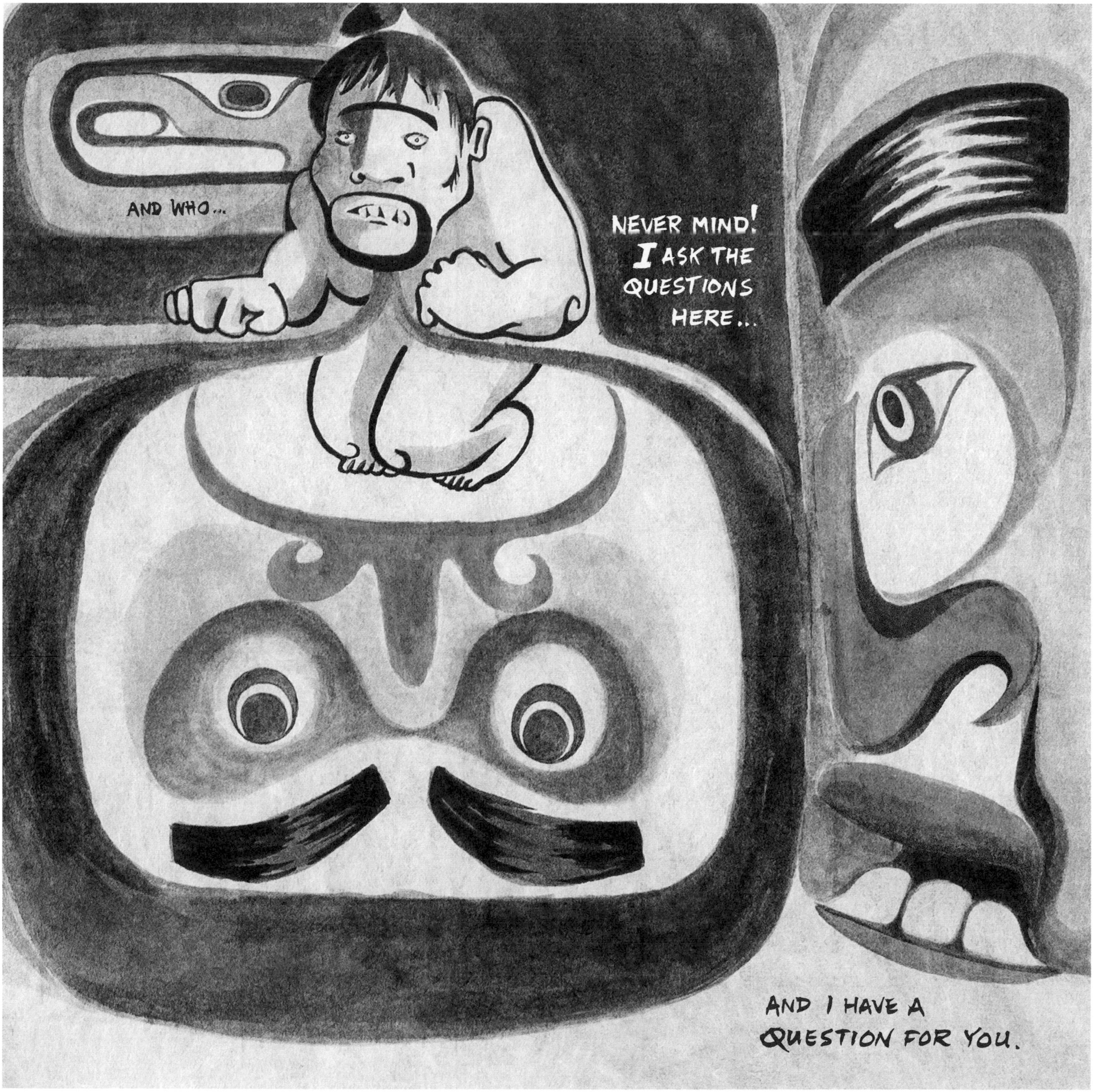
AND WHO...
NEVER MIND! I ASK THE QUESTIONS HERE...
AND I HAVE A QUESTION FOR YOU.

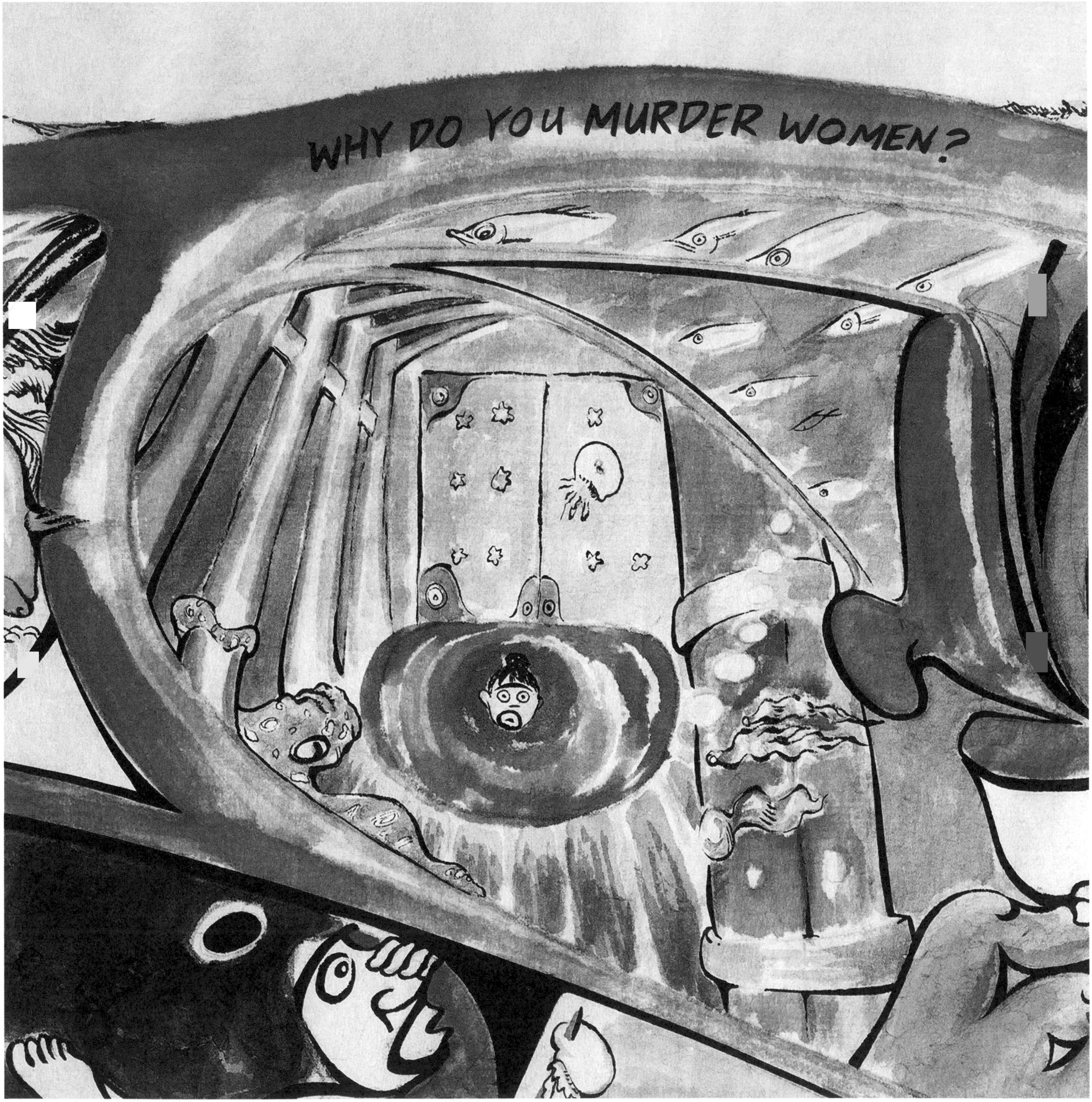
WHY DO YOU MURDER WOMEN?

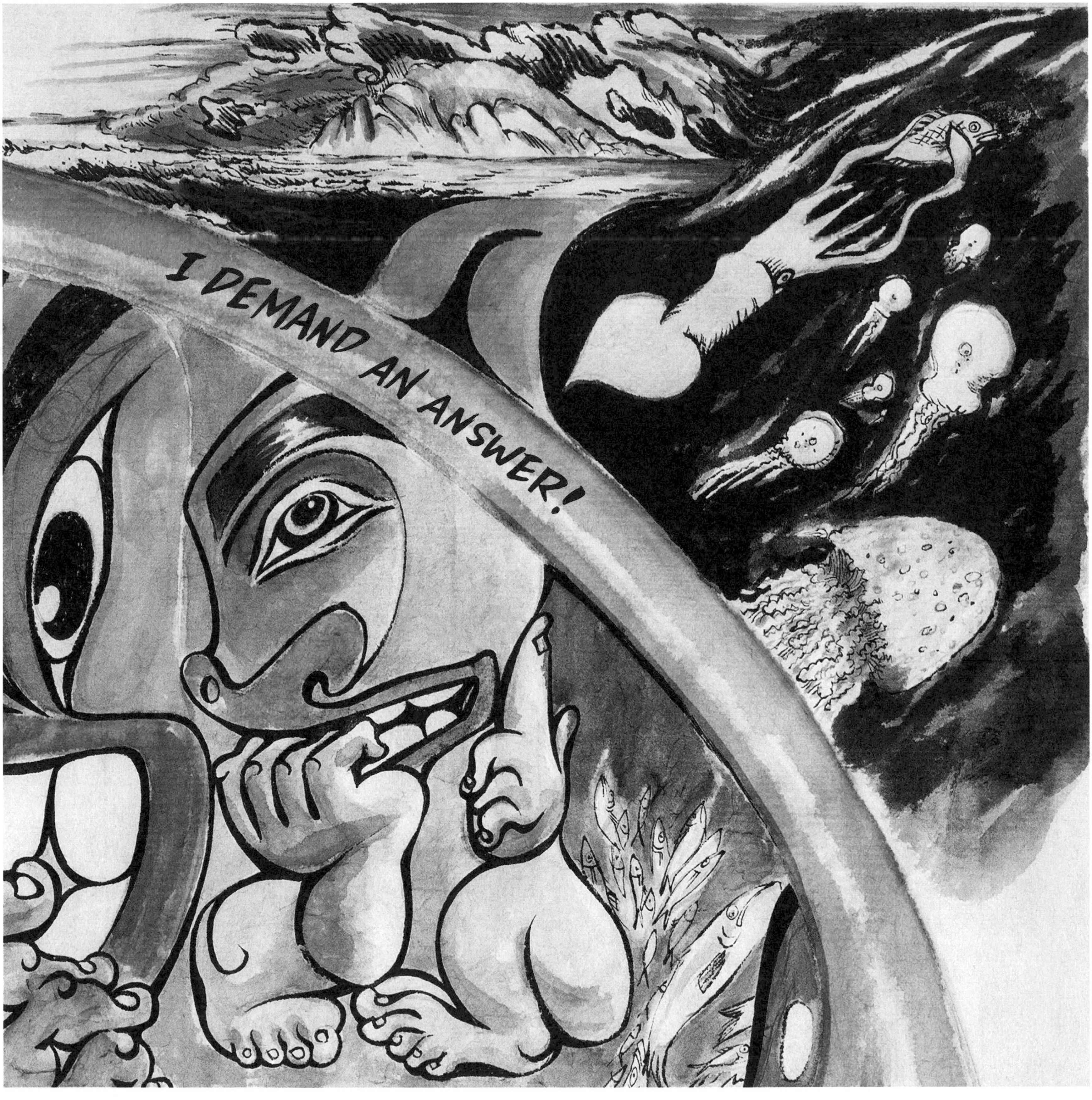
I DEMAND AN ANSWER!

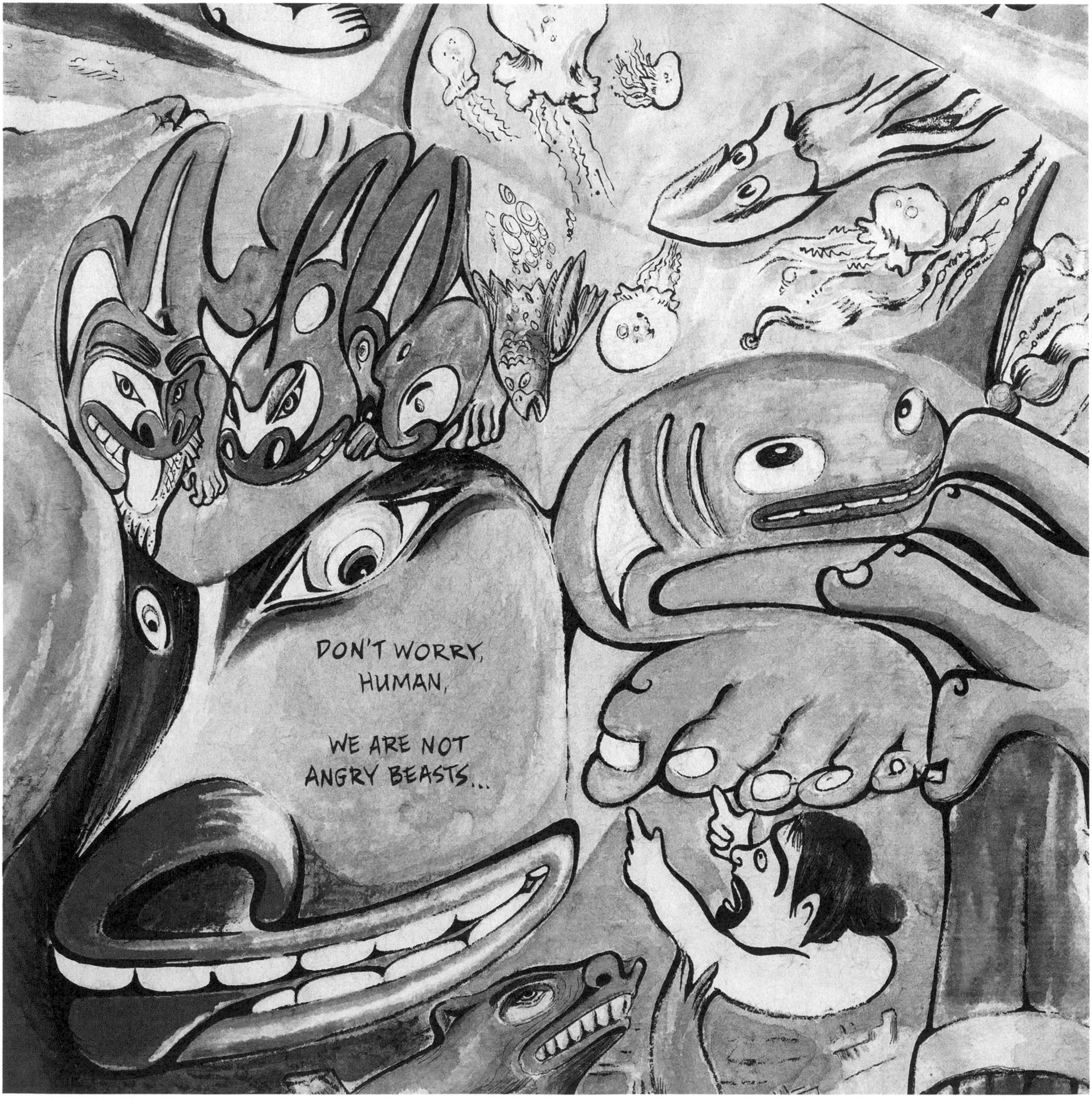
DON'T WORRY, HUMAN,
WE ARE NOT ANGRY BEASTS...

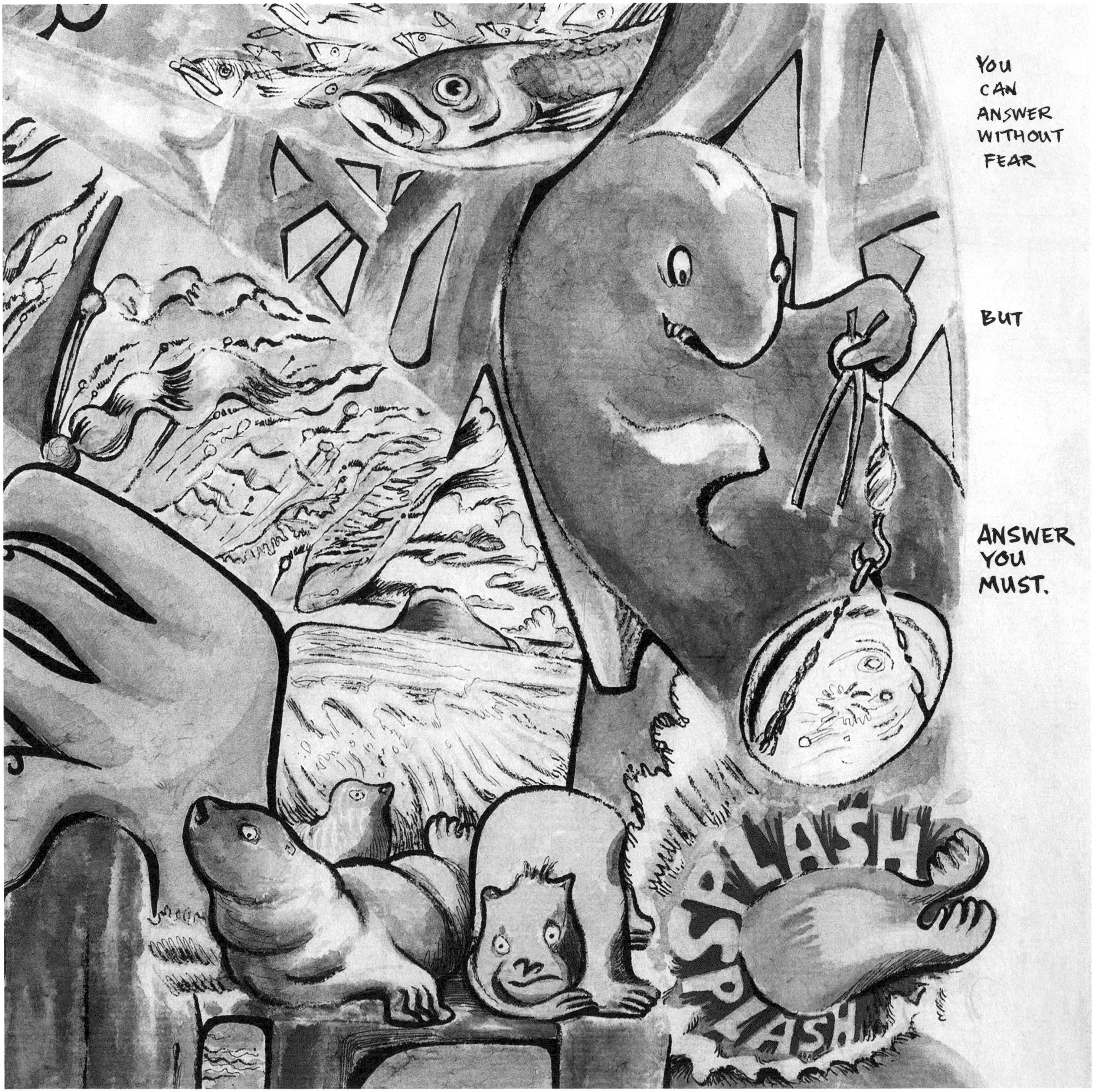
YOU CAN ANSWER WITHOUT FEAR
BUT
ANSWER YOU MUST.
SPLASH
SPLASH!

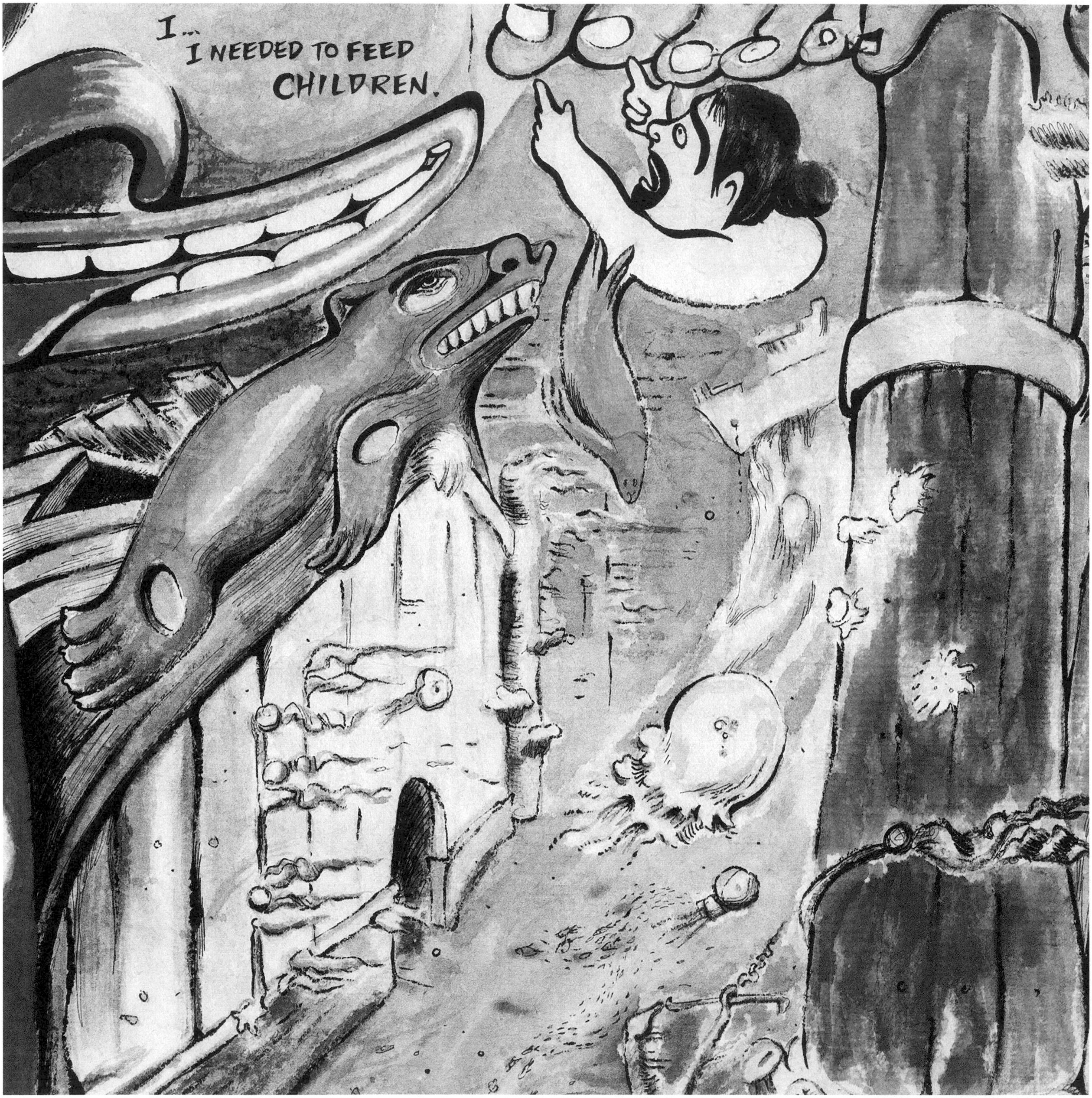
I…
I NEEDED TO FEED
CHILDREN.

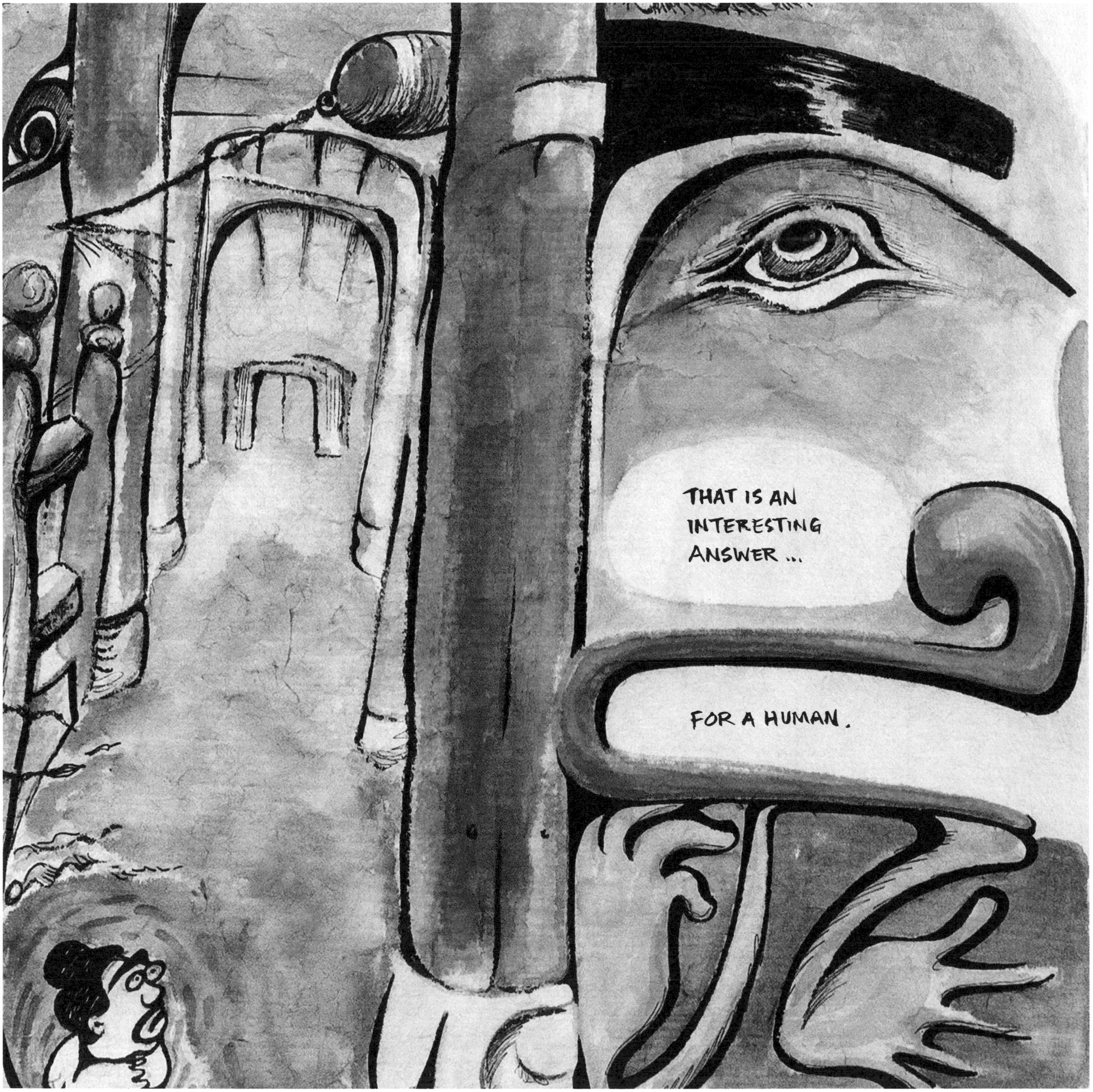
THAT IS AN INTERESTING ANSWER ...
FOR A HUMAN.

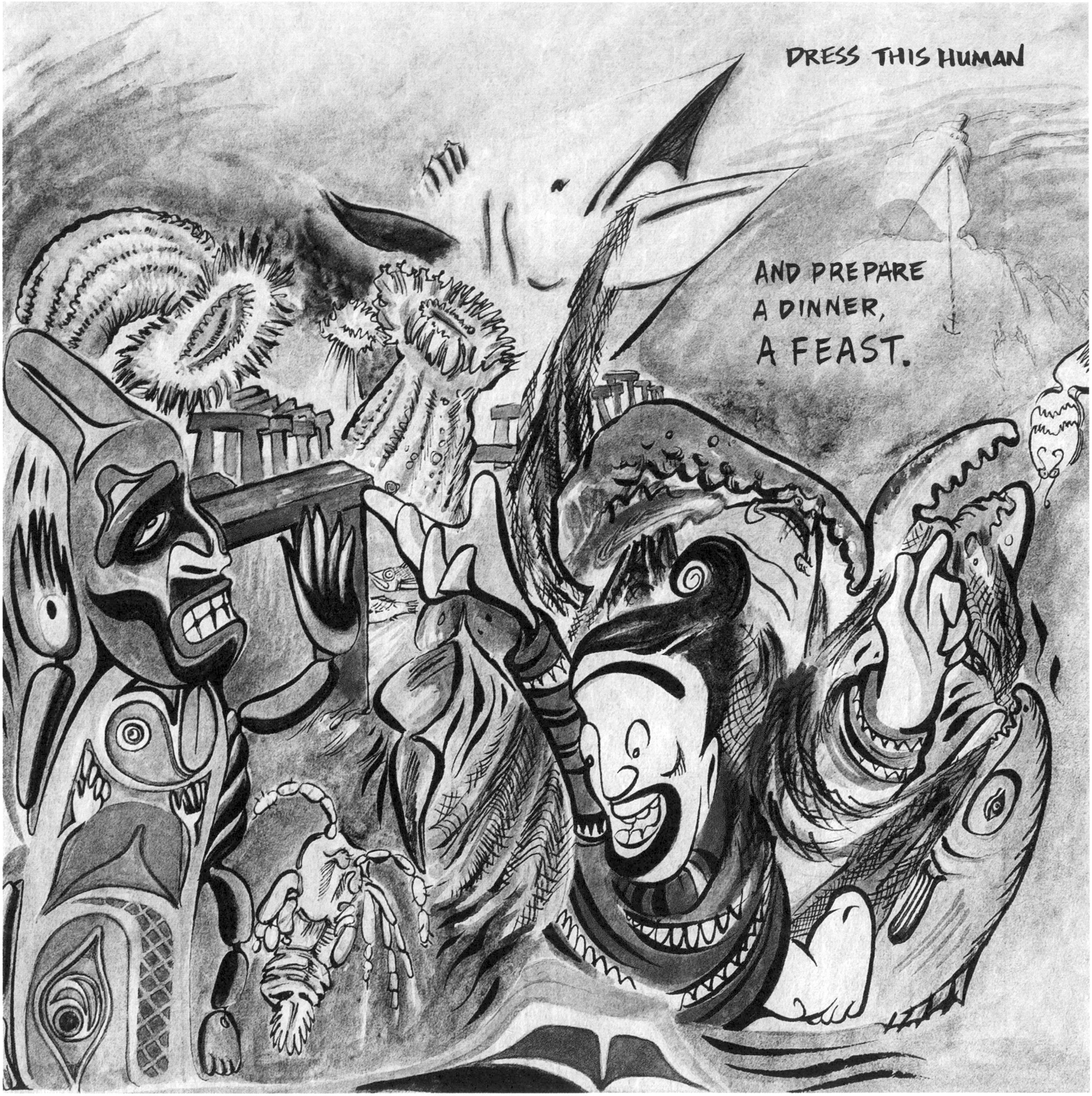
DRESS THIS HUMAN
AND PREPARE
A DINNER,
A FEAST.

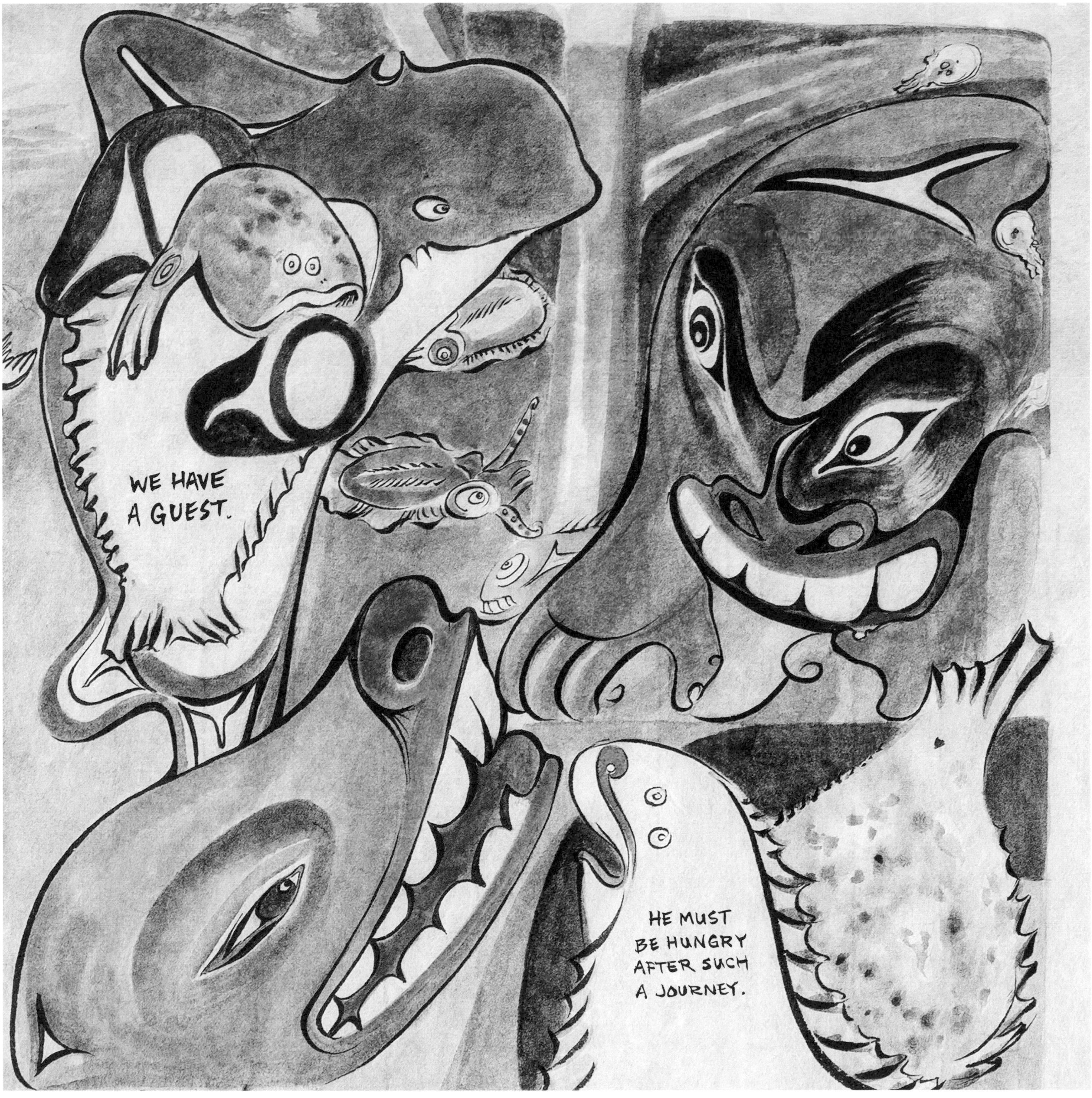
WE HAVE A GUEST.
HE MUST BE HUNGRY AFTER SUCH A JOURNEY.

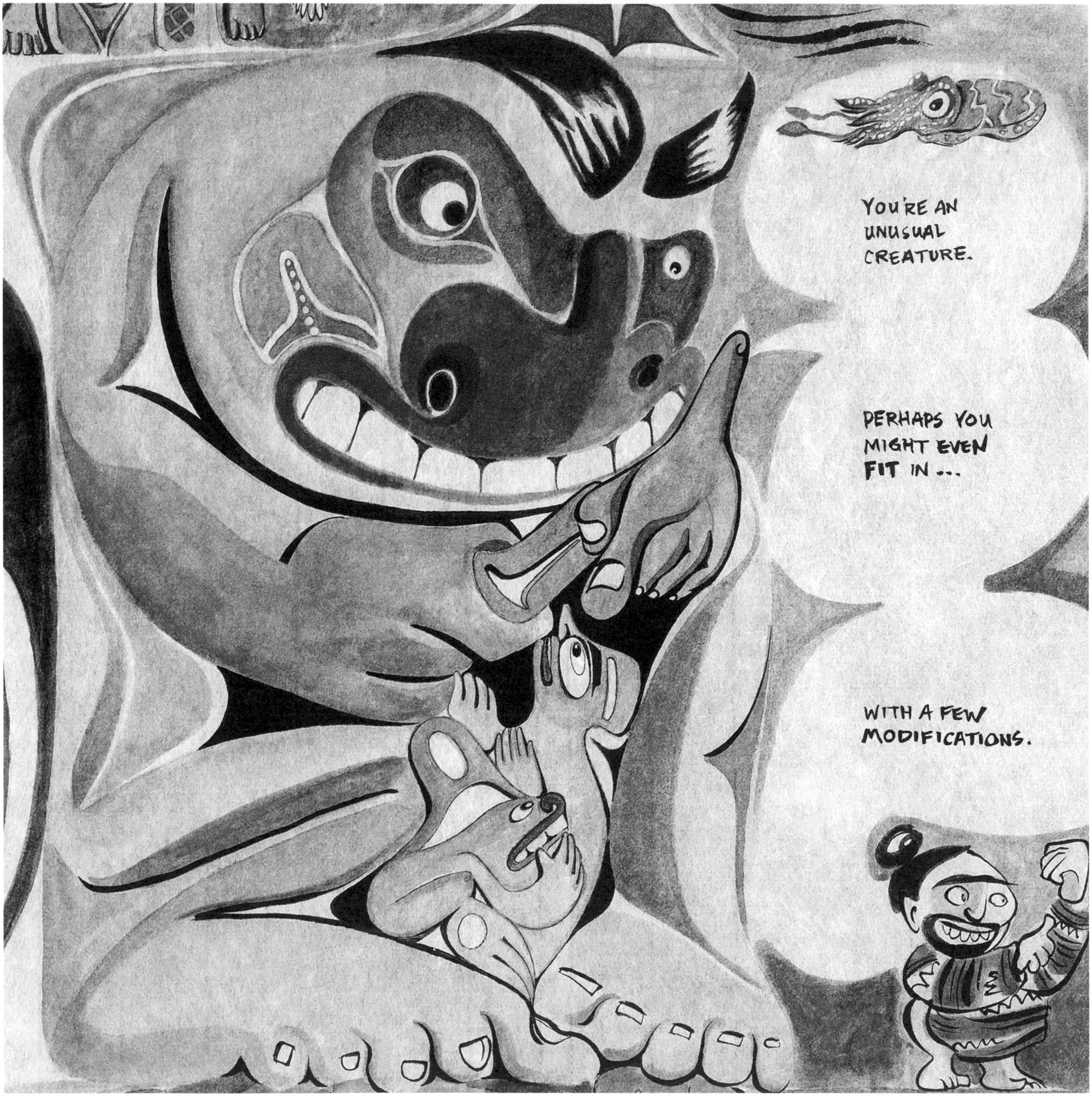
YOU'RE AN UNUSUAL CREATURE.
PERHAPS YOU MIGHT EVEN FIT IN...
WITH A FEW MODIFICATIONS.

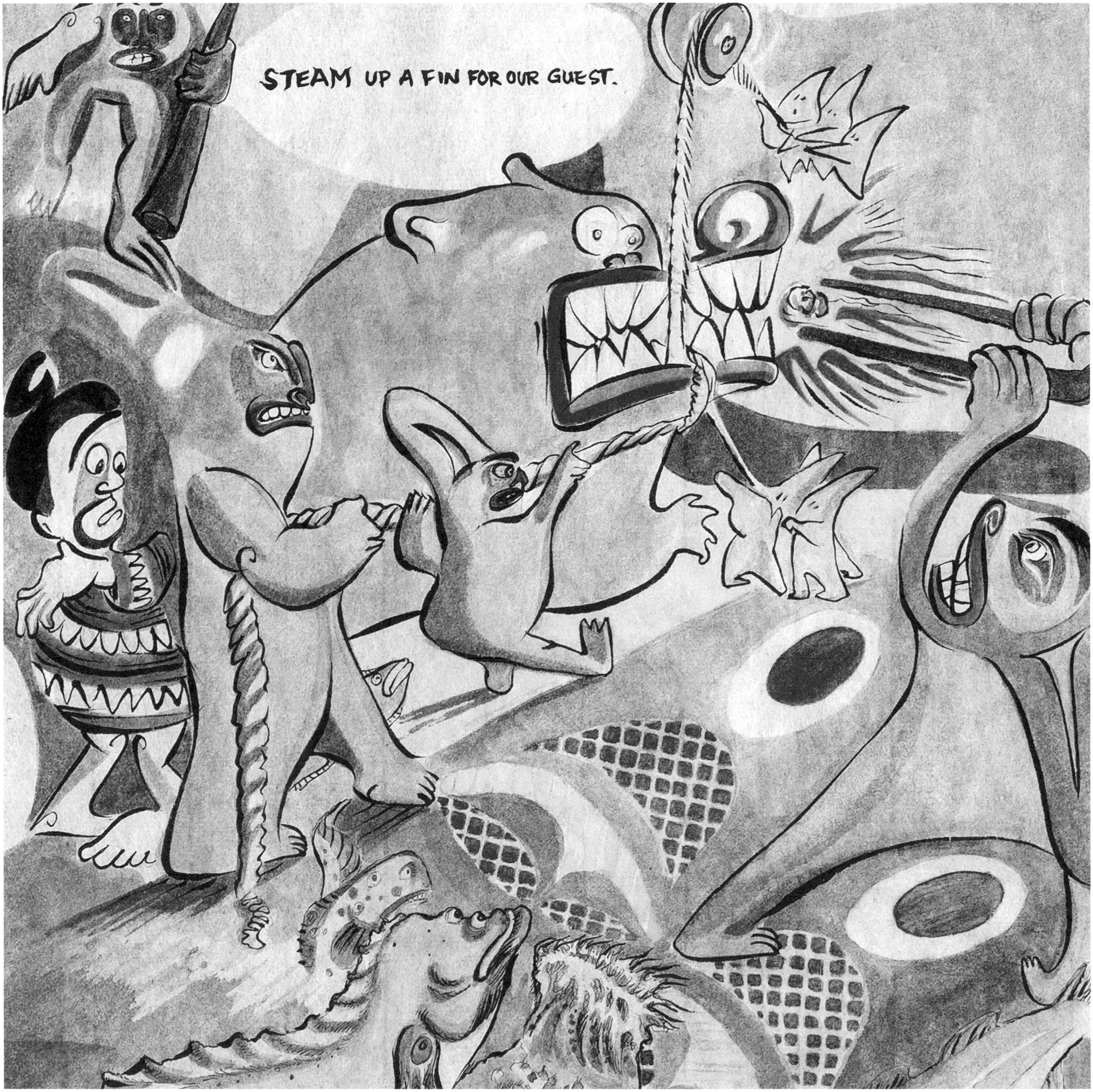
STEAM UP A FIN FOR OUR GUEST.

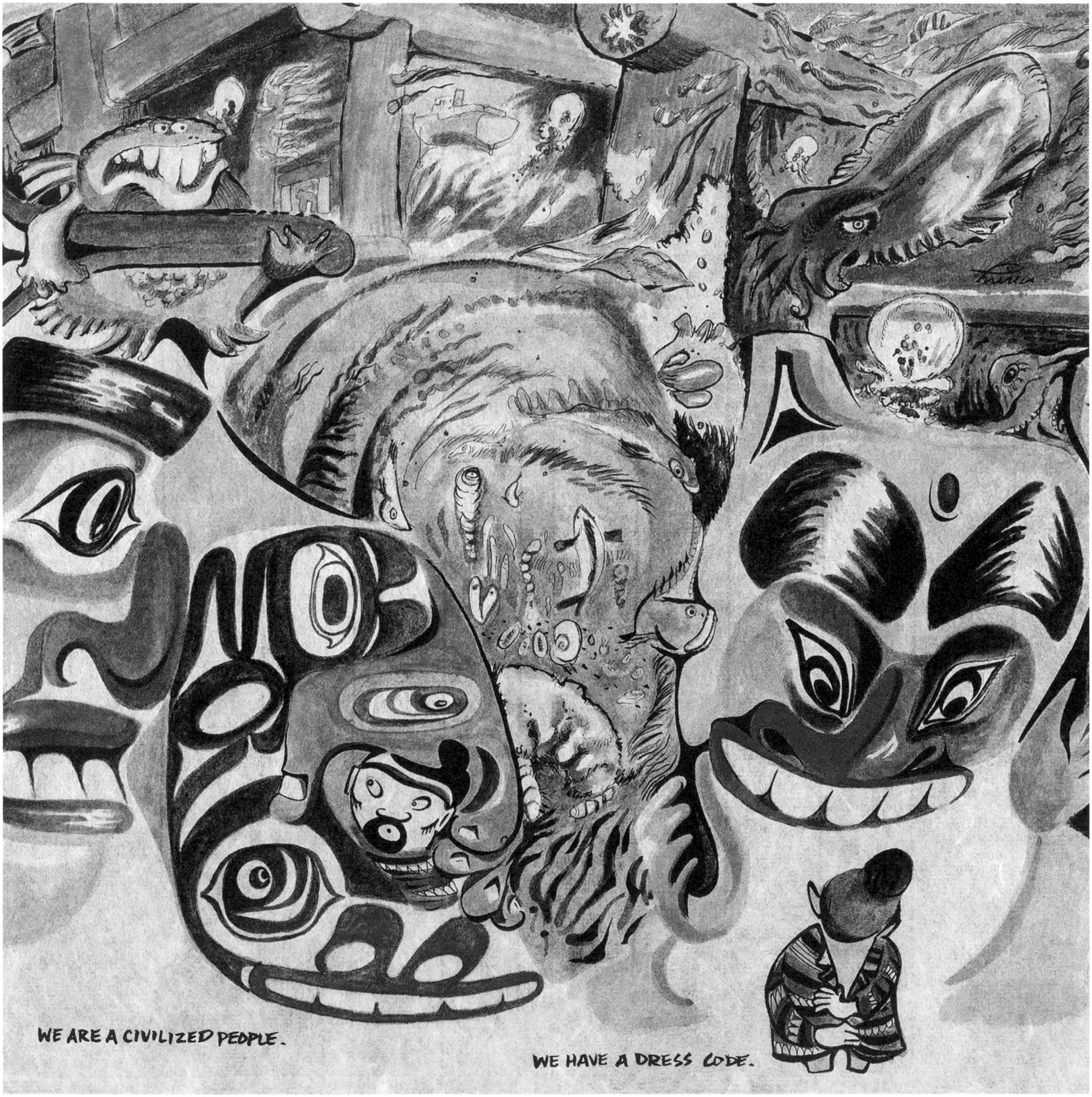
WE ARE A CIVILIZED PEOPLE.
WE HAVE A DRESS CODE.

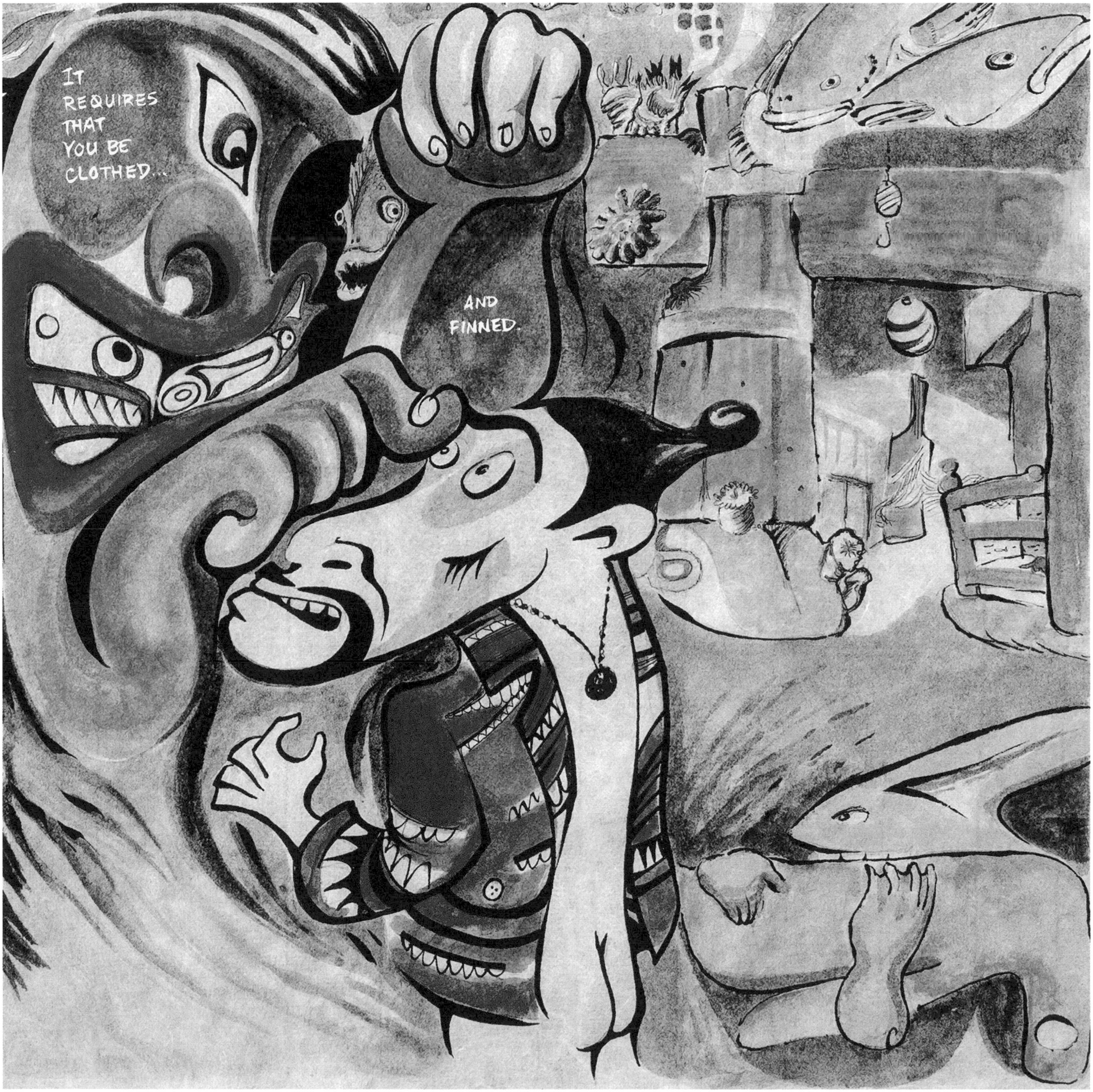
IT REQUIRES THAT YOU BE CLOTHED...
AND FINNED.

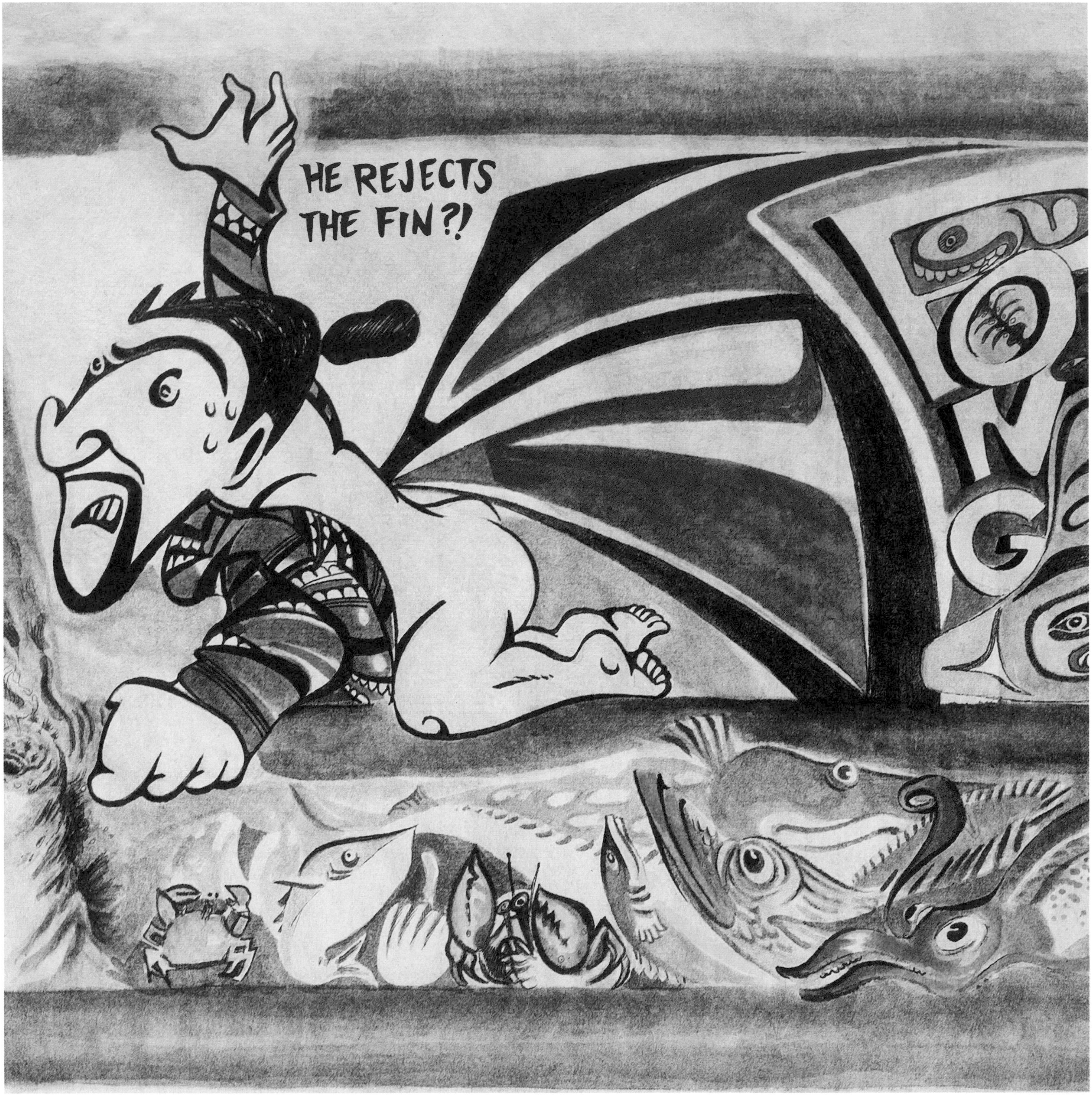
HE REJECTS THE FIN?!

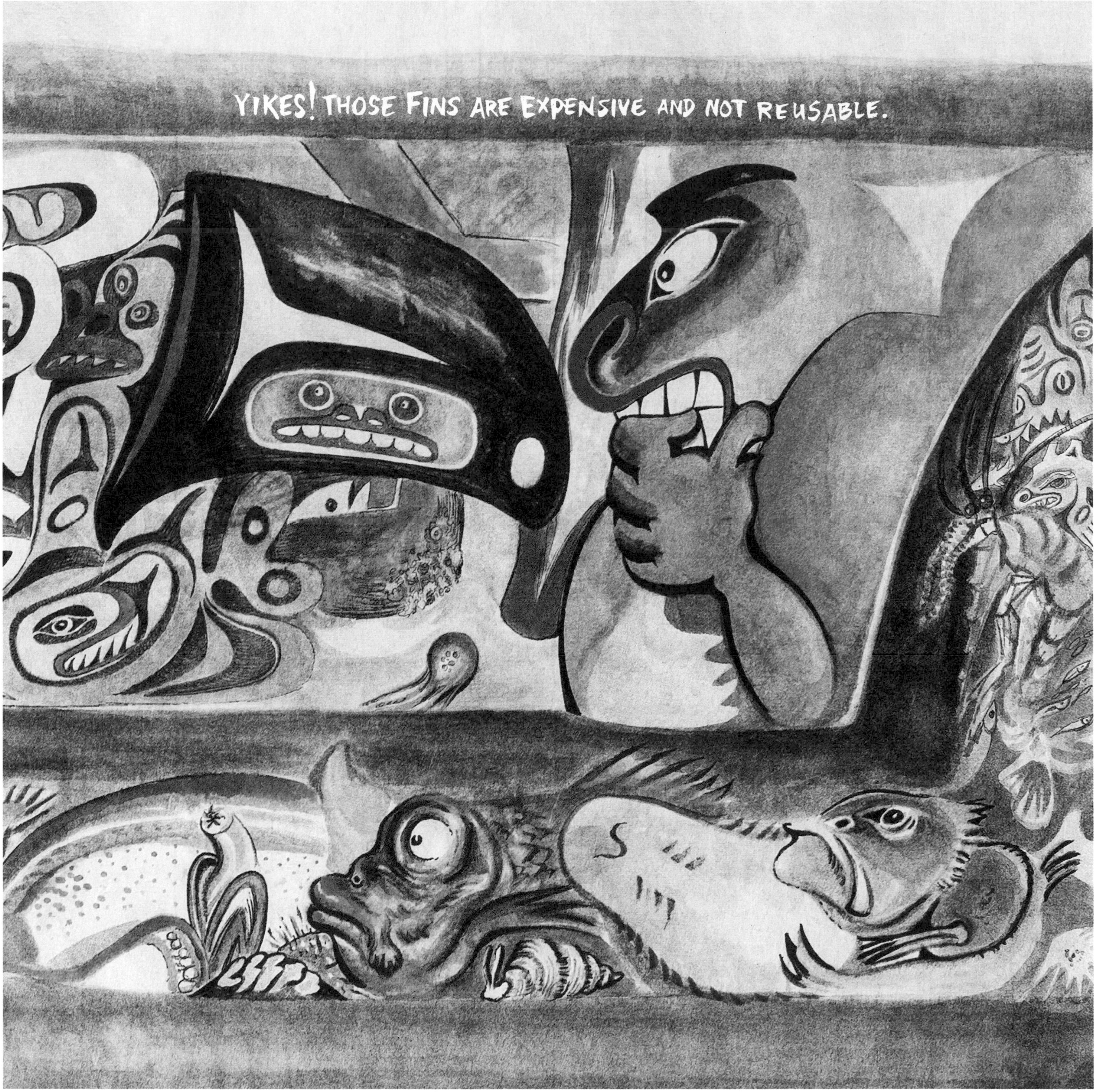
YIKES! THOSE FINS ARE EXPENSIVE AND NOT REUSABLE.

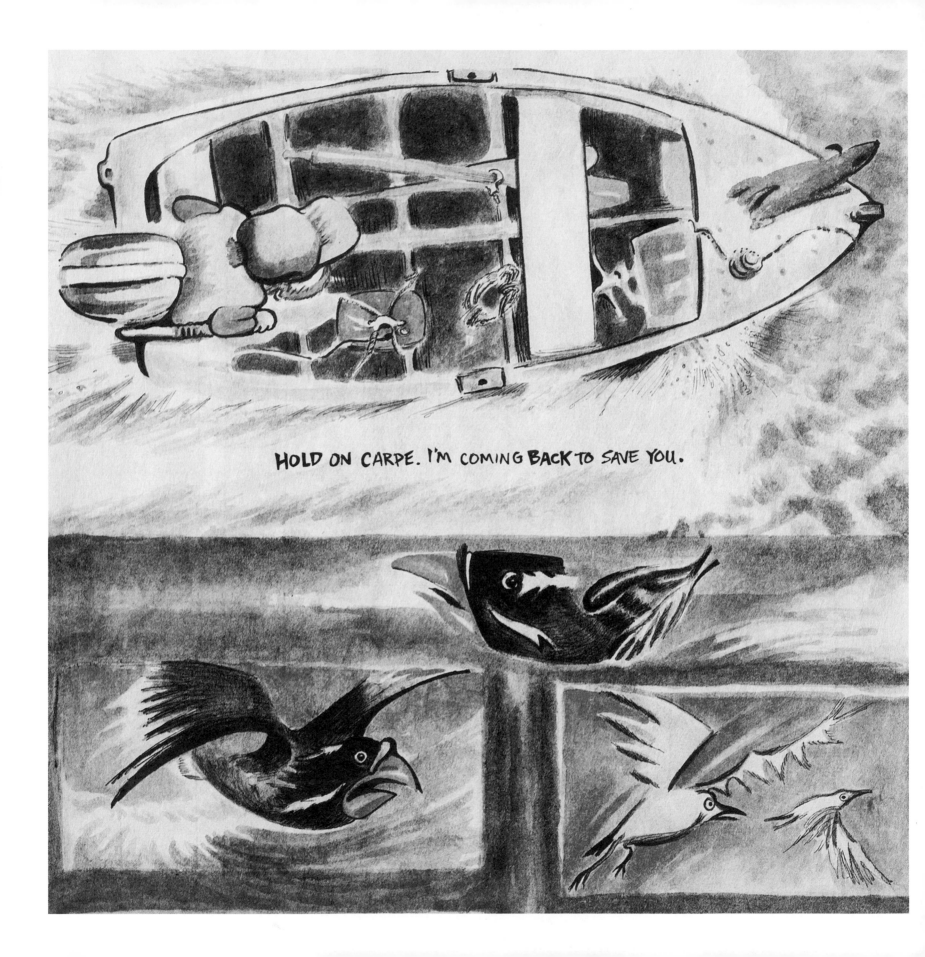

HOLD ON CARPE. I'M COMING BACK TO SAVE YOU.

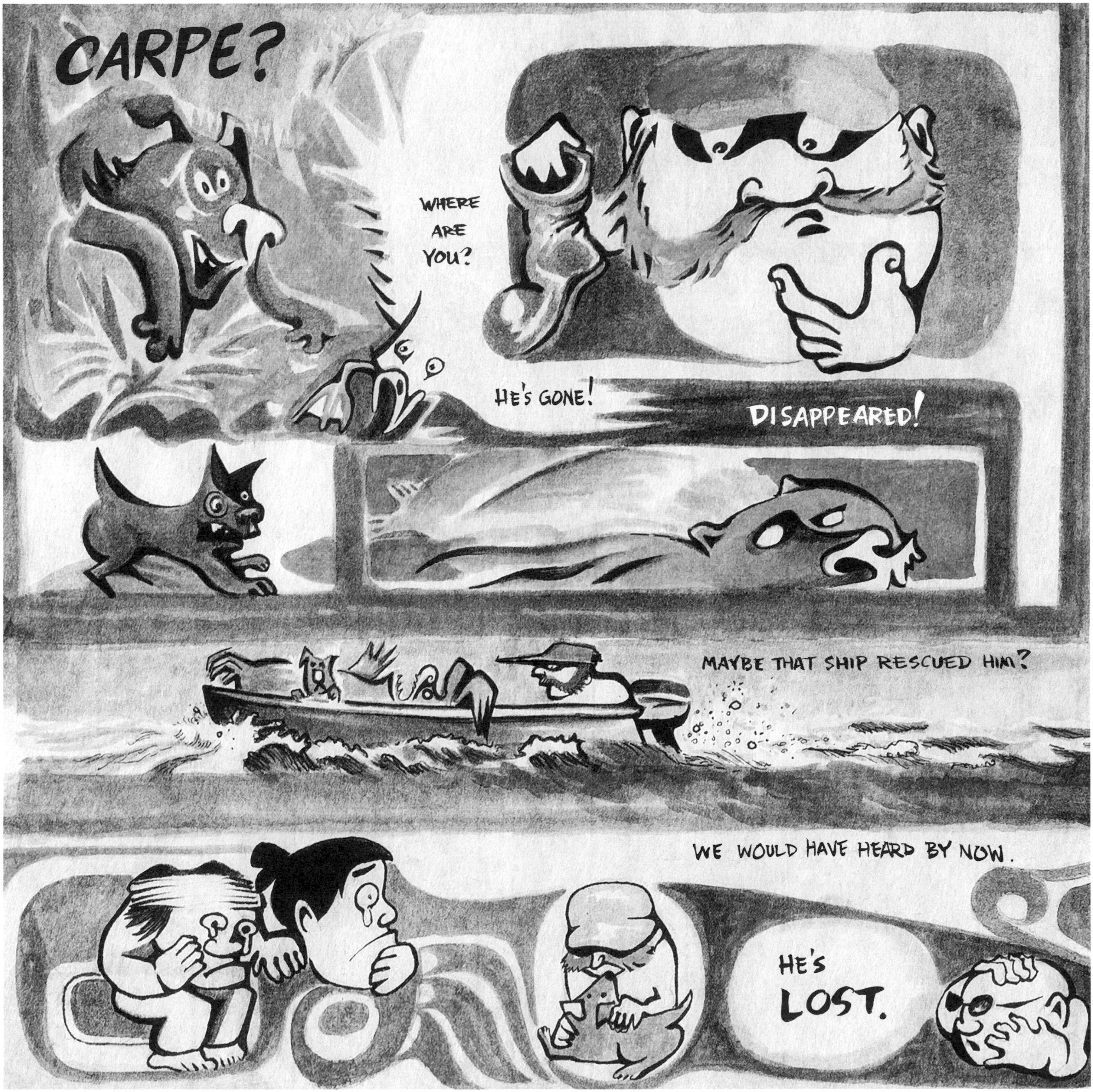
CARPE?
WHERE ARE YOU?
HE'S GONE!
DISAPPEARED!
MAYBE THAT SHIP RESCUED HIM?
WE WOULD HAVE HEARD BY NOW.
HE'S LOST.

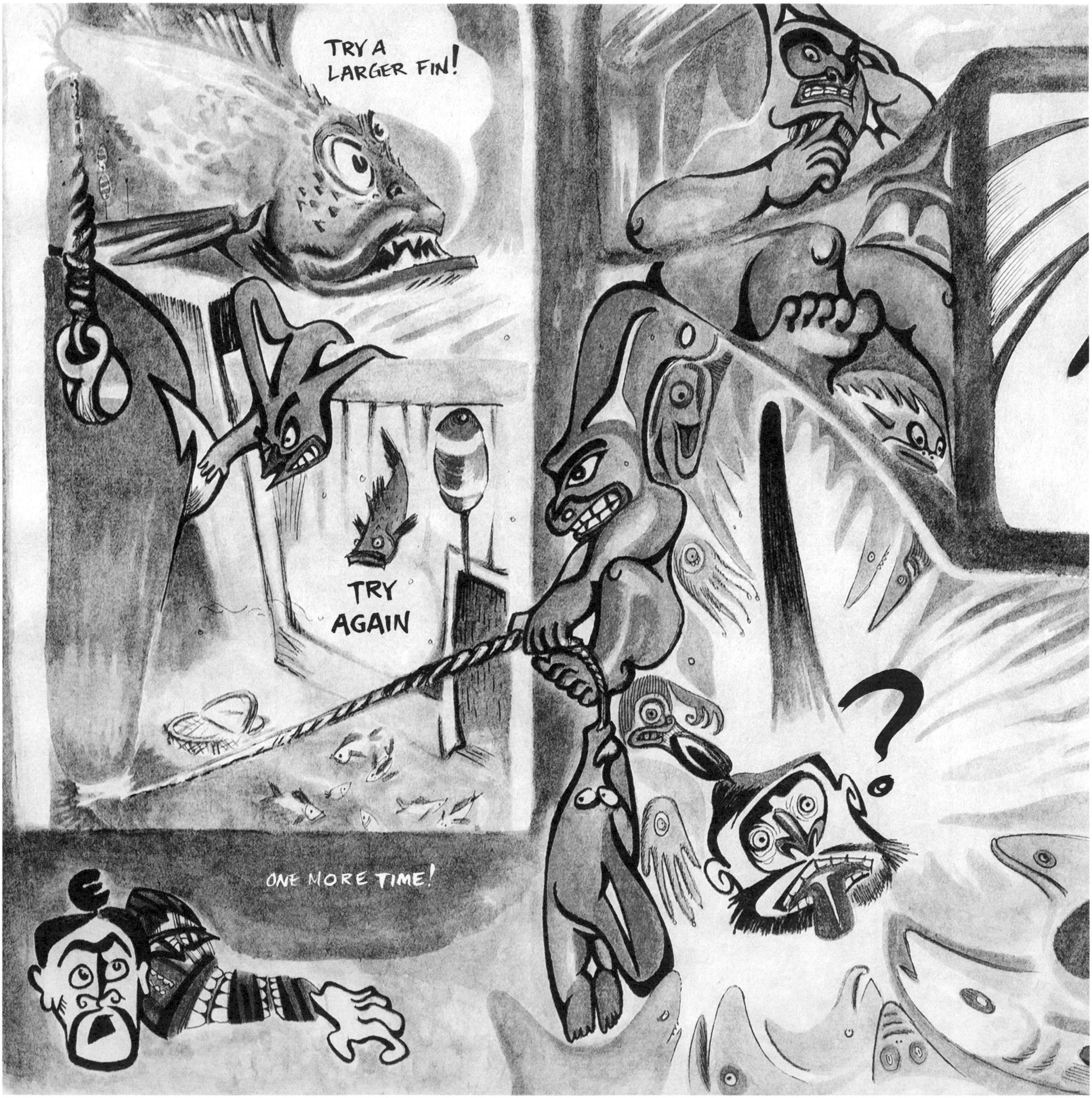
TRY A LARGER FIN!
TRY AGAIN
ONE MORE TIME!
?

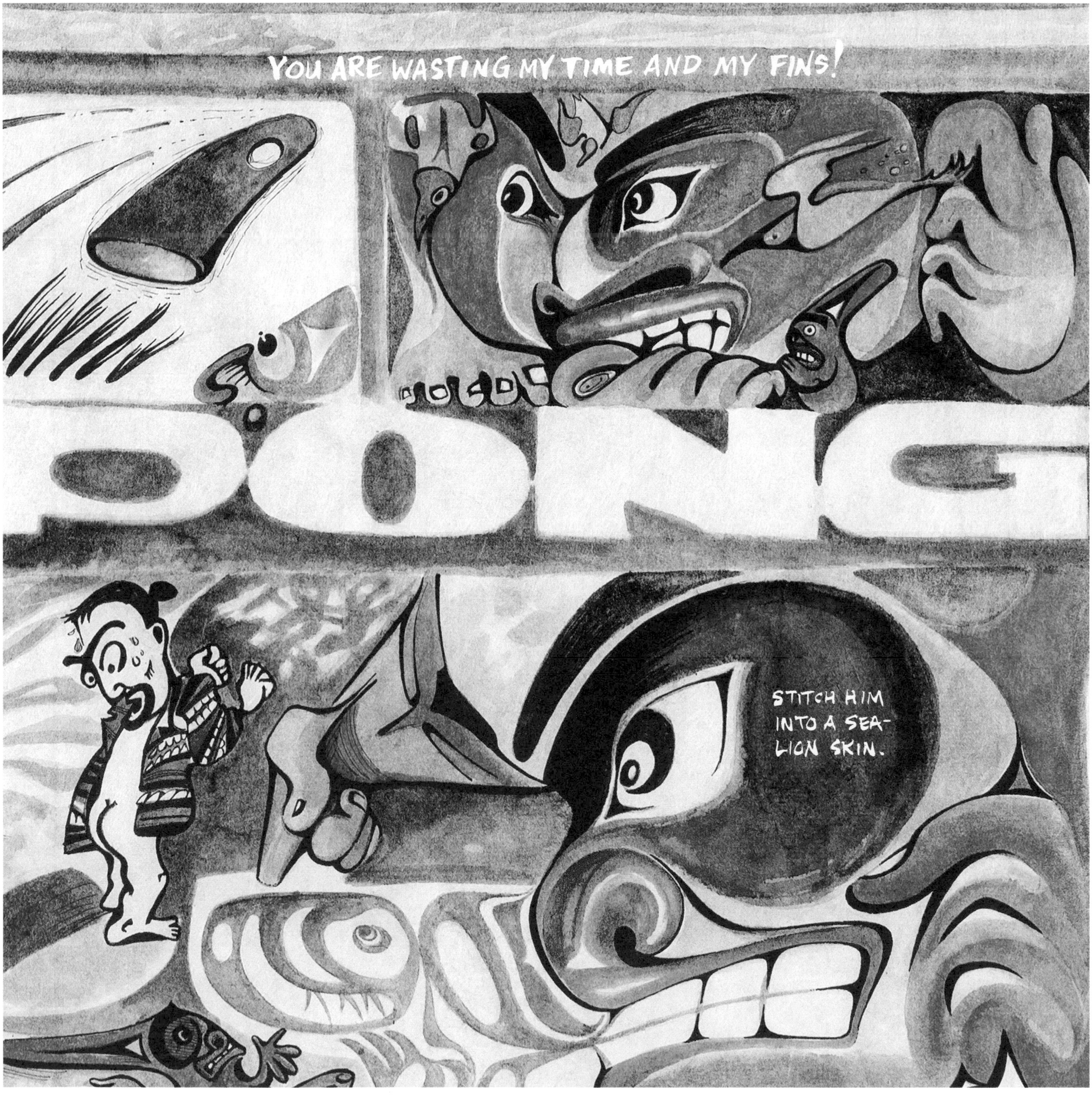
YOU ARE WASTING MY TIME AND MY FINS!
PONG
STITCH HIM INTO A SEA-LION SKIN.

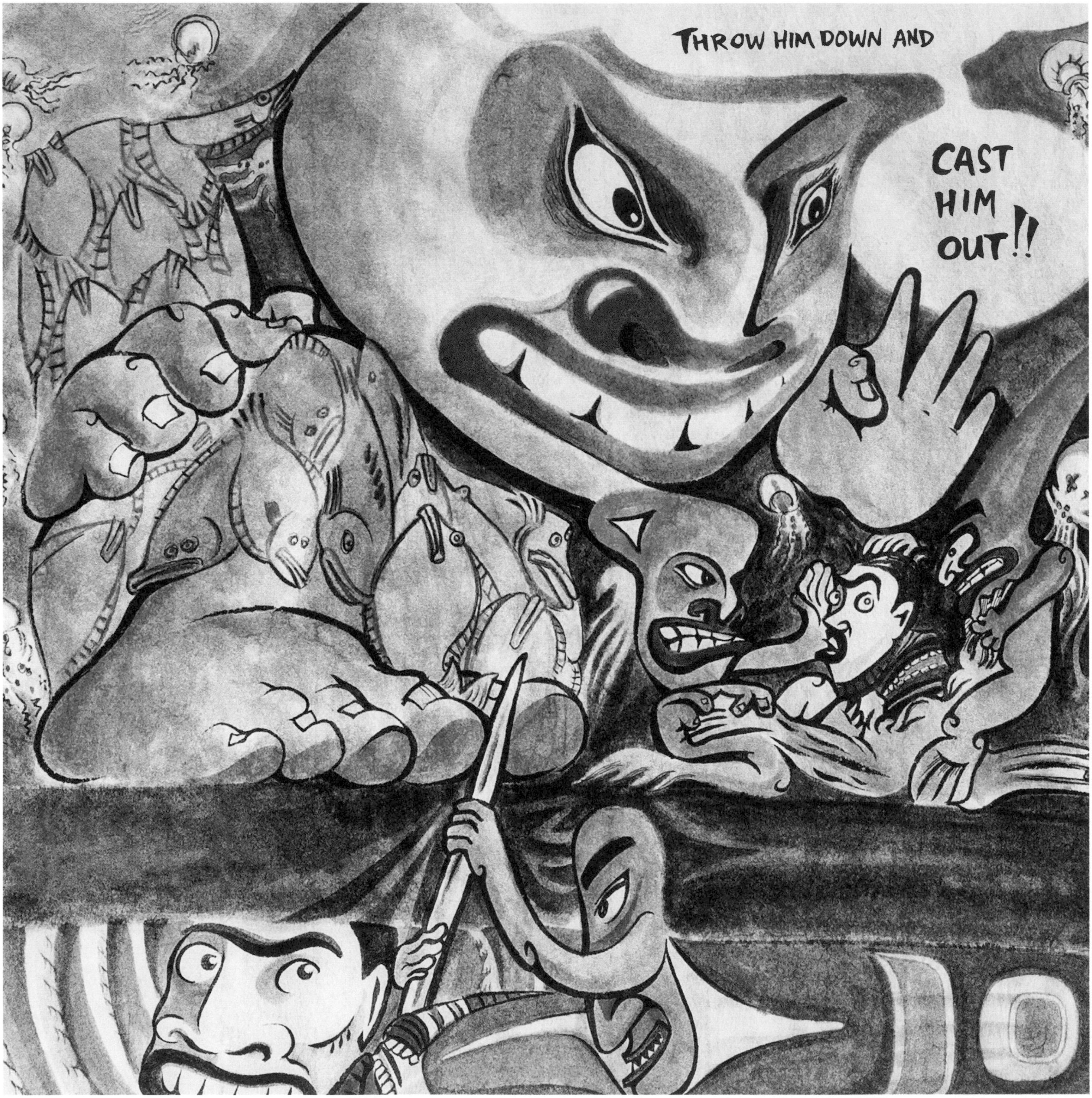
THROW HIM DOWN AND
CAST HIM OUT!!

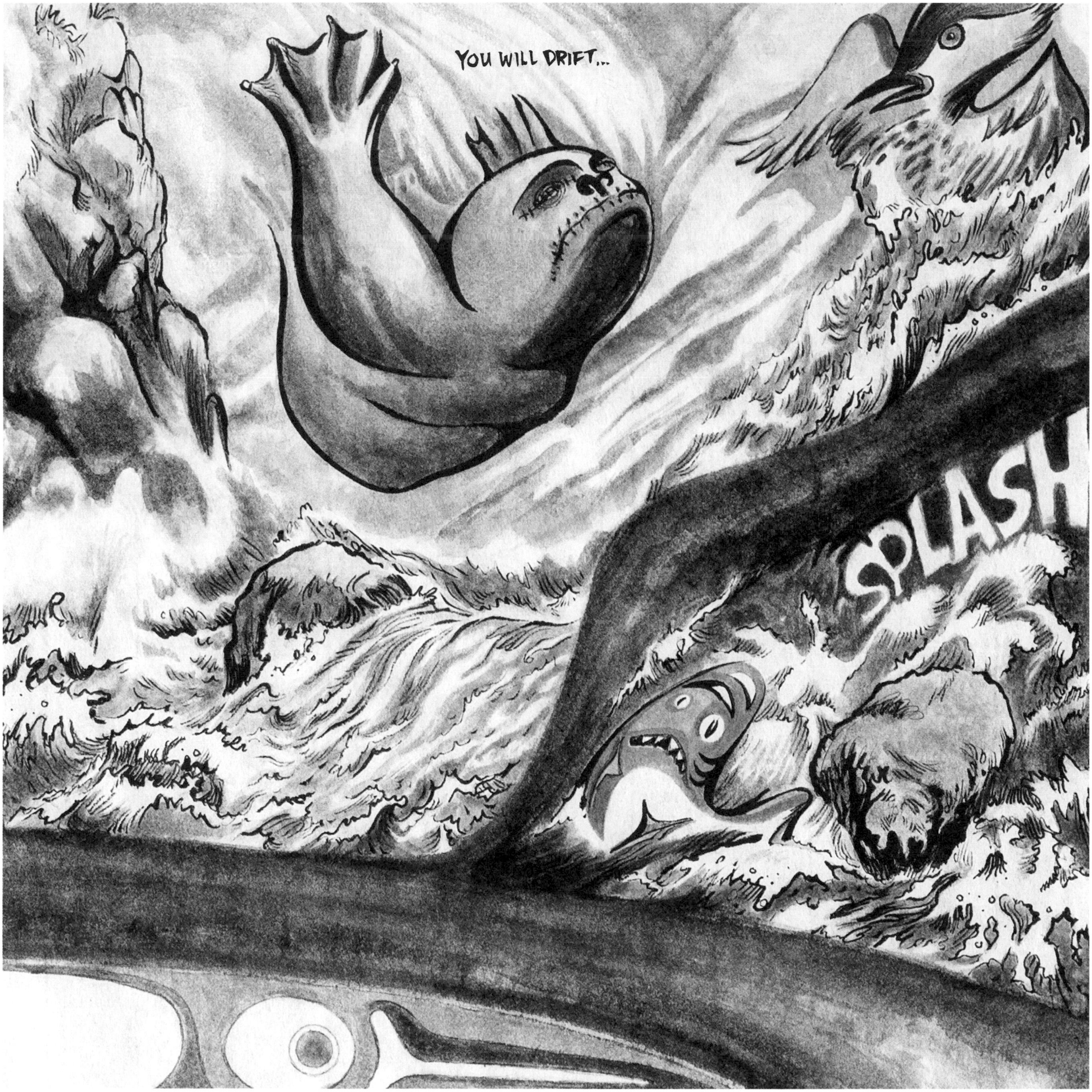
YOU WILL DRIFT...
SPLASH

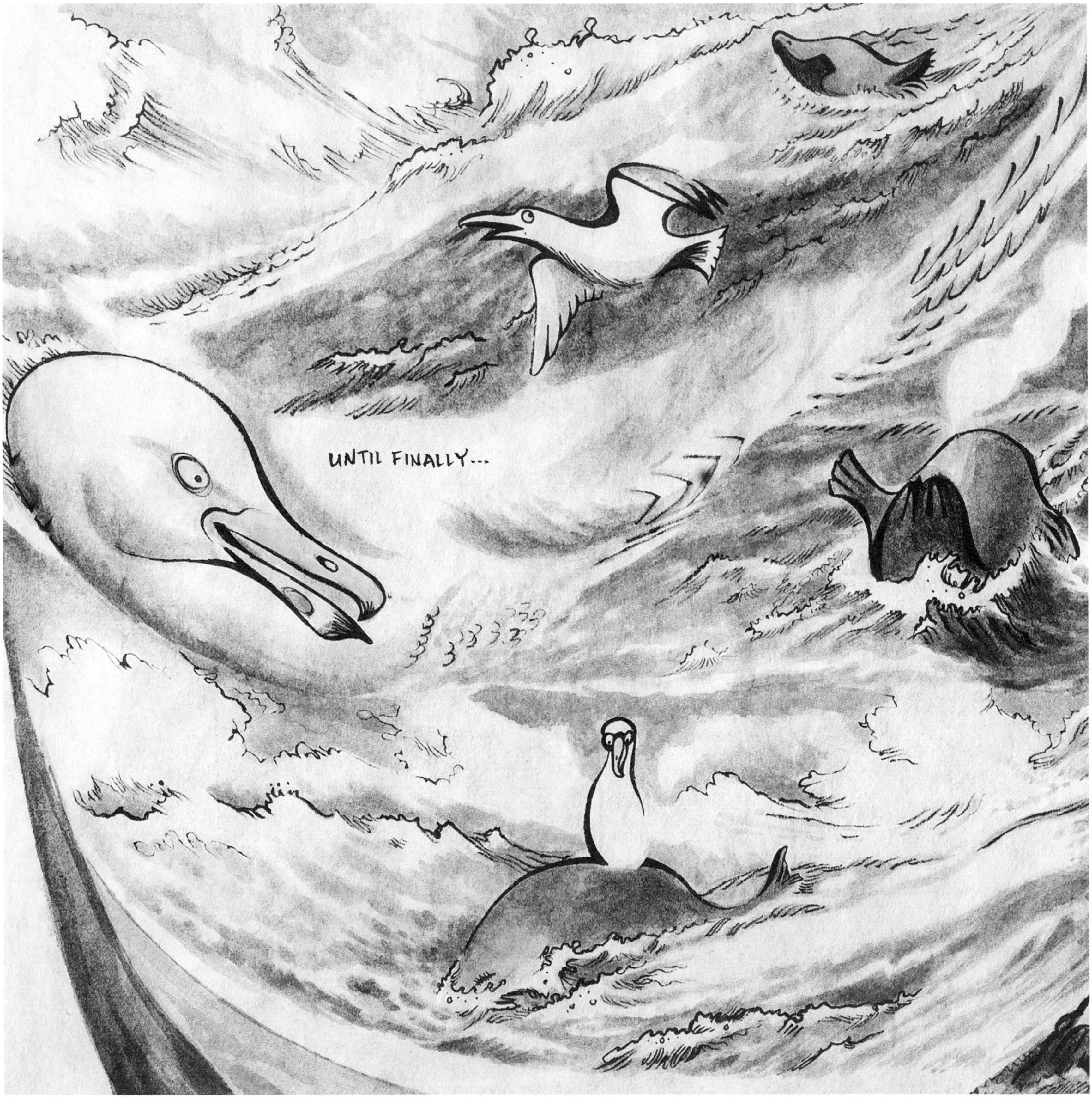
UNTIL FINALLY...

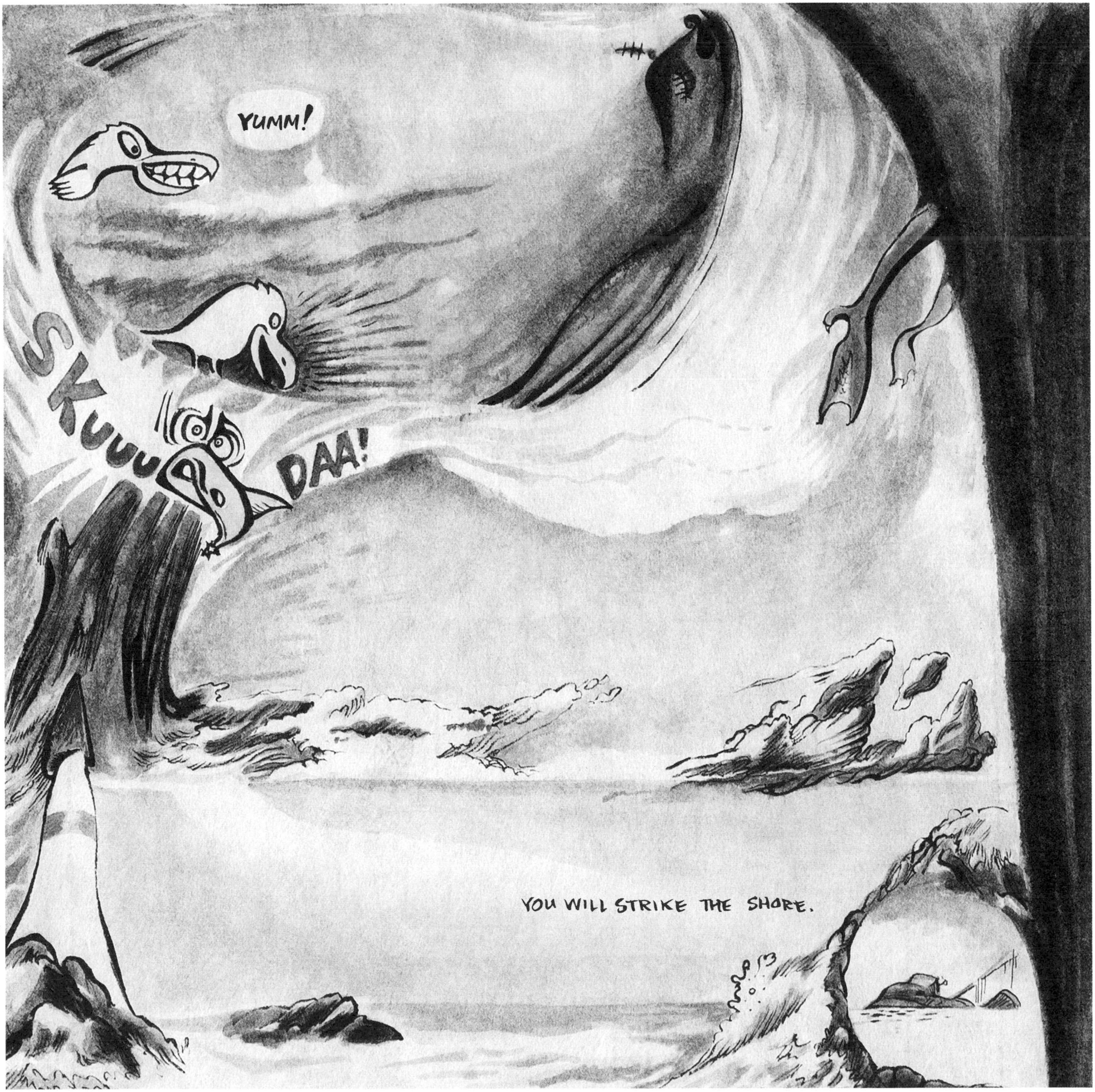
YUMM!
SKUUUDAA!
YOU WILL STRIKE THE SHORE.

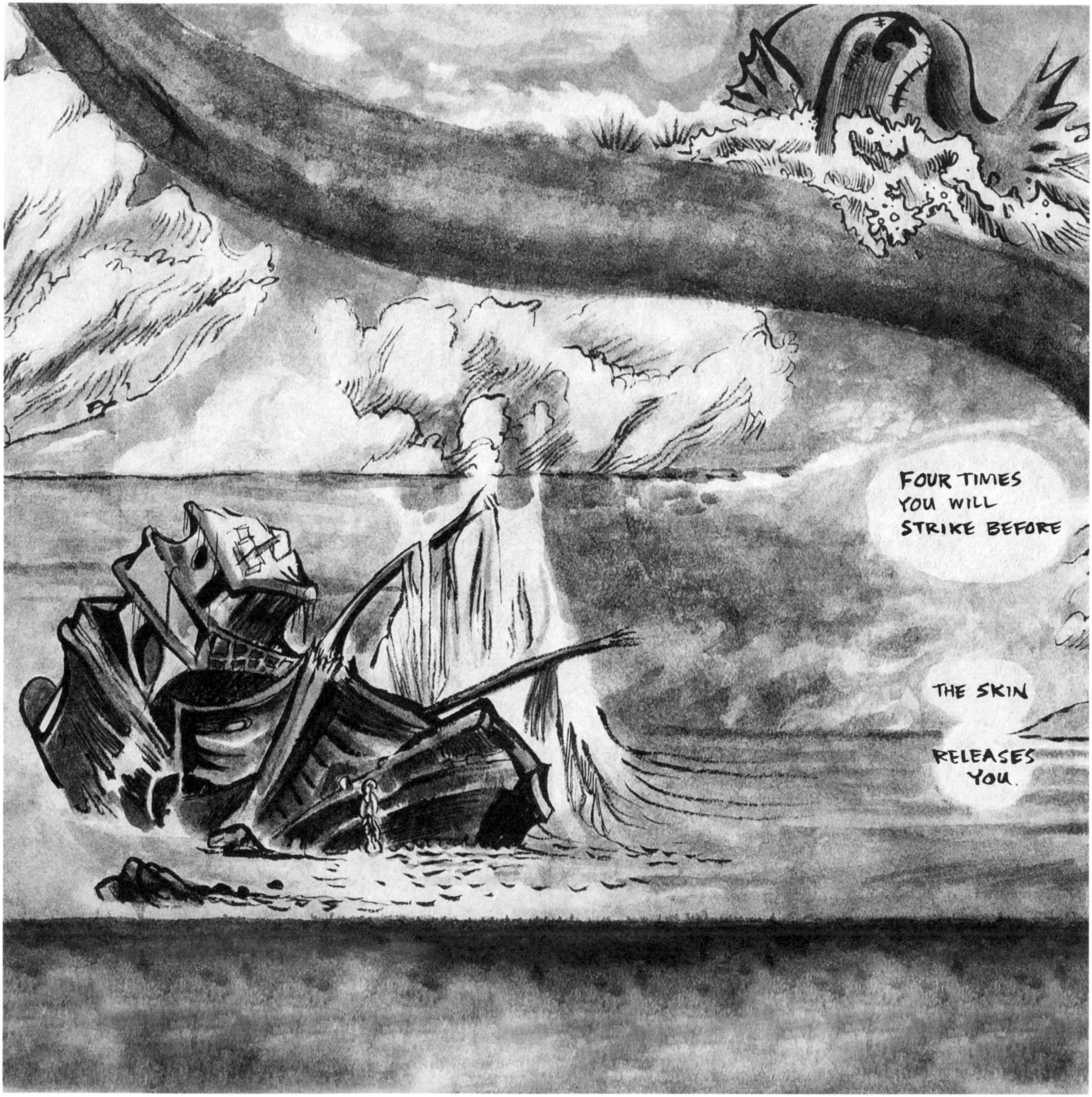
FOUR TIMES
YOU WILL
STRIKE BEFORE
THE SKIN
RELEASES
YOU.

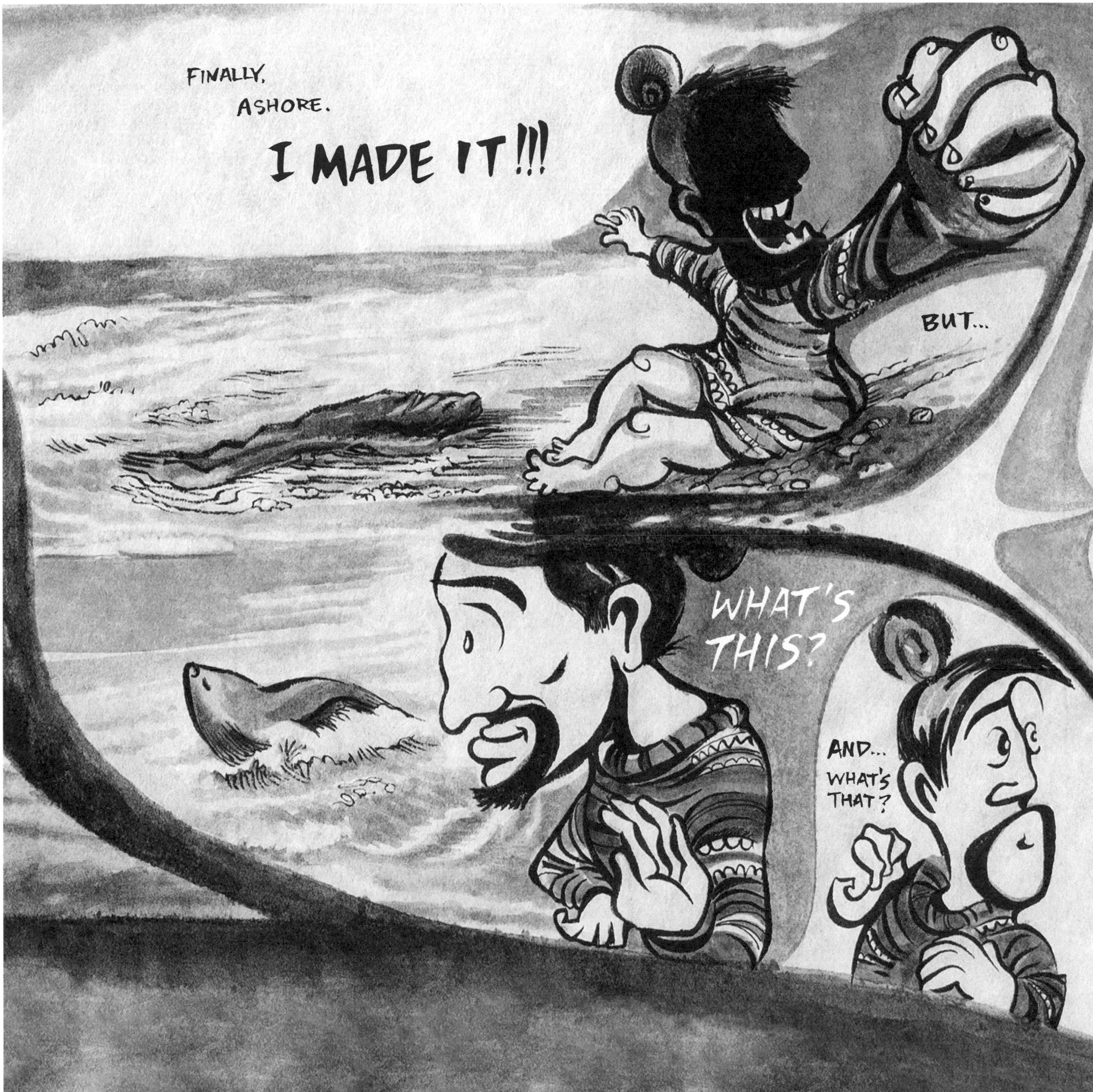

FINALLY,
ASHORE.
I MADE IT!!!
BUT...
WHAT'S THIS?
AND... WHAT'S THAT?

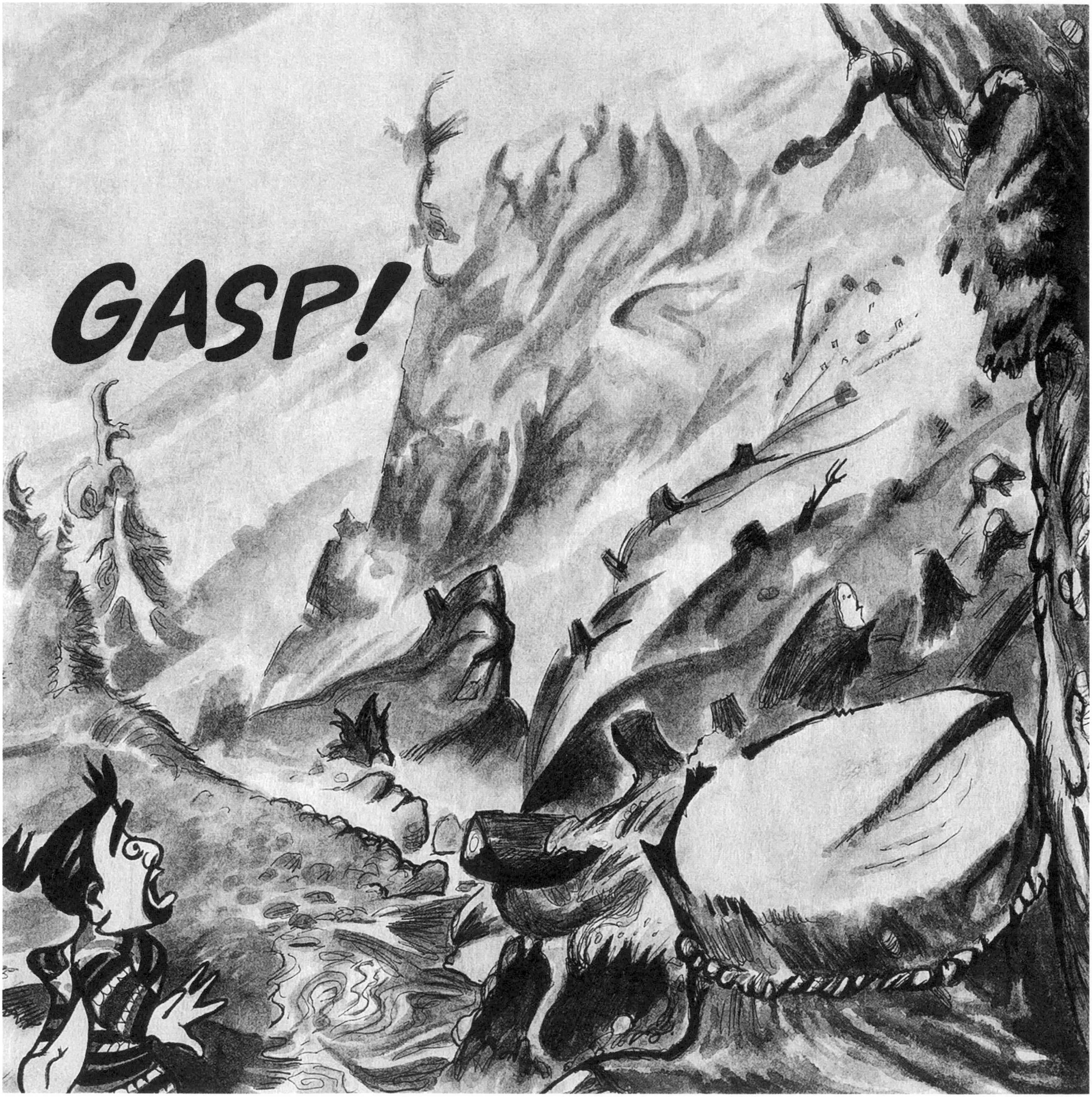
GASP!

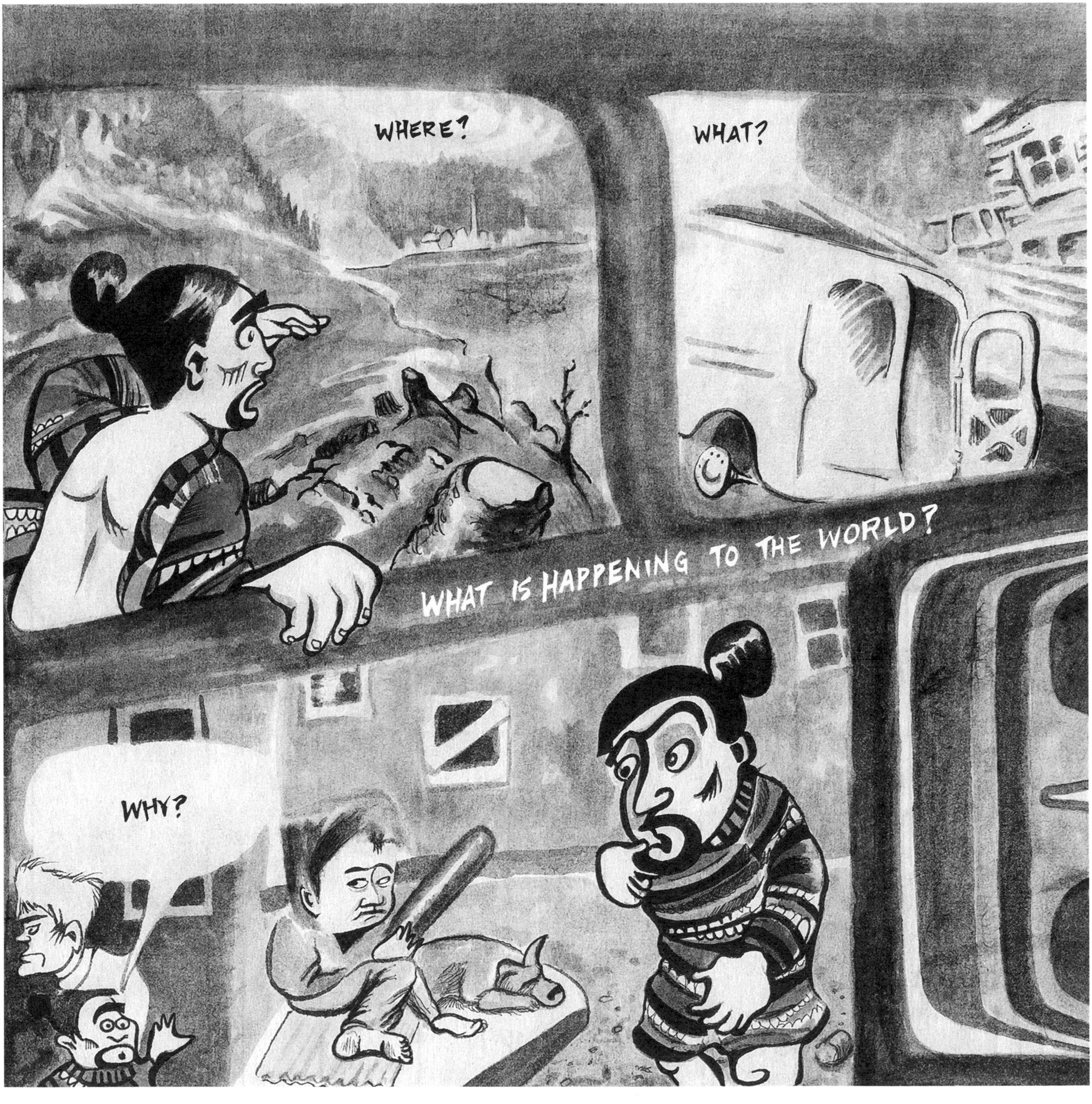
WHERE?
WHAT?
WHAT IS HAPPENING TO THE WORLD?
WHY?

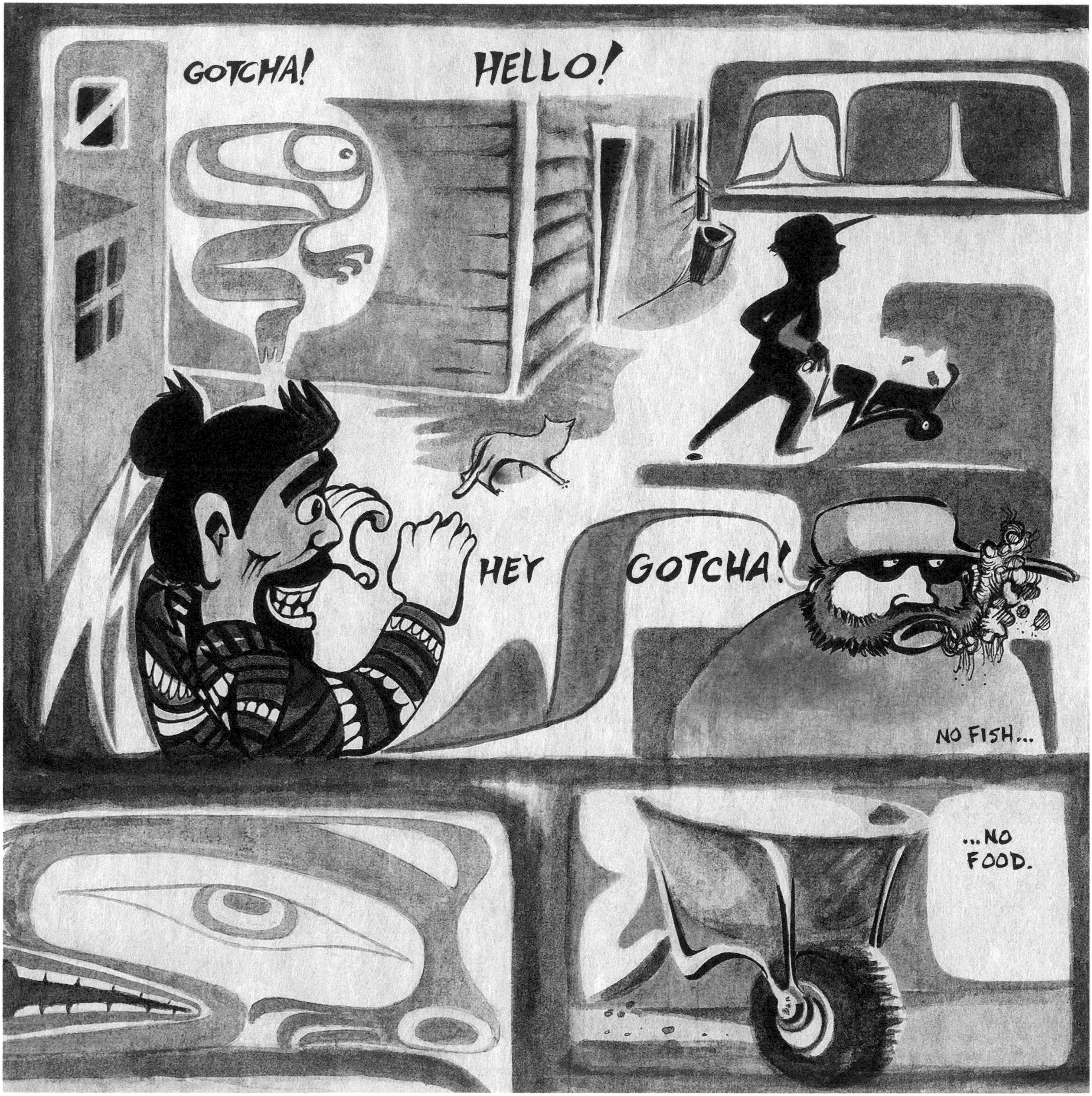
GOTCHA!
HELLO!
HEY
GOTCHA!
NO FISH...
...NO FOOD.

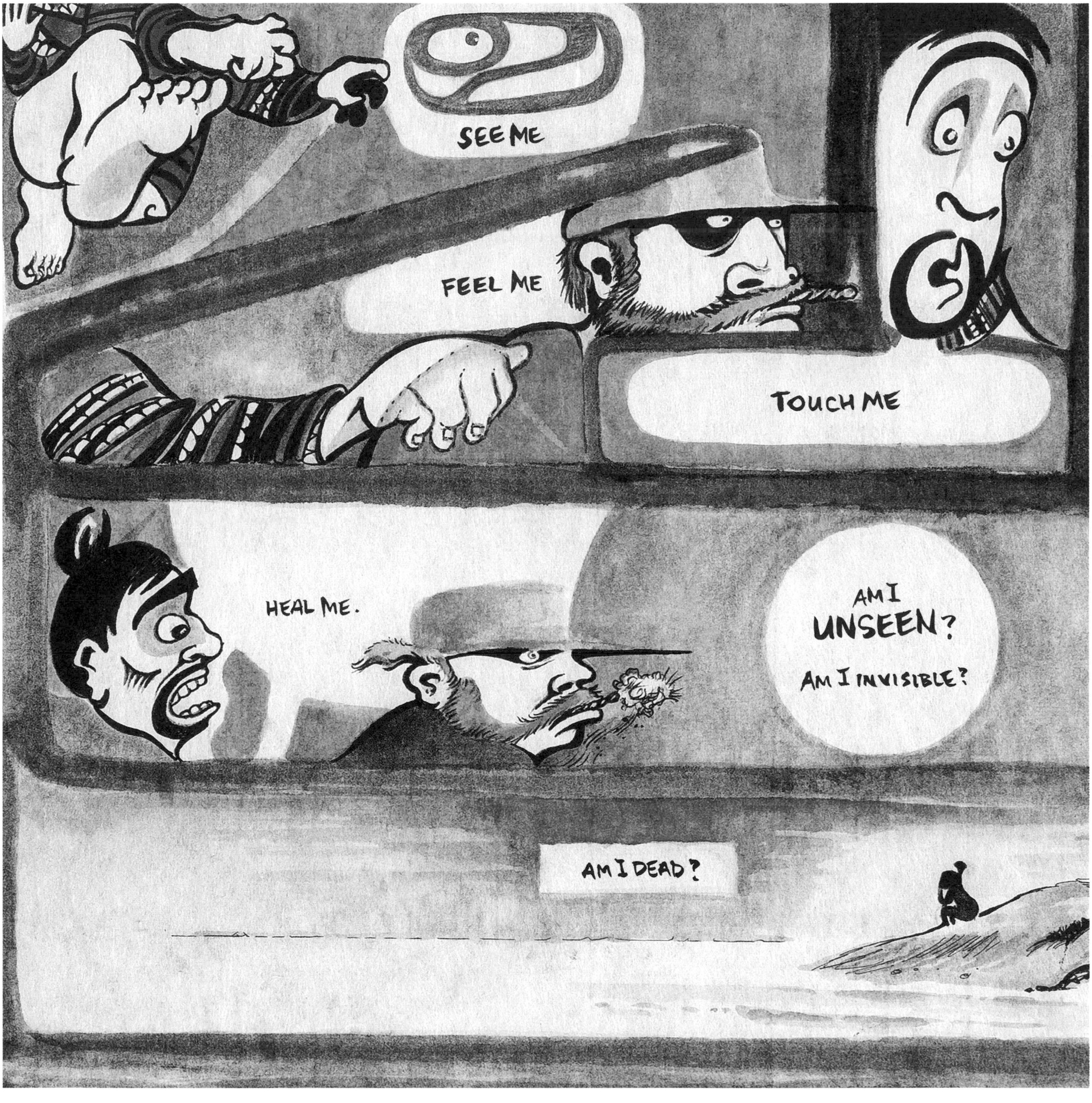
SEE ME
FEEL ME
TOUCH ME
HEAL ME.
AM I UNSEEN?
AM I INVISIBLE?
AM I DEAD?

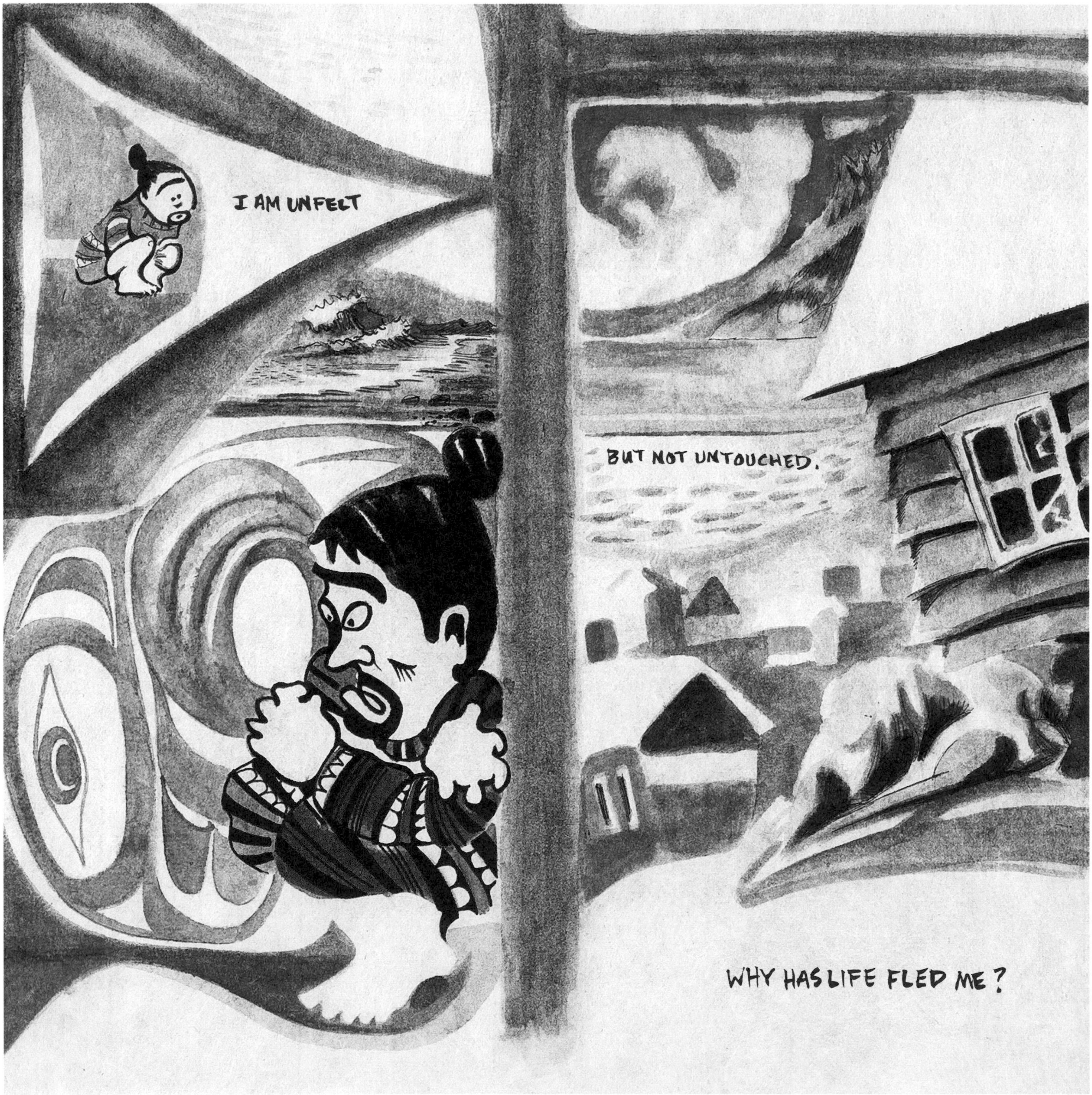
I AM UNFELT
BUT NOT UNTOUCHED.
WHY HAS LIFE FLED ME?

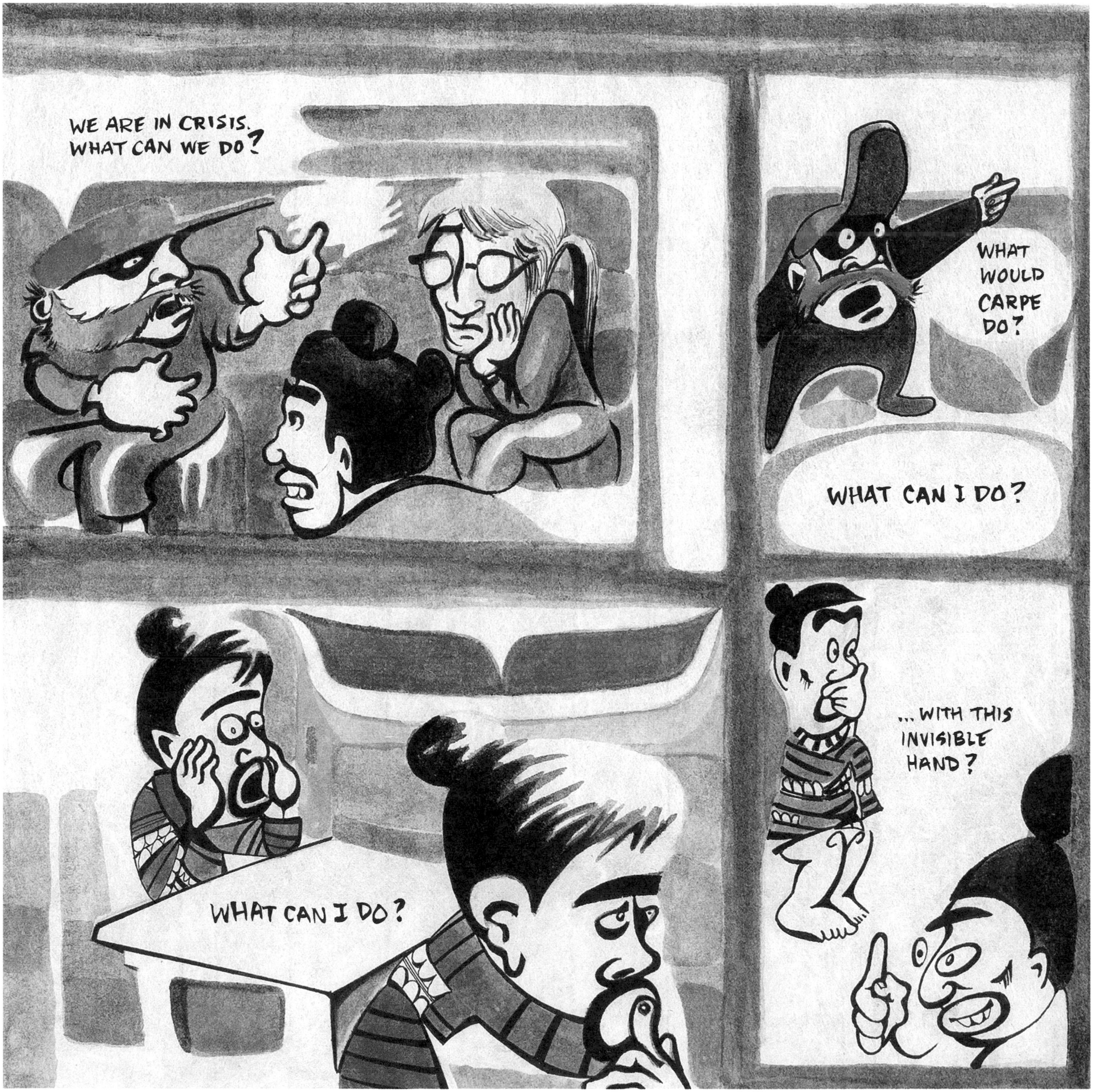
WE ARE IN CRISIS.
WHAT CAN WE DO?
WHAT WOULD CARPE DO?
WHAT CAN I DO?
WHAT CAN I DO?
...WITH THIS INVISIBLE HAND?

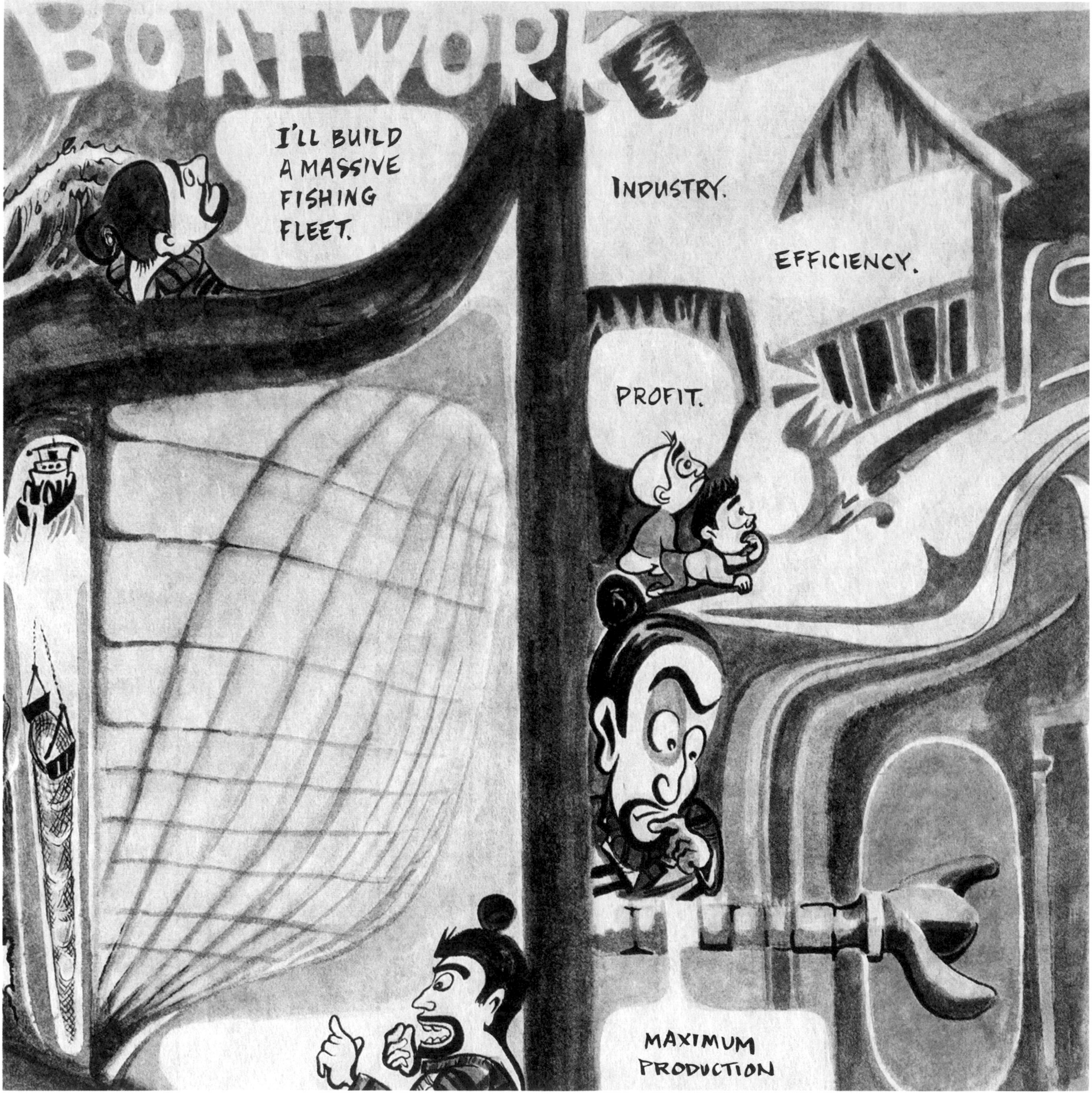
BOATWORK
I'LL BUILD A MASSIVE FISHING FLEET.
INDUSTRY.
EFFICIENCY.
PROFIT.
MAXIMUM PRODUCTION

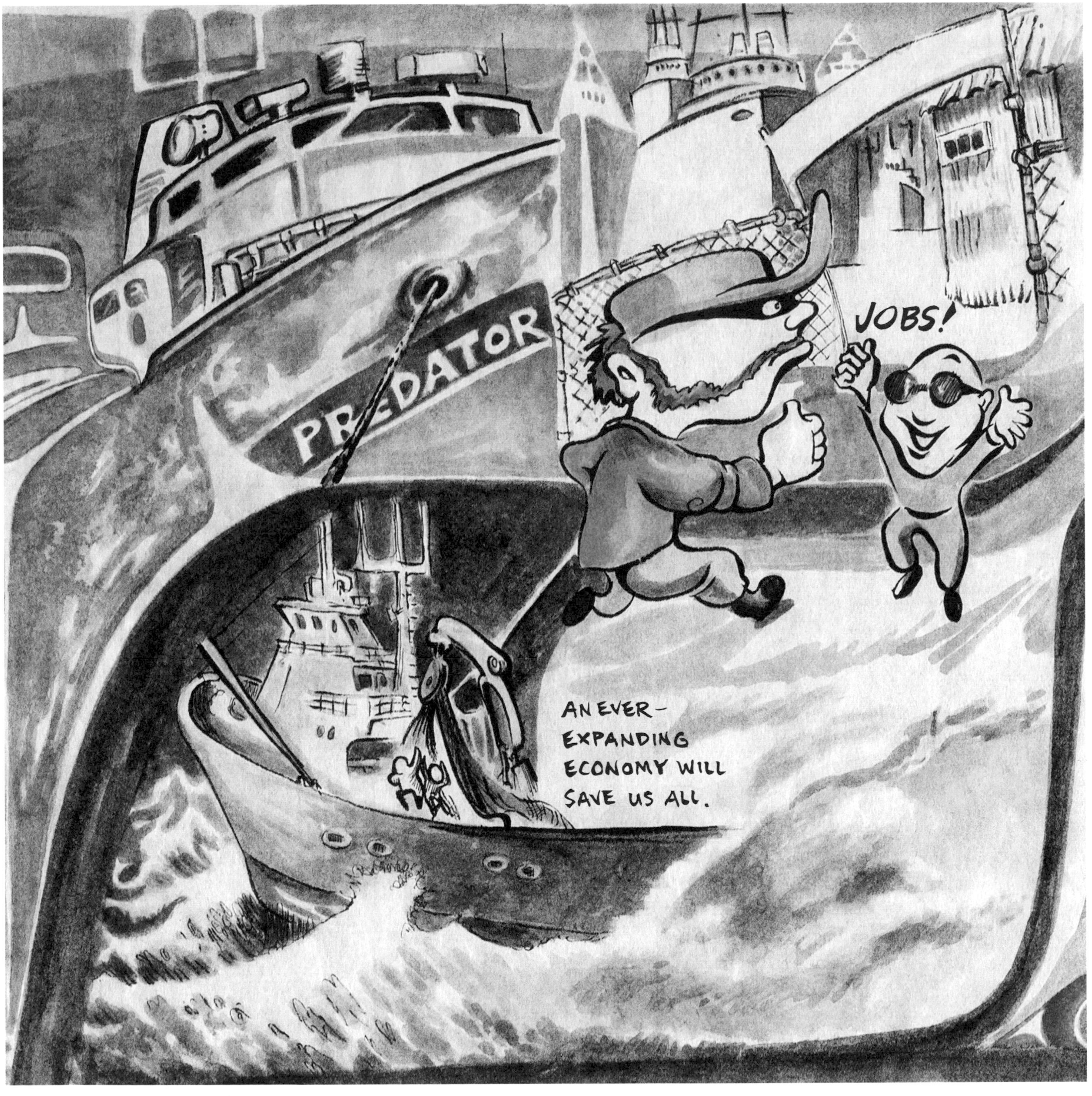
PREDATOR
JOBS!
AN EVER-
EXPANDING
ECONOMY WILL
SAVE US ALL.

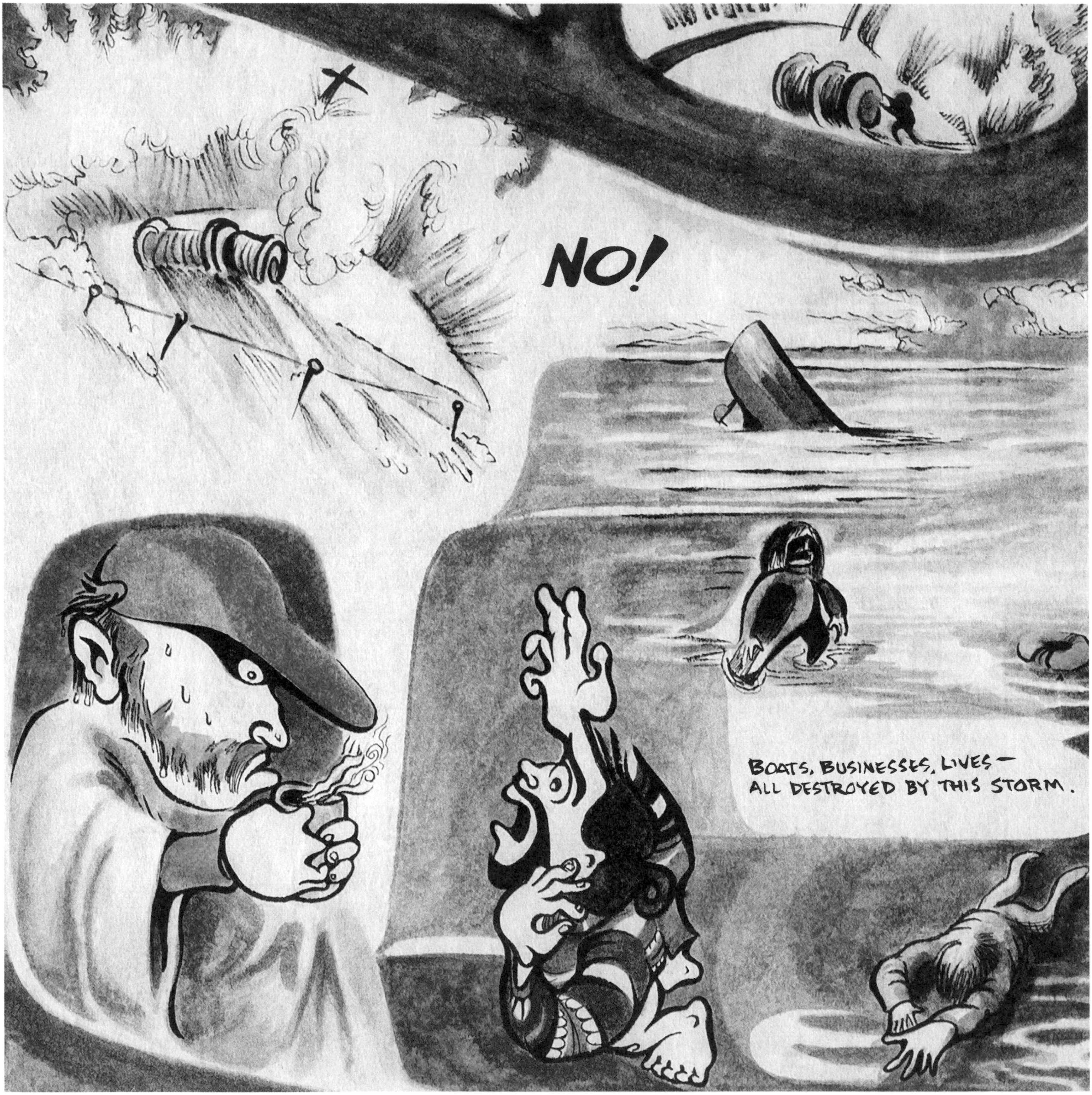
NO!
BOATS, BUSINESSES, LIVES—
ALL DESTROYED BY THIS STORM.

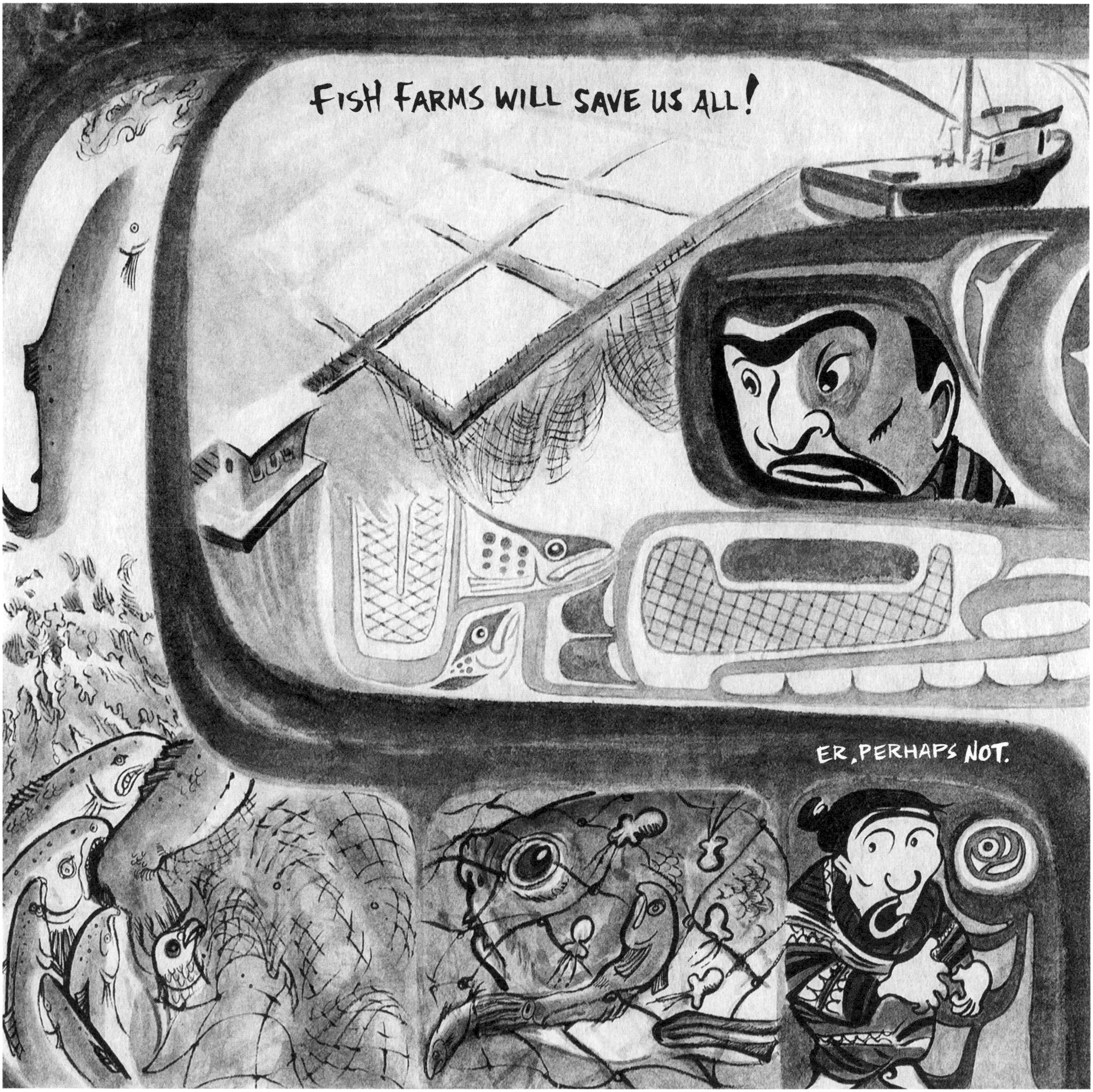
FISH FARMS WILL SAVE US ALL!
ER, PERHAPS NOT.

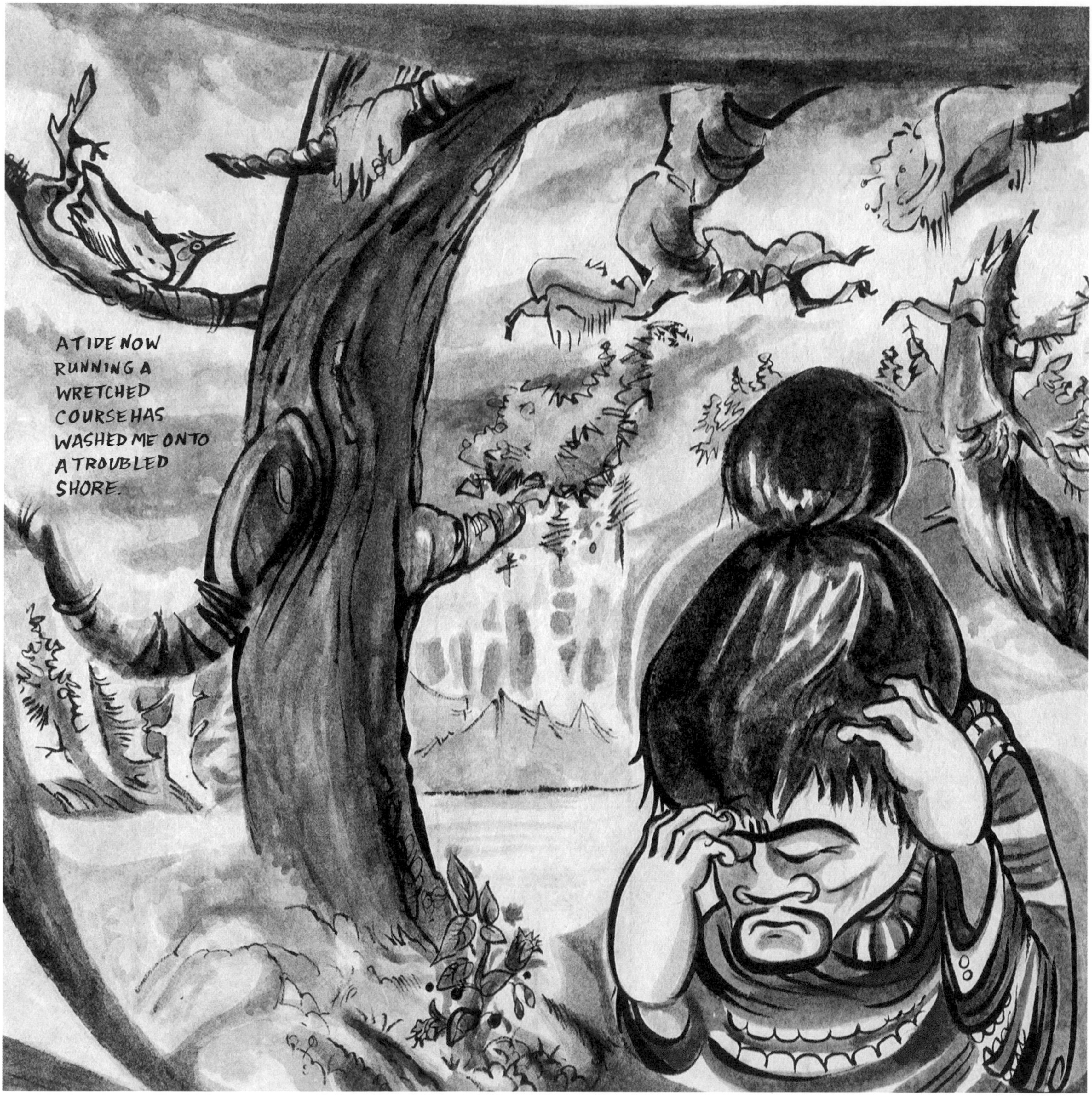
A TIDE NOW RUNNING A WRETCHED COURSE HAS WASHED ME ONTO A TROUBLED SHORE.

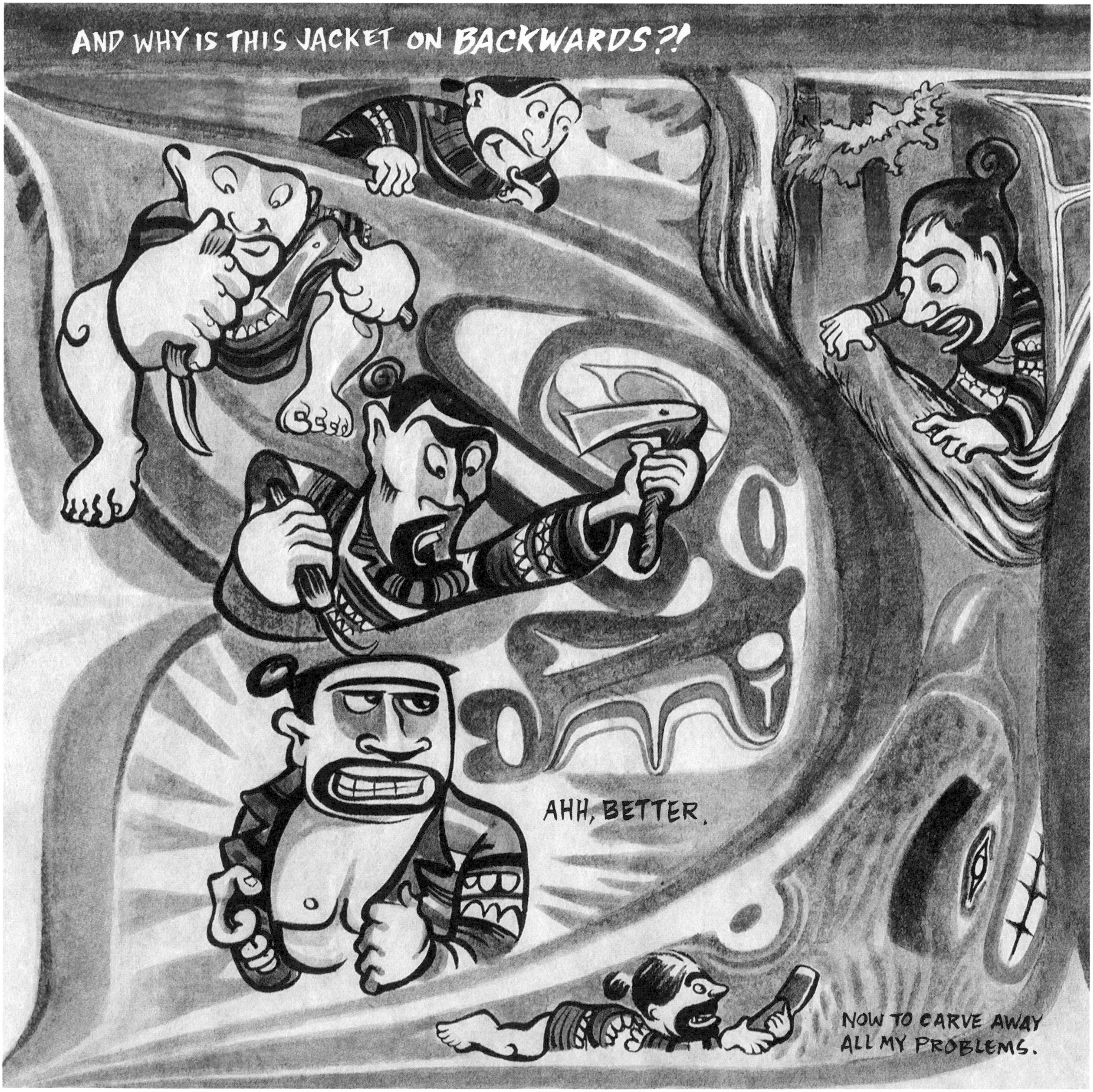
AND WHY IS THIS JACKET ON BACKWARDS?!
AHH, BETTER.
NOW TO CARVE AWAY
ALL MY PROBLEMS.

MY CARVING...
IT'S MOVING?
IT'S BREATHING?!
YOU'RE ALIVE?
SKAANAA, YOU CLEVER WHALE, GO TO SEA AND CATCH A FISH!

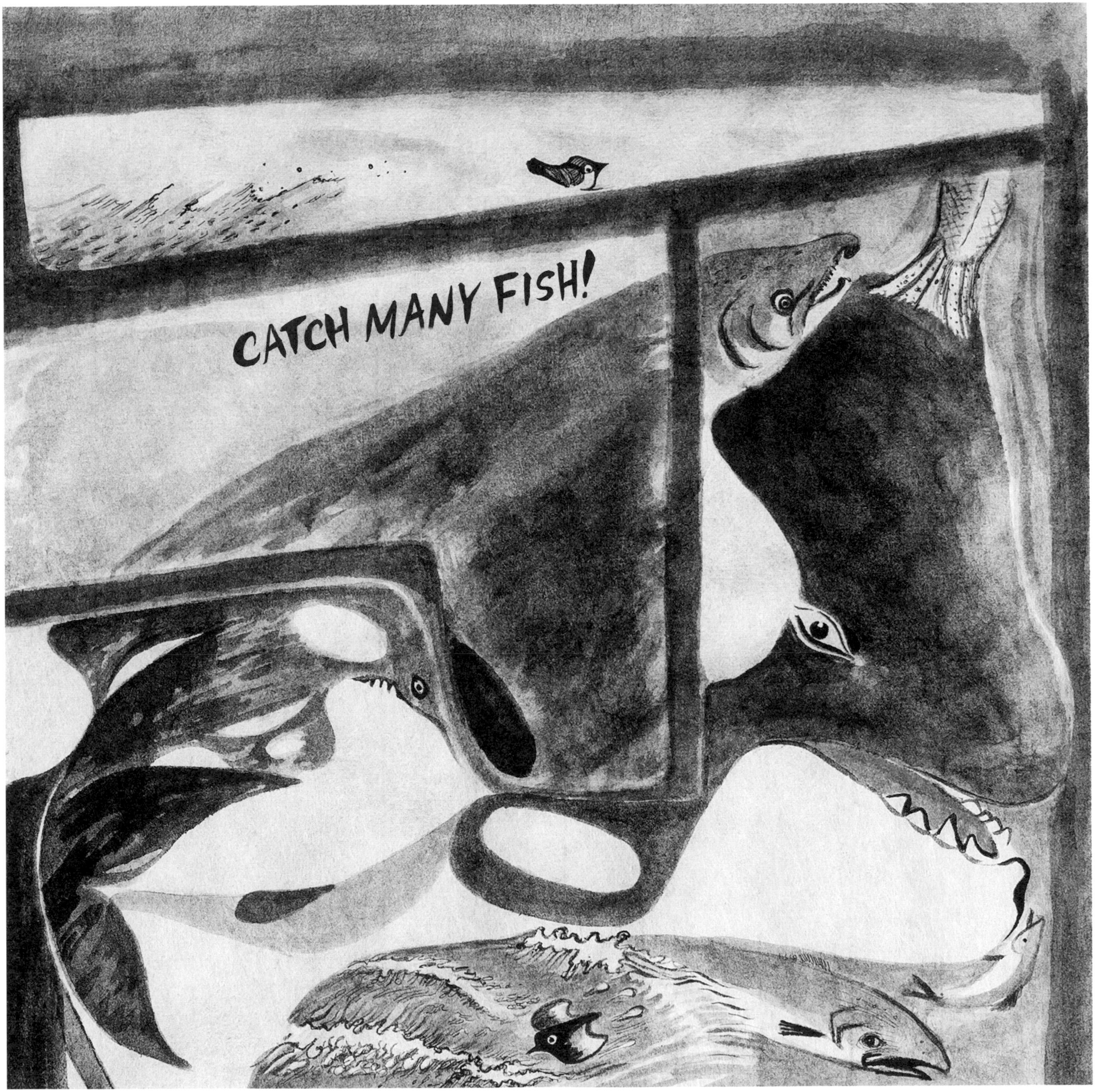
CATCH MANY FISH!

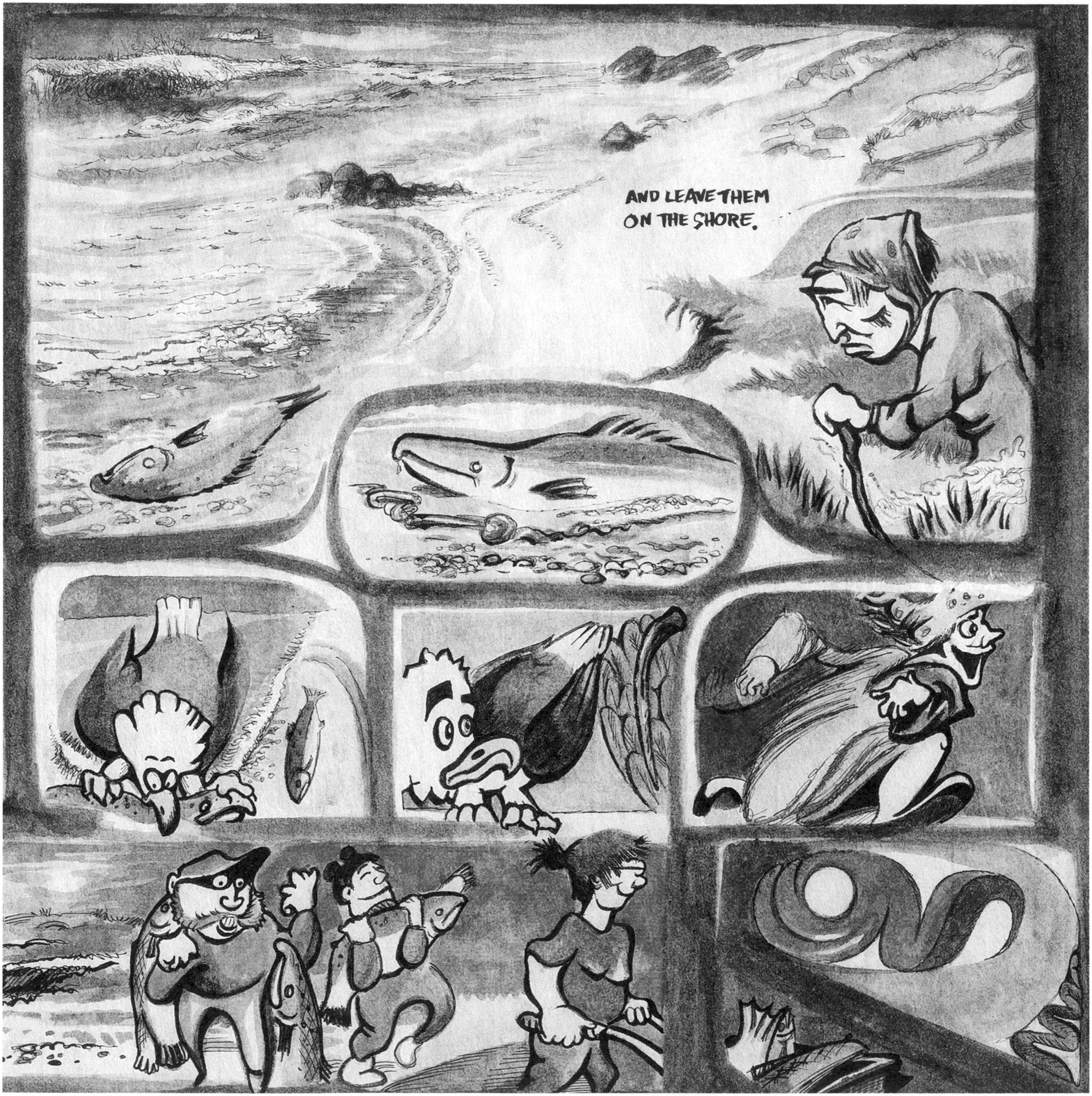
AND LEAVE THEM
ON THE SHORE.

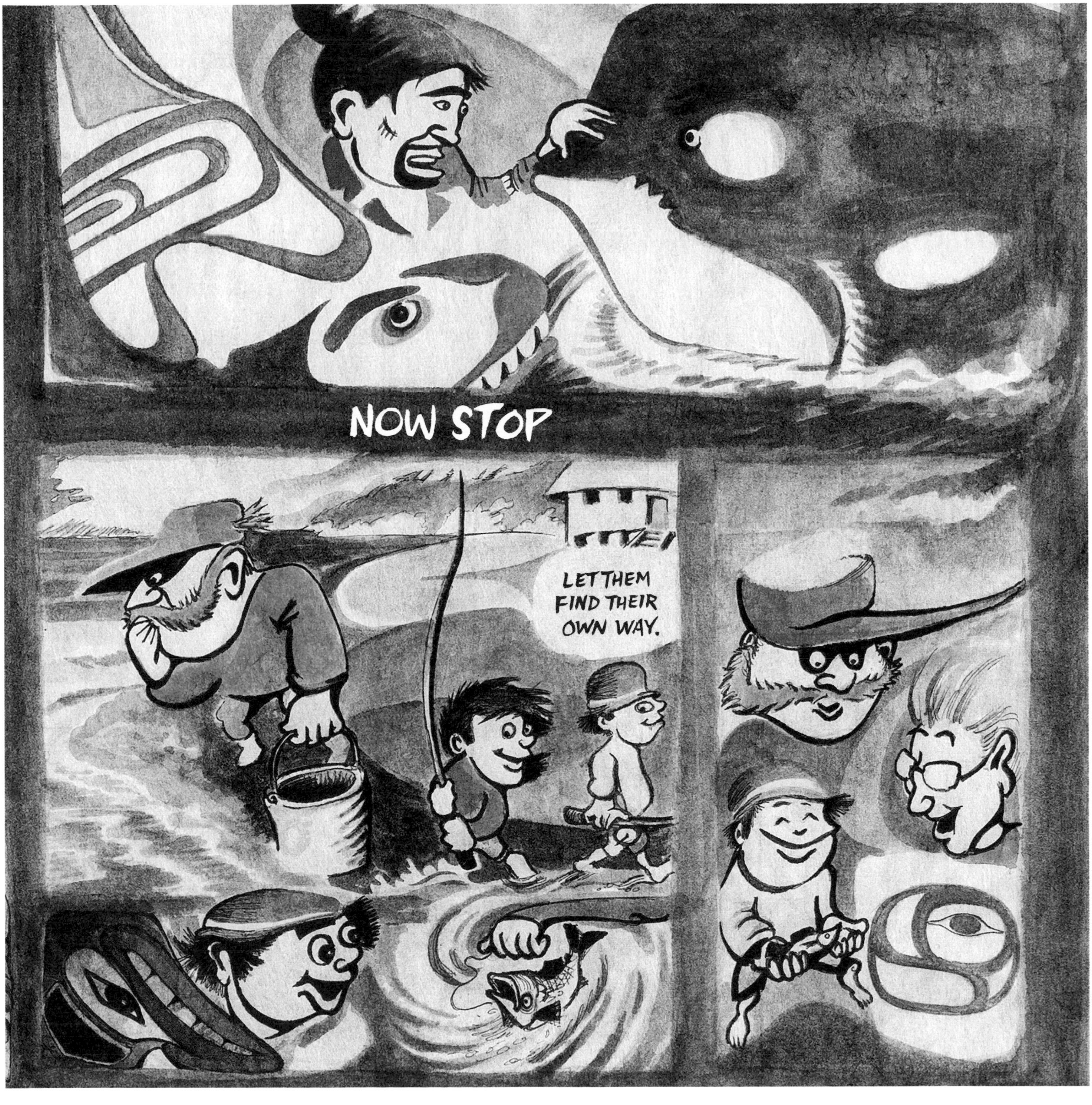
NOW STOP
LET THEM FIND THEIR OWN WAY.

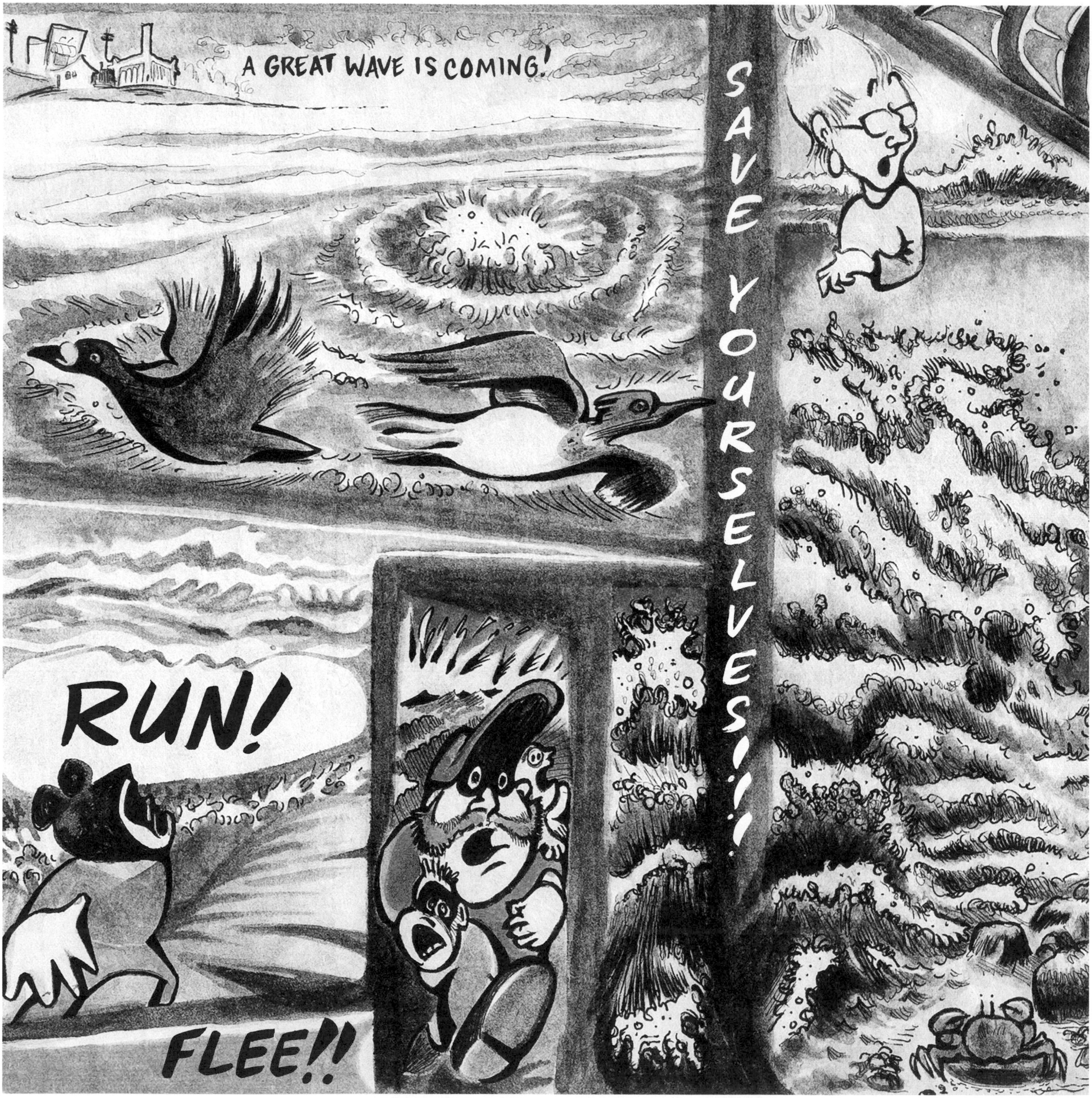
A GREAT WAVE IS COMING!
SAVE YOURSELVES!!!
RUN!
FLEE!!

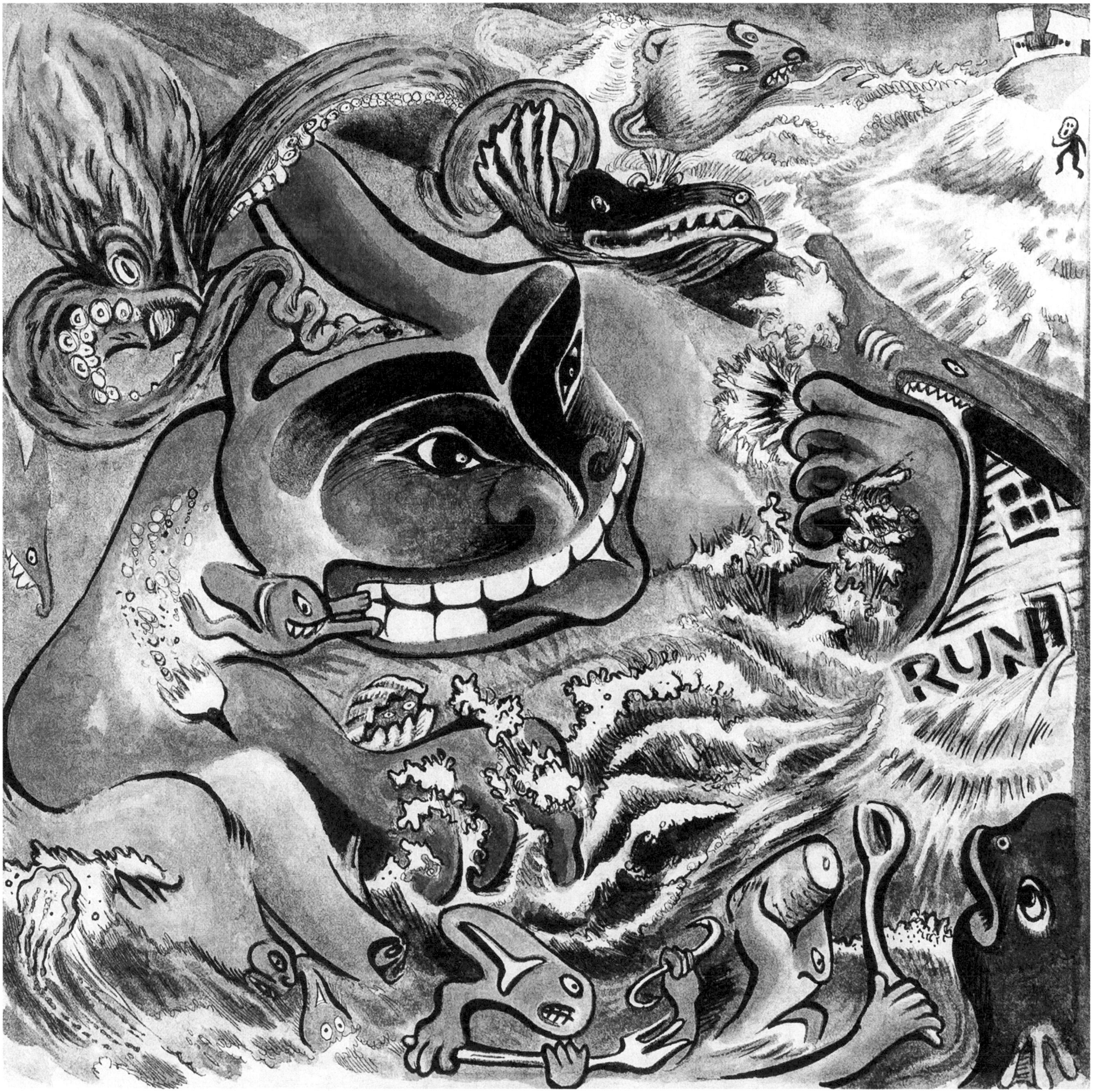
RUN

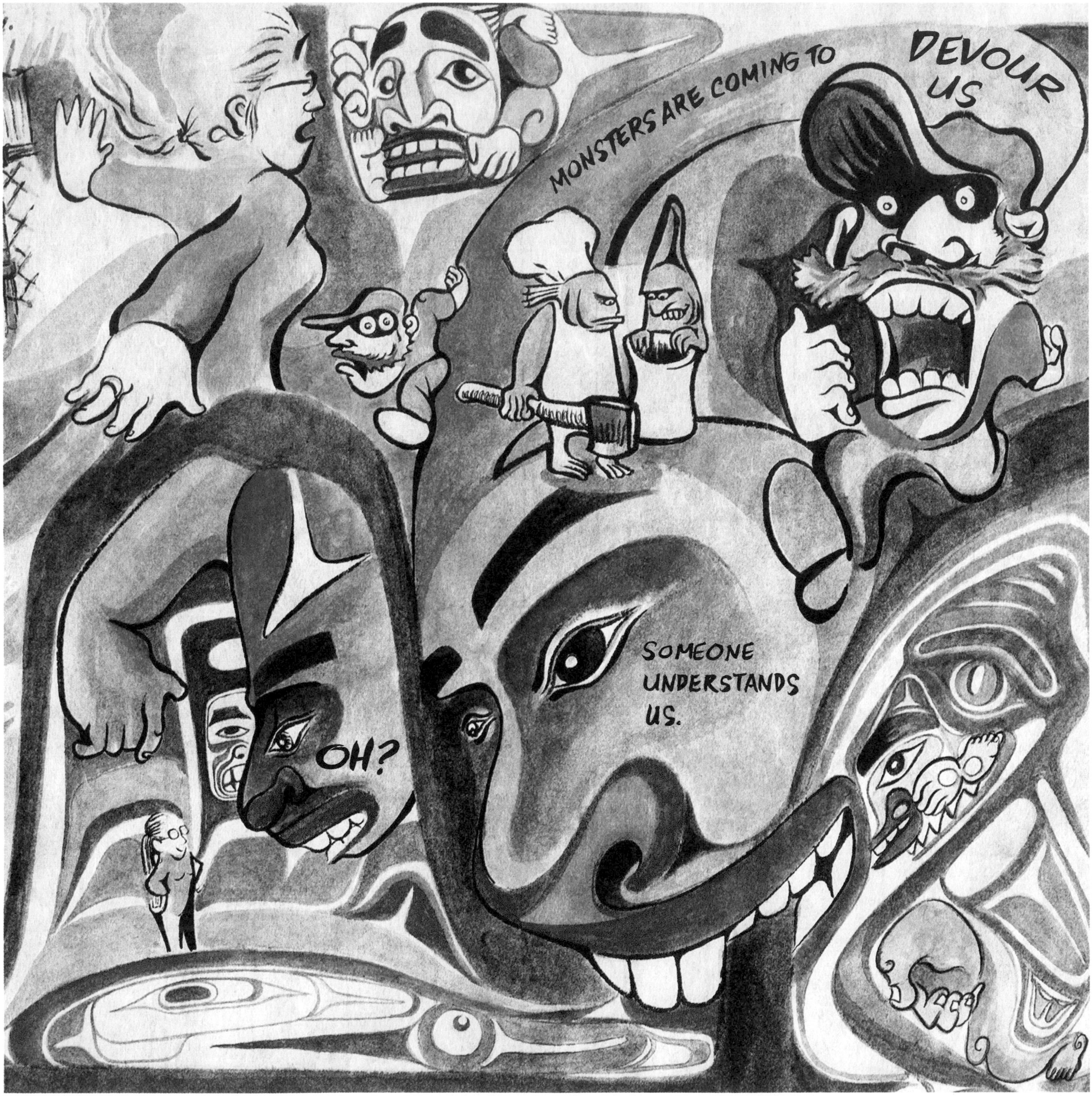
MONSTERS ARE COMING TO DEVOUR US
SOMEONE UNDERSTANDS US.
OH?

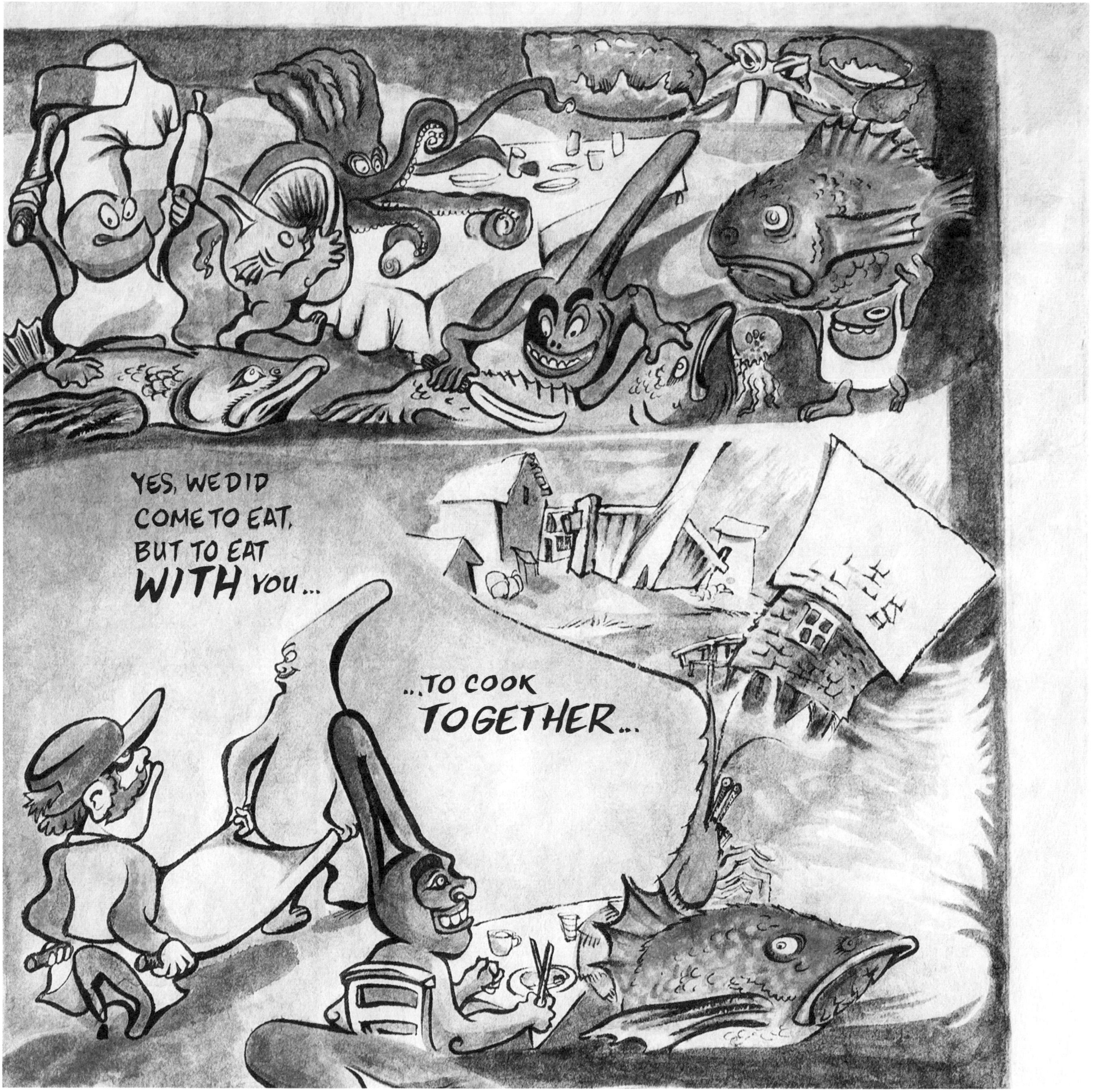
YES, WE DID COME TO EAT, BUT TO EAT **WITH** YOU...
...TO COOK **TOGETHER**...

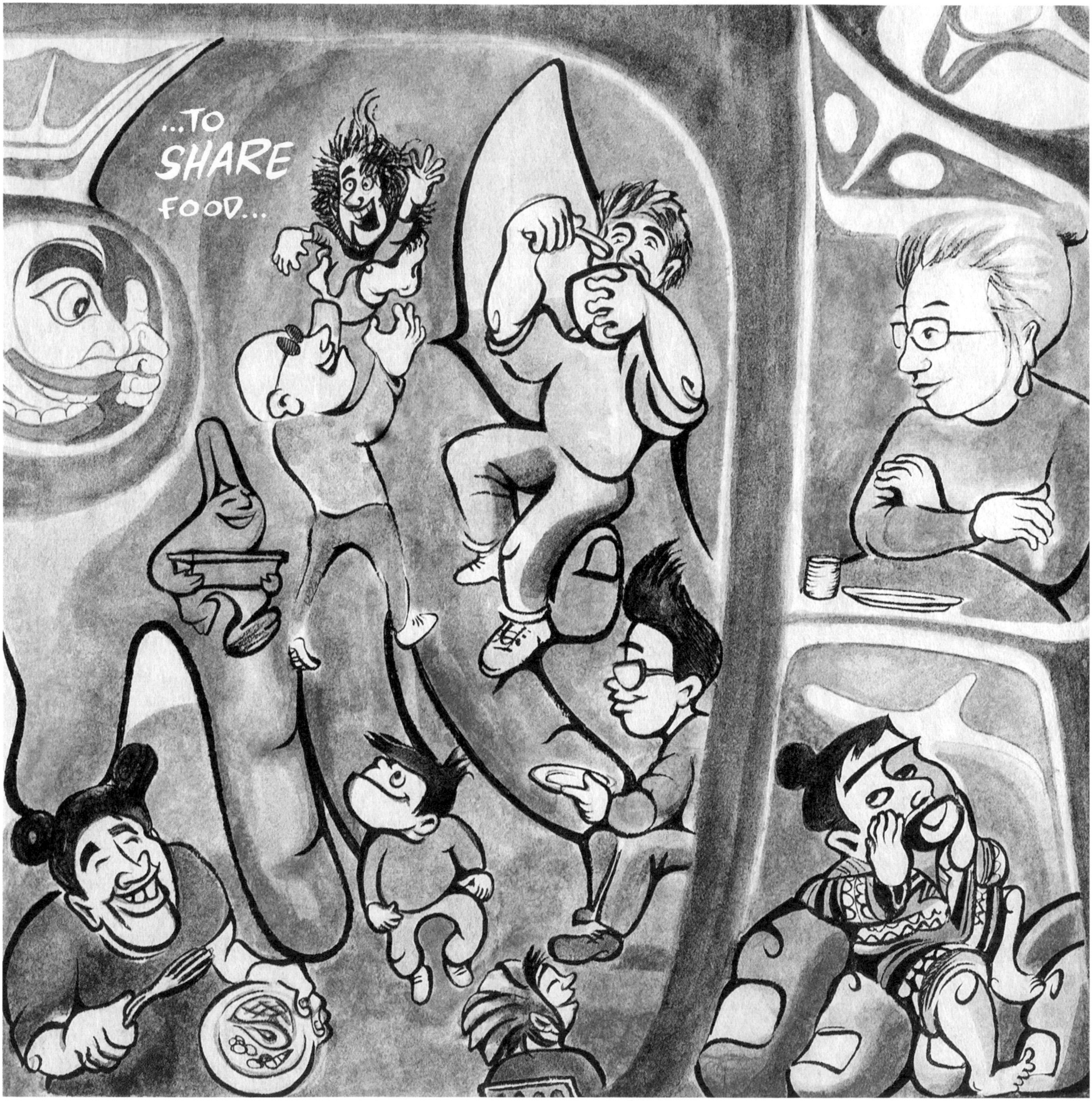
...TO SHARE FOOD...

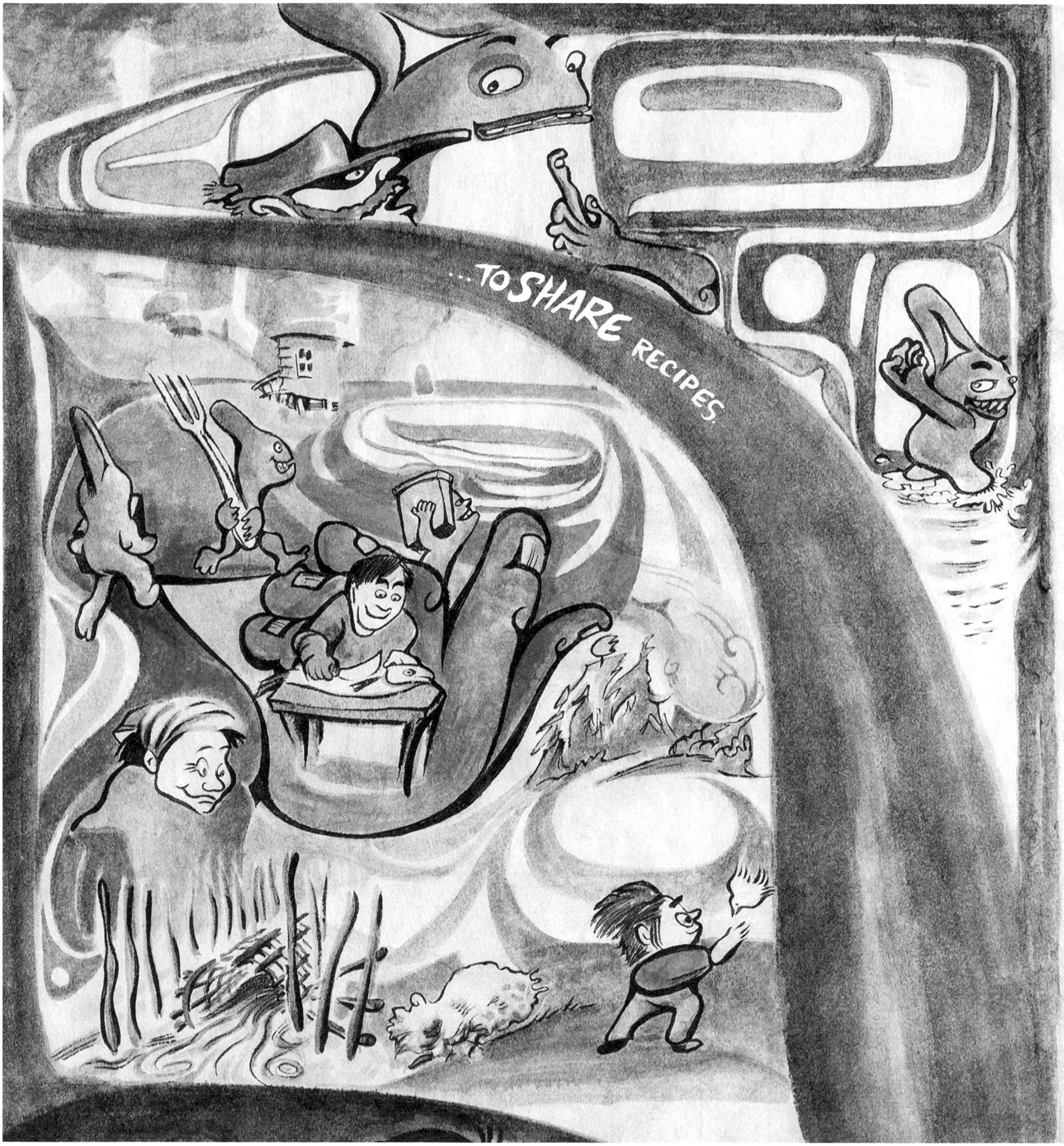
...TO SHARE RECIPES.

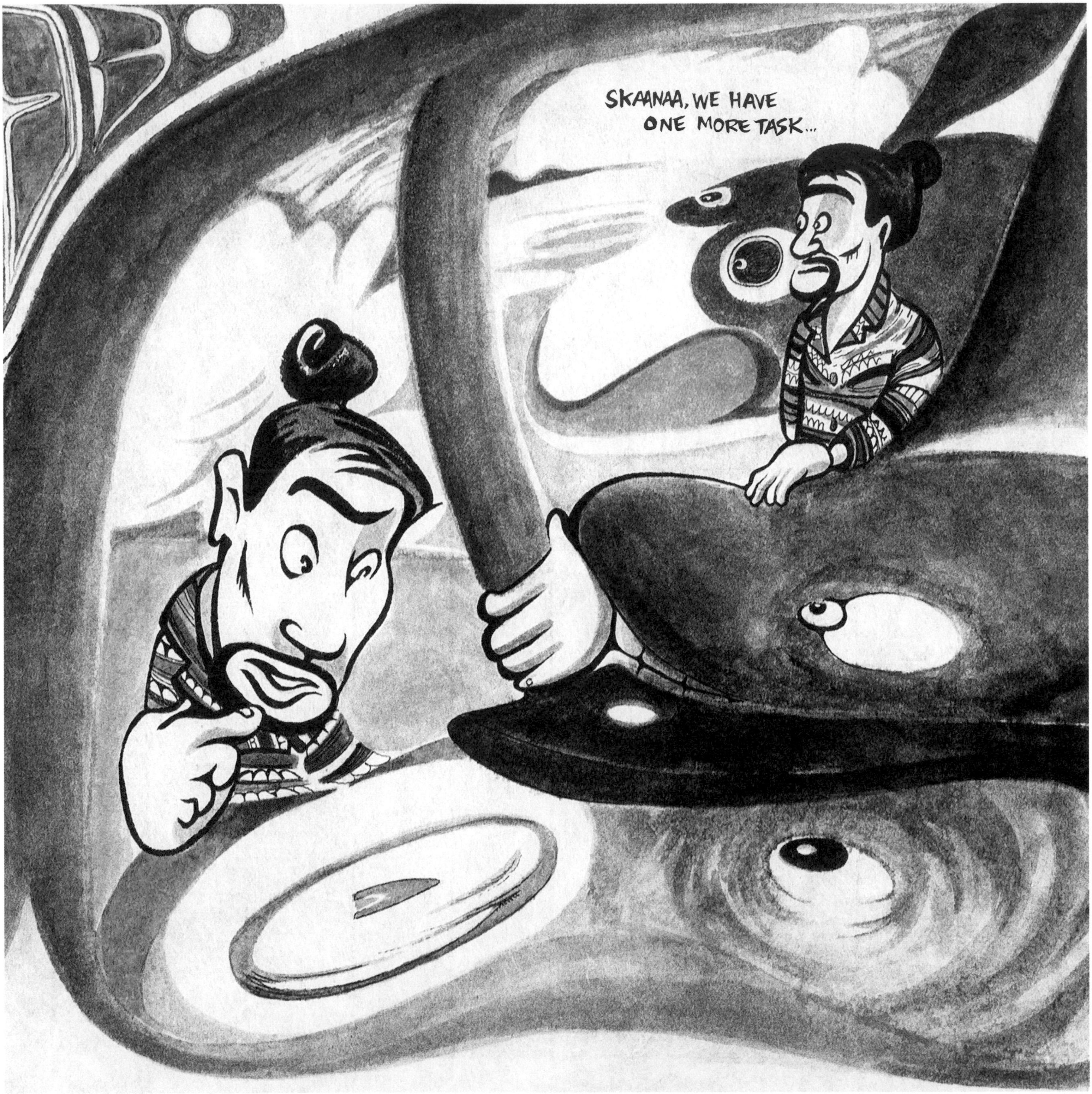
SKAANAA, WE HAVE ONE MORE TASK...

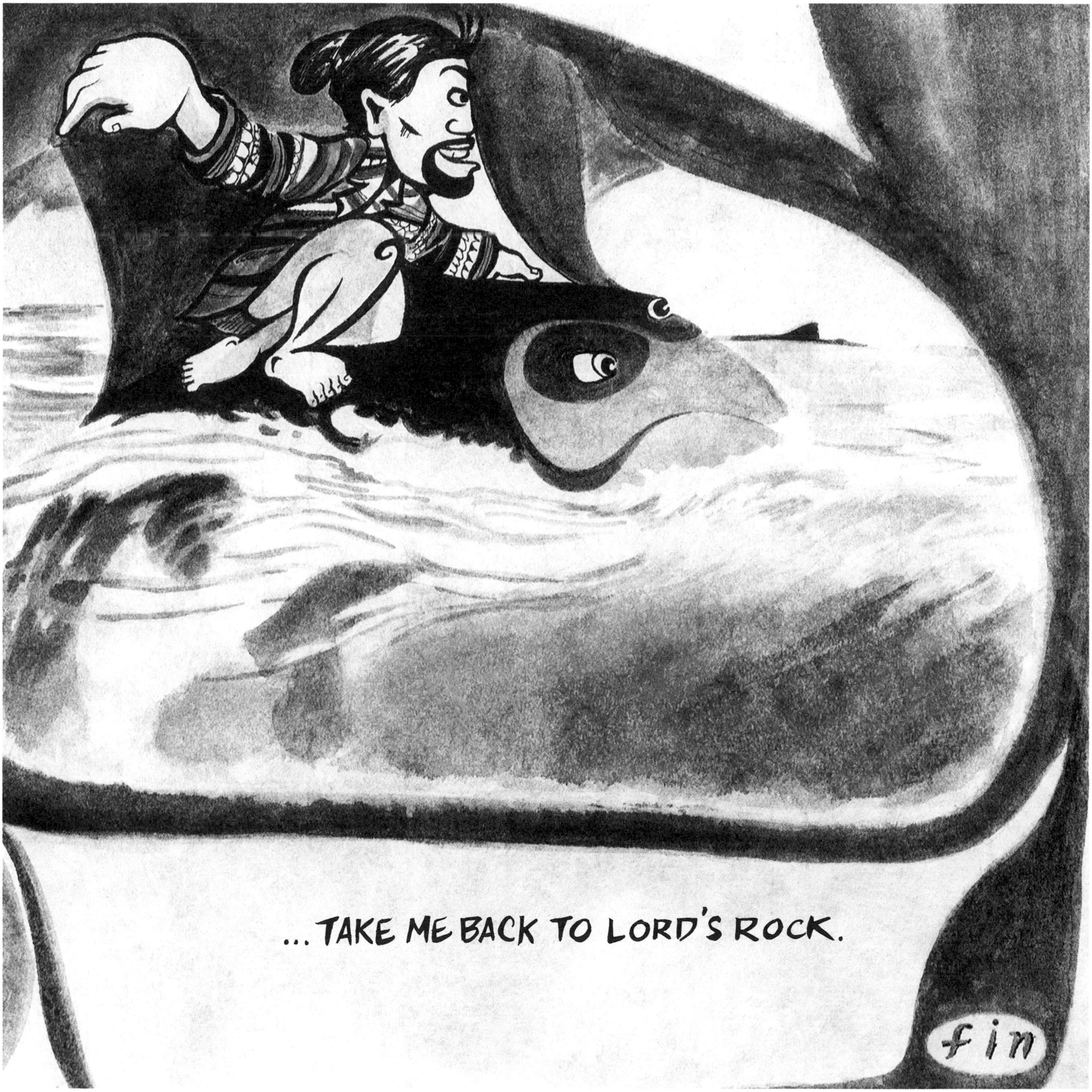
...TAKE ME BACK TO LORD'S ROCK.
fin

1 2 3 4 5 — 23 22 21 20 19

Douglas and McIntyre (2013) Ltd.
P.O. Box 219, Madeira Park, BC, V0N 2H0
www.douglas-mcintyre.com

Library and Archives Canada Cataloguing in Publication
Title: Carpe fin : a Haida manga / Michael Nicoll Yahgulanaas.
Names: Yahgulanaas, Michael Nicoll, artist.
Description: Prequel to: Red.
Identifiers: Canadiana 20190118512 | ISBN 978-1-77162-224-0 (hardcover)
Subjects: LCSH: Haida Indians—Comic books, strips, etc.
LCGFT: Graphic novels.
Classification: LCC PN6733.Y34 C37 2019 | DDC 741.5/971—dc23

Text and dust jacket design by Naomi MacDougall
Copy edited by Caroline Skelton
Printed and bound in China
Printed on acid-free paper certified by the Forest Stewardship Council

Canada | British Columbia Arts Council, An agency of the Province of British Columbia | Canada Council for the Arts / Conseil des arts du Canada

Douglas and McIntyre (2013) Ltd. acknowledges the support of the Canada Council for the Arts, which last year invested $153 million to bring the arts to Canadians throughout the country.

Nous remercions le Conseil des arts du Canada de son soutien. L'an dernier, le Conseil a investi 153 millions de dollars pour mettre de l'art dans la vie des Canadiennes et des Canadiens de tout le pays.

We also gratefully acknowledge financial support from the Government of Canada and from the Province of British Columbia through the BC Arts Council and the Book Publishing Tax Credit.

AUTHOR BIO

Michael Nicoll Yahgulanaas is the creator of Haida manga, a distinctive fusion of pop culture, Indigenous iconography and Asian graphics. His playful practice has exhibited at major institutions and is in the permanent collections of the Metropolitan Museum of Art, the British Museum, the Vancouver Art Gallery, the Museum of Anthropology and the Seattle Art Museum. As the first ever Artist in Residence at the American Museum of Natural History, he reached out to diverse ethnicities, welcoming everyone to more actively enter the in-between spaces that are never as empty as they might first appear.

Michael's previous title *Red: A Haida Manga* (2009) was an Amazon Top 100 book, while *Hachidori* (2005) secured a single-day top three sales ranking on Amazon Japan. *The Flight of the Hummingbird* (2008) has been published in numerous editions and languages and commissioned as an opera. *A Tale of Two Shaman* (2001), a richly illustrated book written in English and three Indigenous language dialects, was reprinted in 2017. Michael's complex and diverse art practice is documented in *The Seriousness of Play* by Nicola Levell. In 2017, Michael was invited to work with a major architectural firm on the design of three high rise towers in Vancouver, BC.

More at YPublicArt.com and at mny.ca.

mny

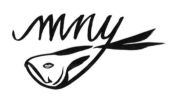